Heart of Granite

A Novel by

Sheryl Y. Battle-Maxwell

SloWriters Publishing, LLC

Heart

of

Granite

PUBLISHED BY: SloWriters Publishing, LLC

Tampa, Florida

Heart of Granite

Copyright © August 2012 by Sheryl Y. B. Maxwell

Library of Congress Catalog Number: 2017912251

eBook ISBN: 978-0-9770434-4-6

Print ISBN: 978-1-944196-75-2

Printed in the U.S.A

Cover Design: SloWriters Publishing LLC

Heart of Granite

Author Sheryl Y. Battle-Maxwell

CHAPTER

ONE

Stepping out of the shower, Garrett grabbed a towel to wrap around his waist. Droplets of water rolled down his chiseled frame, catching in the soft cotton. The lingering smell of coconut oil scented body wash filled the air in the room.

He wiped away the mist from the mirror, preparing to shave the thick beard from his face. Looking at his blurred image, he thought he rather liked the beard. But knew the department had procedures against it. Needless to say, he wasn't one to follow policies and decided to trim it up and keep it. At least for a little while.

Today was officially his first day back on duty, after his unfortunate medical leave. He sighed, at the thought, and couldn't believe how the four-inch scar on his side had gotten there. He had been careless or as Lieutenant Manning put it, reckless. In that split second, he had forgotten just how dangerous his job could be. But this scar would be a constant reminder he would carry for the rest of his life.

Chasing Omar, the neighborhood drug dealer, into the alley wasn't Garrett's smartest move. He hadn't given a second thought, that it could have been a trap. The fifteen-block obstacle course pursuit had Garrett a little winded, but he couldn't let him get away. Omar was in better shape than he thought. He guessed it came from running from his abusive mother, store owners he robbed, and the police. Seems like he had a lot of practice.

Omar was a lot smarter than anyone had given him credit, at least, street wise. Omar had received a tip about the bust, in exchange for some of his high-grade merchandise. The junky failed to mention that he was the one supplying the police with the information and that Granite that was heading the bust. Granite was a household name, and if you knew him by Granite, you were on the wrong side of the law. Omar warned the junky that if he were wrong, he would be coming after him, and his merchandise, or his money.

Garrett thought he had Omar trapped. He tried to follow departmental protocol and convince him to throw out his weapon, and give himself up. Garrett slowly entered the alley, aware that he was an open target. He darted his gaze up towards the surrounding buildings, paying close attention to the windows. He held a firm grip on his gun aimed in front of him. The word, *caution,* rung loudly in his head, and he stopped.

However, Omar had other ideas, and he wasn't giving up. He was determined to put Granite in his place, six feet under. With Granite gone, he could run this town. Take his place as top dog, and be known as the man that single handed took him down. From where he hid, Omar removed his gun from the waistband and took aim.

When the shooting started, Garrett darted behind a dumpster, shouting to the kids playing in the streets to run and take cover. Garrett reached for his cell phone to call for backup and realized he left it on the dashboard in his car. Should he lay low until backup arrives or take Omar down himself? Of course, he chose the latter. He fired a few rounds to pinpoint Omar's' location. Omar fired back, unleashing a barrage of bullets on him.

It wasn't long before Omar ran out of ammo. He ejected his clip from his guns and checked his pockets for another clip. *Damn,* he cursed, but he had another plan up his sleeves and came out with his hands up. "Granite! I give up!" he yelled, stepping into view.

It surprised Garrett that he gave up so easily. He kept his gun aimed at Omar, as he walked towards him. Garrett instructed Omar to turn around, place his hands on his head, and don't try anything. Which probably was the stupidest statement he ever made. After holstering his gun, Garrett in his haste to secure Omar didn't have him lay face down on the ground.

With one handcuffed, Omar unexpectedly stood, throwing Garrett off guard. He managed to reach behind his back for the knife before Garrett realized what was happening. Omar turned, pushing Garrett back, lashing out at him.

Garrett jumped back, as the knife cut deep into his side. Omar was quick but not as quick with a knife as Garrett was with a gun. As he fell backward, he pulled his gun from his holster and emptied the remaining bullets into Omar's chest. He watched Omar fall backward into a pile of trash cans. The expression on Omar's face was of utter shock before he took his last breath.

Garrett tried to stand, but the dull pain stopped him. Grabbing his side, he scooted back against the dumpster. He cursed, tugging the hem of his shirt out of his waistband. Looking down, he thought it didn't look good. He applied pressure with his shirt, but the blood still flowed from the wound, covering the fabric at an alarming rate. His pulse raced, as he tried to slow his breathing in hopes that it would slow his heartbeat, which in turn slow the bleeding.

Apparently, someone had called in the shooting. Garrett could hear the sirens in the distance, thank God. The EMS team reached him shortly after a uniform officer arrived. As the attendant worked on him, another rushed to check Omar. What was the use, no one could survive that many bullets to the chest? The attendant shook his head, which confirmed it.

Garrett wanted to close his eyes, but voices yelled for him to keep them open. He remembered being lifted and placed in the ambulance. When he opened his eyes again, he saw his mother rushing beside him calling his name. He tried to raise his arm to stroke the side of her face, but the straps hindered him. Straps, why was he strapped down? He looked at his mother for answers, but the double doors closed before she could. But he would never forget the look on her face, as long as he lived.

This was the first time in the line of duty he had been severely wounded. And in his line of work, may not be the last. Nevertheless, this was the career he chose for himself, and he had to admit, he loved every second of it.

He returned to work, even though, he was stuck on desk duty until he was cleared physically, and mentally to go back in the field. He didn't care what the doctors said; he knew he was as ready as the first day he signed up for the force. Dressed in a crisp white dress shirt, black tie, and black dress pants, he slid on the black leather jacket to hide the Glock-19, resting in his holster. In doing so, he flinched from the soreness and wondered how long would it take for it to go away. Pushing the pain aside, he checked his backup gun, strapped to his right leg, a custom Kimber. In the waistband at his back as his second backup, a Colt. Garrett's way of thinking was you can never be overly armed, and then he headed out the door.

He pulled up to the station, parking in his usual space next to Lieutenant Manning's. He laughed as he thought back on the day the Lieutenant asked why he always parked next to him. He replied, so he wouldn't have far to move into his place when he took over his job once he retired. The lieutenant grunted then reminded him that he had a hell of a long wait.

He walked towards the building just like any other day, but today wasn't like any other day. It was going to be tough just sitting at a desk all day doing paperwork. He didn't want any special treatment but knowing the other detectives, they were going to make this day a living hell for him with their practical jokes. Hell, if it were up to him, he would hit the streets and show everyone that he was back to his old self and ready for action.

Walking down the hall to his desk, he thought, *"So far so good."* Well, maybe he spoke too soon seeing his desk covered with a welcome back banner, confetti, and balloons. "SURPRISE!" They greeted him with applauds and pats on his back. They knew how much he hated surprises, but he smiled and thanked everyone as he pushed the balloons and confetti to the floor. When he opened his desk drawer to secure his gun, more confetti popped out into his face. Everyone laughed as he brushed the red and blue paper from his bald head, face, and clothes. He knew it was all in fun and decided to let them enjoy the moment, but reminded them that payback was a mother.

Reviewing the daily reports at his desk, Lieutenant Manning concentration was interrupted by an outburst outside his door. Most days he could turn out the occasional noise, but not today. He had too much work to do. He stormed from his office, looked around at all the decorations, and bellowed, "Who the hell is going to clean up this mess?" With that said, everyone hurried off leaving Garrett to fend for himself. "Garrett, I want to see you in my office as soon as you all are finished with this little celebration.

"Yes, sir. Right away." Garrett answered, securing his guns in the drawer, then headed to the lieutenant's office. He lightly tapped on the opened door and waited for a signal to enter.

"Sit down Garrett. I'll be with you in a moment." Manning instructed, and continued to look over the papers in front of him. Garrett shifted his weight in the chair feeling uncomfortable. He remembered the last time he was in this office, and when the lecture was over, Manning had chewed him a new butthole. The lieutenant removed his reading glasses, sat back in his chair asking. "How are you feeling Granite?" He only addressed him as Granite when they were alone. They had known one another for as long as Garrett could remember. He and Garrett's father started on the force around the same time and were good friends.

"Well sir, I'm doing fine, but it could be a lot better if I weren't stuck behind a desk." He stated, trying to gain some sympathy, but the lieutenant was a real hard nose and had none.

"Well, if you want, I can recommend that you return home until you are fit to resume your duties in the field?" He added knowing he wouldn't last another week recovering at home.

Shifting in his chair, he cleared his throat replying, "No sir. Desk duty will be fine."

"Okay then. Now, what I wanted to talk to you about the Omar case. As I recall, it was supposed to be a routine pick up for questioning." Manning opened one of the files on his desk and asked, "You were to pick up Omar and bring him to the station while the Fed's raided his stash house. However, you chose to do your John Wayne act. You go charging in with all guns blazing and of all things, followed him into an alley. Then proceeded to have a gunfight with him. Am I correct so far?" Garrett opened his mouth to answer, but the lieutenant stopped him with a stern gaze. "And, to say the least, you didn't think to call for backup, which…" Holding up his index finger, "As I recall, is a routine procedure?" Garrett didn't know if he should respond, so he kept quiet. "This little stunt almost cost you your life. And as if I didn't already know, it was brought to my attention by Internal Affairs, there are quite a few John Wayne stunts in your file." Leaning back in his chair, he pushed his glasses up his nose then continued. "Now Hart, I like John Wayne as much as the next guy. But I will not tolerate this behavior in my department, not even from you!" He shouted, banging his fist on the desk.

"Lieutenant, let me say in my defense that most of those things were not my fault. I go in with every intention to bring a suspect in as procedure states. But as soon as they see me, they take off running or want to fight their way out of going to jail. It doesn't leave me with any other choice but to do what I do." He explained but knew the Lieutenant wasn't buying any of his explanations.

"Look Garrett. The Board will be evaluating you to determine if you can return to street duty. You are one of my best detectives, and I would hate for you to be stuck behind a desk. So, to show you in a more positive image, I'm assigning the new detective to you. It's temporary - until you are ready to resume your field duties." Manning stated, judging Garrett reaction, "You'll be driving Detective Bradley around to get familiar with the district. So don't give me any grief over this, and until then, catch up on your paperwork. Any questions?" He asked but didn't want an answer.

"No, Lieutenant." He left the lieutenant's office feeling like a scolded kid. He should have been commended for getting a dangerous criminal off the street, not punished by babysitting some wet behind the ears detective.

After clearing off his desk, he commenced looking over the case files. But there was no sense stalling. He dreaded typing these reports into the system. Hell, he couldn't read half of the handwriting of some of these detectives. He found that after a while he was a good typist, and at the end of the day, he had successfully keyed in most of the files. As he gathered his things to leave for the day, the clerk laid another stack of files next to them. She smiled and shrugged her shoulders, walking away with the completed folders. He was mad to the point that he wanted to shoot something. But that would ensure he would be glued to this desk the rest of his career.

CHAPTER TWO

It's a wonder Vonda made detective with her life in such an uproar. The divorce had been a nasty one despite that they didn't have children. It's a good thing there hadn't been. Not that they hadn't tried. They wanted a family from the beginning. But it never happened. For some reason, Vonda couldn't conceive. The way she looked at it now, not having a child with her ex-husband was a blessing.

The property and other assets had a substantial valued, and she deserved more than her share, since the money her grandfather had left her funded their investments. Jerrod's high-priced lawyer had no supporting arguments, and the courts ruled in her favor. She thought of leaving the country and starting over, but she loved living in the states and loved more being a police officer. Now that she made detective she considered about leaving New York and starting a new life away from the painful memories.

Detective Vonda Bradley sat in her lieutenant's office. It seemed this was becoming a habit with her lately. She wiped at the bleeding cut above her right eye, with a gauze she took from the first aid kit. Vonda chastised herself for not seeing that punk rush her from that vacant building. He had tackled her, knocking her to the ground before she could react. She bumped her face on the concrete floor but recovered quickly. He thought it could stun her long enough for him to get away, but apparently, he didn't know Vonda. She ignored the pain and chased him as he exited the building. He didn't get far before she tackled him, returning the favor, pushing his face into the gravel. Now, he wanted to holler excessive force. This kind of shit would have never happened to her six months ago. She was fed up with this city and hoped one of her transfer requests to another state would come through.

Lieutenant LaPointe entered her office and dropped a file on her desk. "Well Detective Bradley, this is the fourth complaint against you this month," The Lieutenant complained. "I know you're going through a tough time right now after your divorce, but your work performance has been less than standard." She pointed out her disappointment.

"Lieutenant, what was I supposed to do? Let him beat the crap out of me. Then ask if he would mind coming down to the precinct and telling his side of the story?" Vonda knew she was walking a thin line with the lieutenant, but at that moment, she didn't care.

"Watch that mouth with me, Bradley. I'm on your side, and for that reason, I pulled some strings and got you temporally reassigned to Florida."

"Florida? I don't want to go to Florida." She said, jumping to her feet in protest. "There's nothing but a bunch of old retired folks living in Florida. I submitted my requests to Atlanta, Louisiana, and Los Angeles."

"Sit down Detective before you find yourself on suspension for the next few weeks!" She demanded, taking her seat. "I would think the way things have been going; the old folks would be a welcome change." Vonda knew not to call her bluff, so she sat back down with tightened lips, and kept quiet. LaPointe liked Vonda. She knew she was an outstanding detective before she caught her cheating husband with her best friend. She refused to seek to counseling, and it looked like she was taking her rage out on the job. She knew how she felt because she had gone through a similar situation a few years back herself. Nevertheless, Vonda needed to pull it together and move on with her life. "Now as I was saying, this will be only a temporary assignment until an opening comes through at your selective precinct. You had better thank your lucky stars that I was able to pull this deal together. Lately, with your record, you would be back working traffic or assigned to desk duty." LaPointe crossed her arms over her chest and asked, "So it's your choice Florida, or a desk?"

At the suggestion of the Lieutenant, Vonda hesitantly agreed to take a much-needed vacation before she moved. She had plenty of vacation time coming, and if she didn't use it before she left, she would lose the majority of it, as well as her sick time. She never took a vacation because Jerrod never had the time, and she didn't want to go without him. After the divorce, she couldn't stay home with nothing to do. That was out of the question. Within a few days, she would be out of her mind of boredom, or deeper into depression, thinking about how unfair her life was.

With the last of her things packed in the rental truck, she took one last look around the home where she had built all her hopes and dreams on with Jerrod. She would miss her New York apartment more than anything. She and Jerrod had found it after looking at what seemed like hundreds of apartments in New York and the surrounding areas. It had everything they were looking for, spacious rooms, a fantastic kitchen with all new appliances, a cozy fireplace in the master bedroom and a balcony with a magnificent view. It was just what they were looking for.

They had a perfect life, so she thought until that summer Tierra unexpectedly came to visit for two weeks. Tierra didn't give a reason, just said she needed to get away for a while. They had been friends forever, and Vonda would never turn her friend away. Nor did she want her to fend for herself, as she was going through the ordeal. Vonda worked nights, and due to her schedule, she managed to take a couple of days of vacation. She had no choice but to plead with Jerrod to keep Tierra company. To Vonda's surprise, he agreed to take good care of Tierra. She should have suspected something wasn't right.

She and Tierra hit the clubs her first weekend just like in their college days. Lately, they use their time catching up on their lives, and the latest gossip. Much to her surprise, when she returned to work, Jerrod kept his promise.

The following mornings, Tierra would tell her over coffee where her and Jerrod dined and the sites he took her to tour.

However, while she was out protecting and serving the city neither cared to mention the part about Jerrod serving her up with all ten inches of his dick, in her home. What you do in the dark always comes to light. When she entered the house, the vibe of the place didn't feel right. There was a faint hint of her scented candles in the air, and the soft sound of music could be heard coming from the bedroom. The closer she got to the bedroom door, the harder it became for her to breathe. Slowly pushing open the door, it took her sight a second to adjust to the dim lighting. When they did, she was speechless as the realization washed over her that their marriage was over.

Naked, wrapped in each other's arms, careless and content. By the condition of the bed, the two lovers must have been going at it all night. They had fallen asleep. The same bed, she and her husband made love on many nights and tried to start a family. In a rage, she pulled her sidearm, aimed it at them, and slowly put her finger on the trigger.

Tierra stirred, then kissed Jerrod on the lips. Sensing a presence in the room, she hazily turned to the sight of Vonda standing in full gear, with a loaded Glock pointed at them. Her screams brought Jerrod fully awake, and once he saw her, he immediately started explaining what she thought happen, hadn't. Tierra, on the other hand, kept repeating how sorry she was and pleaded for Vonda not to kill her. Vonda never felt such hurt and betrayal in her entire life. How could her best friend and husband do this to her? Two people whom she loved dearly, and would have given her life for without a second thought. Her hands shook, tears welled up in her eyes, the air lodged in her chest, as she hyperventilated. Her mind raced with thoughts of what to do, pull the trigger and send them to hell or not? The entire scene moved in slow motion right before her eyes. She couldn't hear their pleas; only see their reaction play out in front of her.

The man who once vowed to love, honor and cherish her until death do them part, now pleaded for his life. Well, it looked like the parting part of the marriage had come. She took aim, pulled the trigger, and fired two shots over their heads. Lowering her arms to her side, she turned, leaving the place she once called home. She hadn't been back until now.

****

Vonda held her lower back, rubbing at the dull pain. She finished unpacking the last of her things, then stacked the empty boxes in her outdoor storage unit. She stored most of her furniture in New York until her permanent assignment came through. Which she hoped didn't take long. She wouldn't be wasting her time getting to know the locals and vice versa. All she wanted was to do her job then get the hell out of dodge when the time came.

Her cell phone vibrated in her pocket. She looked at the display and sighed. It was her mother. She decided to let it go to voice mail and call her back later. She didn't feel like answering twenty-one questions about her move. Or if she needed her to come and help her get everything in place? She loved her parents, they were an enormous comfort helping her through this divorce, but right now she needed to take a moment for herself. She opened the box of delivered pizza and placed a slice on a plate. It was cold, but what the hell, she ate cold pizza before. She took a bite and wished it were the New York Style Pizza she enjoyed from home. Because there was nothing like a big slice of New York Style Pizza, cold or hot.

Chapter Three

As in the past, she already knew her new partner wasn't going to welcome a female partner. Even on a temporary basis. She wasn't thrilled having him, or anyone else as a partner. She liked working alone, things just run smoother that way. But if she had to have him as a partner, she wanted to know as much as she could about him. Lieutenant Manning hadn't given her much information. Other than the Detective Harts name, and a brief resume of his accolades. She knew everyone had a dark side, and Hart was no exception.

Google, the all-knowing, super information highway was the best place to start. Lying in bed, with her favored cup of tea, she booted up her computer, typed in his name and waited. All the information on him was laid out in front of her. Even his nickname, Granite was intriguing.

High School All-Star athlete in football, basketball, and baseball, Garrett Hart was destined for a great career in any sport of his choosing. However, only one thing held him back, his uncontrollable temper. Most of the time, he was as gentle as a lamb, but when his anger rose, he was a force to be reckoned with and was the source of many fights during and after the game. Everyone had hopes that after high school, he would be chosen as the top draft pick in the state, but most of the top colleges wouldn't recruit him because of his reputation. They didn't have the time or patience to babysit him. Not wanting to take second place in anything, he decided to follow his father's footsteps, and become a police officer,

then work his way to detective. He gave it his all, excelling at the
Academy as he did in everything. His first years on the force, he
achieved the highest arrest record in the district.

Nothing she had read could have braced her for a bigger than life images of him. Garrett Hart was one magnificent specimen of a man. His apple-butter complexion and deep-set brown eyes mesmerized her from the computer screen. His regal set nose and delicious full lips could kiss a woman into submission. She licked her lips thinking about it. His nearly bald, haircut with that five o'clock shadow beard, gave him a rugged mountain man look that just added to his charm. Parts of her were starting to heat up as she flipped through the gallery of photos. There was one picture, in particular, that caught her eye. A victory shot of him shirtless in the team locker room, holding the game football high in the air. His six-pack abs were very impressive, as well as the size of the bulge under the towel in front of him. Vonda couldn't believe she was eyeing this man like a piece of prime cut meat, and the dinner bell had rung.

There was a Bio of his family, but she wasn't interested in any of that. This man had her full attention in more ways than one. Her nipples harden against her nightshirt just looking at him. If she were wearing panties, they would be damp with her sexual juices. She reluctantly powered down her laptop and placed it beside her on the bed. She looked up at the ceiling, taking a deep breath then sighed as she thought of her life up to now.

Vonda worked on the police force for ten years and was a beat cop for eight of them. After the incident, she needed to get away from New York as fast as she could. She didn't need anything to remind her of her cheating ex-husband, Jerrod, and Tierra, her best friend of twenty-five years. Even after a year, it still hurt to relive that night.

It all happened so fast without any warning signs. Jerrod was her husband, he vowed to love and honor her forever, and Tierra had been the sister she never had. They shared everything, but that wasn't supposed to include her husband. "Well to hell with both of them!" She shouted, and turned over on her side, switching off the light. Pulling her pillow close to her body, she refused to shed one more tear on either of them. Tomorrow was the start of a new beginning, and she wasn't going to waste another thought on them.

Unable to sleep, Vonda crawled out of bed. There was no use in lying around. She showered, ate breakfast, and turned on the TV to look at the local news. She shook her head at the broadcast, thinking she had relocated to a quiet retirement state. But from the looks of it, she had her work cut out for her. Crime was up by five percent from last year, mainly in the St. Petersburg area, and of all things, cops seemed to be the target. In her career, she had met her share of dirty cops but, for the most part, they were there to serve and protect. People didn't realize if there were no law enforcement, the city would be in worst shape than it is now. The cities would be overrun with gangs; drug dealers and God knows what else.

Looking at her watch, she turned off the TV then finished dressing. Tucked away in her closet she removed from her safe, a small arsenal of weapons. She purchased a Walther P22, a Ruger LCP, and a Glock-19 when she arrived. She placed the Glock in her holster, the Ruger in her ankle holster and the Walter behind her back. She hoped the department would allow her to keep her babies, and not issue her their standard firearms. Closing the safe, she grabbed her keys and headed out the door.

She turned the key in the ignition to her rental car, then activated the GPS. The friendly female voice greeted her, and her first thought was to change that as soon as possible. She didn't need that cheery voice this early in the morning. She didn't have a damn thing to be cheery about.

Vonda parked at the far side of the lot. There were plenty of closer vacant spaces, but she could view everyone entering the station lot undetected. This would give her an idea of the type of people she was working with and maybe get a glance of Detective Hart. She leaned her seat back a little and waited.

She slightly raised her head when headlights came into view. A 2010 Cadillac STS Luxury Sedan, 4-door, dark gray, pull into the Lieutenant's reserve parking space. She had only spoken with Lieutenant Manning on the phone a few times. He appeared to be a reasonable man; then again, you can never tell. Her previous boss, Lieutenant LaPointe, knew Manning and his family years ago when she lived in Florida for a brief time. She said they were good people.

"Not bad for an old man," she thought, as he exited his car. From where she sat, he looked to be at least five feet eleven, maybe a little taller. Medium build, one-hundred-eighty, maybe one ninety. The scowling expression on his brown face worried her a little. Nevertheless, she watched him enter the building with his shoulders erect, like he may have been in the military at some point in his life.

Moments later, another car pulled in, parking next to the lieutenant's car. A Mustang GT 2005, maybe 2006, 2-door coupe, black exterior, nice expensive rims. A real chick magnet. Then the living legend appeared, Garrett Hart. Gripping the steering wheel, she sat up straight and peered out the windshield like a child looking through a window of a candy shop. The dawn was just coming over the horizon, but the well-lit parking lot allowed her to see him. Man, she had to say he was better looking than his picture. Tall, six plus, broad shoulders, very well built, one-ninety – two hundred pounds, slightly bow-legged and very well dressed.

From what she could tell, he was packing three guns. One in his holster, one behind his back, and, by the way, his pants leg on his right leg fit, he had one strapped there also. She smiled thinking he was a man after her own heart. His computer photo didn't do him any justice - at all. He paused, looked in her direction surveying the area. As if he could see her, she ducked down low and watched him enter the building. Her heart thumped wildly just looking at him. She realized her mouth gaped open in awe. She closed her mouth, swallowed the lump in her throat, and prepared herself to meet Granite Hart face to face.

Chapter

Four

Garrett arrived at the precinct at 5:00 am. As he walked towards the building, he had an eerie feeling of being watched. But thought otherwise looking around the nearly empty lot. He shook it off and continued inside.

He removed his guns and secured them in his desk. He began looking through the ever-growing files and completing the paperwork to close the case. About an hour later, the other detectives slowly started arriving. He nodded his greetings to a few of them. He looked up from a file he was reviewing and cringed when he saw the Lieutenant headed in his direction. Thinking, he could possibly make his way to the exit, without having to have the same old conversation. Then he had remembered that today he was assigned to taking some new detective out with him.

"Good morning, Garrett. Are you ready to meet your new partner?"

Wide-eyed, Garrett was shocked, outraged in fact to hear that word, *partner*. No one said anything to him about getting a partner. The lieutenant knew as well as everyone in the department, he preferred to work alone. Always have.

He jumped to his defense. "Hold up Lieutenant. Partner?" Garrett looked around the office to see if anyone was listening, "You didn't say anything about a partner. I thought I was supposed to just take this Joe out and show him around for a few days. You know, to make a good mark on my record."

"I know, but that's not the way things work around here. I decide who or who doesn't get a partner. I didn't want to give you the opportunity to try and talk your way out of it. Which wasn't happening anyway. Besides, I think you will like Detective Bradley, you two have a lot in common." The lieutenant turned, walking back to his office.

Garrett caught him by the arm to stop him saying. "Look Lieutenant. I work alone, and have since I became a detective." Manning looked at Garrett's hand, and he quickly removed it and replied.

"You only worked alone because none of the other detectives would risk working with you. You're too reckless. But starting today, you don't." Manning didn't give him a chance to answer, and continued to his office, with the furious Garrett in tow.

Detective Vonda Bradley sat in Manning's office waiting for him to return with her 'partner.' Just saying the word, left a bad taste in her mouth. She was nervous but would die a thousand deaths before letting it show. Looking around the office, she saw several plaques hanging on the wall along with pictures of him shaking hands with some dignitaries, at different stages of his life. On a table behind his desk, sat an eight by ten framed picture of a beautiful woman. She assumed it must be his wife since he was

35

wearing a wedding ring. There were other family photos of Manning with her and two kids, who appeared to be twins. Other than that, it was a typical office.

She started to wonder what was taking them so long when the door abruptly opened. By the tight expression on Hart's face, he wasn't very pleased with the news. The Lieutenant had warned her, that Detective Hart didn't know he was being assigned a partner. He went on to explain Detective Hart *situation,* either way, she didn't care because she didn't want a partner either.

Manning entered his office and made the introductions. "Detective Hart, this is Detective Vonda Bradley, your partner. Detective Bradley, this is Detective Garrett Hart."

Garrett stopped in his tracks, looked at Bradley, then at the Lieutenant as if he had lost his mind. He didn't like the idea of having a partner, and to make matters worse Detective Bradley was a female.

As a courtesy, she stood and extended her hand to Garrett, but was only met with a blank stare. She could see where this was going, another chauvinistic pig to deal with. Well, she wasn't having it. She had worked too hard to make detective. She demanded to be treated like every other detective, and not be judged by what didn't hang between her legs. If you asked her, she had more balls, than half the men on the force and was willing to prove it, anytime, anywhere.

Manning took his seat, saying, "Detective Hart will be showing you around the city to get you familiar with the area." He glanced up at her and asked, "Any questions?"

She looked at Manning to Hart. "Yes, sir. Is he gonna stare at me like this all day, or what?" Looking in Garrett's direction, she noticed he diverted his eyes. She was sure he was unaware that he had been staring at her.

"I don't know. Detective Hart, are you going to stare at her like that all day or what?" Manning repeated her question.

Finding his voice, "No, sir, I was just caught off guard. I didn't know my – my partner was a woman." He replied with a strained smile on his face. But his eyes told a different story.

"Okay, now that we have that cleared up. Detective Hart will take you out to the south side after you go to Human Resource. You have a few other forms to complete and take your picture." He replied. "And Detective Bradley welcome to the precinct." Manning shook Vonda's hand.

Turning, she came face to face with Garrett, who couldn't seem to move. From a single head to toe glance, she could see why he was known as Granite. Underneath his crisp white shirt, she could tell he had a rock-hard chest and a powerful set of arms. She only hoped that all she read about him wasn't just media hype, and he lived up to the articles. From what she read, he was almost some type of Hero. It didn't matter to her one bit. She needed all that hype where it belongs, on the street watching her back, not her ass.

Garrett opened the door, stepping aside for her to pass. Being the man that he was, he quickly gave her the once over glance and liked what he saw. She appeared to be in great shape, but it was hard to tell under the suit she wore. The slacks were loose in the legs but fit snugly across her hips and ass. However, there was no hiding the full rack of double D's beneath her blouse. Her fragrance teased his senses as she stormed passed him. She stopped just outside the office door remembering she didn't know the way to Human Resources and allowed Garrett to walk ahead to lead the way. By the smirks on his fellow detective's faces, it looked like the joke was on him.

Heading towards the elevator, he noticed the desk across from him had been cleared off. If he remembered correctly, it was used as the catch-all desk since the last Detective left. It was a breeding ground for piles of old office equipment.

They stood side-by-side waiting for the elevator to arrive, and when the door opened, they stepped in. Once the doors closed, Vonda was up in his face, which caught him off guard.

"Okay, let's get something straight Hart. Don't underestimate my abilities to do my job just because I'm a woman. Now, I expect to be treated like any of these other detectives, and if you have a problem with me then you can..." Vonda searched for the right word to relay her point.

"Hey hold up!" Garrett emphasized, by pushing her back with his finger on her shoulder. "I don't know what your problem is, but I don't give a rat's ass if you're a woman or not. All I expect from you is that you hold your own and have my back out there. Is that understood?" His chest swelled with anger as he held her gaze. No one had ever gotten in his face like this, and for the life of him; he couldn't understand why he was aroused by it. Damn, he had never met any woman like her. It took all the self-control he could muster to not grab her, and slam her against the wall and fuck her mindless.

Other than his family, most people wouldn't dare approach him in this manner, and not expect to be greeted with a fist to the mouth.

Now that they understood one another, she turned to face the door as if nothing had occurred, saying, "Don't worry, I can hold my own. I just expect you to do the same."

The elevator door opened, and Garrett led the way to the glass doors of the Human Resource's Office. Without looking at her, he told her he would meet her back at his desk, then turned and walked away.

♥ ♥ ♥

Vonda didn't ask many questions as Garrett pointed out some of the known thugs in the area, and the gangs they were associated. He gave her the rundown of the who's who, and what crimes they were known for committing. She seemed to be taking it all in, but only time will tell.

By two o'clock, Garrett was hungry and knew she should be too. Since they were in the neighborhood, he had a taste for some of Baby Girl's delicious fried fish.

She thought that was an odd question when he asked if she ate fish. She was from New York, not Mars. She grunted her reply. He gave her a sideways glance, then headed to his favorite lunch spots on the east side.

Friendly Fish Market, a local black-owned business, served up some of the best fried fish in town, as well as a sold variety of fresh seafood. It also, served as the neighborhood corner store, selling everything from cold sodas to beer, canned goods to fresh delivered bread. He just hoped they hadn't sold out of the mullet because he sure could go for a hot tasty piece right now.

Vonda had never witnessed anything like this in New York, as she looked at the small blue colored building with a variety of sea creatures painted on it. There were a few cars parked out front, but Garrett chose to park across the street in a vacant lot. At first glance, she thought how could this little place be as spectaculars as Garrett bragged about. Until he opened the door, and the delicious aroma engulfed her every sense. The owner, Doris, was there taking inventory while daughter, Christa, ran the day-to-day operations, and chef, greeted them warmly. Cris inquired how was he doing since the incident, and was glad he was back to work.

He introduced Vonda to Mrs. Doris and Christa, also known as Baby Girl or Cris to her friends and family. Both women greeted her with a warm smile, and welcome her to their city. Cris asked him if he wanted the usual. He replied that he did, then she asked Vonda what she wanted, then gave her a rundown of what they had available. Vonda opts for the same as Garrett; then Cris went to work on the orders. With orders placed, he continued his friendly conversation with Mrs. Doris as Vonda walked over to the drink cooler. Looking over the selection of cold beverages, she noticed they had cream-flavored soda. Thinking it had been ages since she had a cream soda, then took the last two cans from the rack. Garrett asked if she could grab him a strawberry-flavored drink.

Mrs. Doris market was a neighborhood fixture for as long as he could remember. She and her husband had opened it many years ago to serve the black community. When most of the small black-owned businesses were closing, due to many of the larger food chains opening in the areas. The chain's stores were able to carry seafood, and other merchandise at a much cheaper cost, making the smaller businesses a dying breed. However, their market stood the test of time and pulled through the hard times. Garrett was looking forward to going there for a very long time.

Vonda sat back in her chair, and couldn't believe she ate the entire fish dinner. Her side of the table was loaded with napkins, from wiping away all the mustard and hot sauce from her fingers. She was surprised, included with the big piece of fish, were hush puppies, a small salad, and a stack of fries. Man, she never in her life had fried fish that tasted like this. If she kept eating like this, she would have to find a gym to work off all those calories. She looked up and noticed Garrett looking at her smiling. She asked him,

"Is there a problem?"

"No. No problem at all," Garrett said, trying to wipe the smile off his face while enjoying watching her eat. "It's just that most women don't enjoy their food as much as you seem to." There was a moment of silence as he looked at her. He couldn't resist reaching over and wiped a smug of mustard from her cheek. She couldn't move, as he gently rubbed her cheek with a clean napkin. His touch was gentle, as his fingers brushed her skin. She closed her eyes to shield the lustful glare in them and pulled back from his touch.

She suppressed the heat building, replying, "Well, you will learn that I'm not like most women," The simple act of him wiping her cheek, seemed as natural as breathing. Moreover, the thought of her letting him scared her more. What was wrong with her? Since Jerrod, she hadn't let any man get this close to her. She sat back; finished cleaning her mouth, then took her container to the garbage can. Garrett sat for a moment; surprised at his own actions. He lowered his gaze to his own empty container, then took the last sip from his second can of drink to calm the fire building in him. He took a moment to get his shaft under control, stood to place his container in the trash. He turned to her again, asking her if she was ready. Before leaving, he went to the market's door, said his goodbyes, and told them lunch was excellent as usual and promised to be back soon.

Back in the car, he was more in control of himself. He decided to make a detour down Lake Avenue, to 22nd Street. He had heard one of the local hotheads, Jay-Boy, was back on the streets, and he wanted to verify the information. Jay-Boy was supposed to be doing ninety days in county lock-up. But instead, he was released early due to overcrowding. Ain't that a bitch. He may be back on the streets, but he was still on probation, and he would be keeping an eye on him.

He parked the car in front of the apartment number Jay-Boy gave upon his release, which was his mother's address. Getting out of the car, they took a moment to look around. Most of the neighborhood thugs knew Garrett's car and fled the area once they spotted him. Ms. Boyd liked Garrett and knew he had tried to help

Jay-Boy in the past before something serious happened to him in the streets. But to no avail, Jay-boy had other ideas of his own. As they approach the door, loud music and talking could be heard coming from inside, which indicated Ms. Boyd wasn't home. They knocked on the door several times. They both caught a faint smell of marijuana coming from inside, then Garrett banged harder.

"Hold the hell up! I'm coming!" Jay-Boy yelled, opening the door with a joint between his lips. He must have been expecting some of his old crew to stop by to celebrate his homecoming. "Nigga, why you banging on my doe-like that?" He laughed, opening the door. He froze, seeing Garrett and the lady cop. He cursed, then yelled, "5-0!" And took off running towards the back door, with Garrett on his heels. Vonda wasted no time in the pursuit. She ran around the outside of the building to cut him off. She wasn't sure where she was going but knew there had to be a shortcut. Most of the areas were closed in with six-foot fences, and from what she could see; the only exit was an opening on the south end.

'Damn, Jay-Boy was faster than a jackrabbit,' thought Garrett. As he closed the distance between them, out of nowhere, Vonda tackled Jay-Boy, taking him down hard, like an Offensive Linemen. He was impressed. He hadn't seen tackling like that since he played in school. In an attempt to escape, Jay-Boy hit Vonda in the face with the back of his head. What he would soon learn was a big mistake. Garrett watched as she forcefully placed her knee on his back while smashing his face against the concrete sidewalk. She twisted his arm behind his back and cuffed him. He screamed for Garrett to call off his 'bitch,' as he put it. He didn't like being cuffed, especially by a woman cop.

"Granite, get this girl pig bitch off me!"

"Who you calling a girl, you low life thug?" Vonda replied flipping him over to look him in the face. Garrett couldn't believe what he just witnessed. He thought he just may enjoy having her as a temporary partner. He asked as he helped lift their prisoner off the ground.

"Are you okay? That was quite a blow he delivered to your face." Noticing an old cut above her eye.

"Yeah, I'm all right. I've had worse."

Jay-Boy complained more as a crowd gathered, as they led him back to the car. He never learned when to keep his mouth shut. Garrett called for a patrol car to pick him up, and take him to the precinct.

"Granite man, look at my face. She smashed my face into the concrete. I can feel it burning. Take me to the hospital! I may need plastic surgery!" He rambled on.

"Jay-Boy, shut up. If you hadn't run, this wouldn't have happened." Garrett said as he leaned him against his car, and checked him for weapons.

"Granite what are you doing with the girl cop anyway? You supposed to be the lone ranger." Garrett looked over at Vonda, as she wiped at her forehead.

"Well, things change, and don't call me Granite," He stated, as he put him in his car. He walked to the back of the car, opening the trunk, then took out the first aid kit, and handed it to Vonda.

The patrol car arrived, and Garrett turned Jay-Boy over to them. Vonda was still fuming, as she helped put Jay-Boy in the patrol car. And by chance, he smashed his nose on the hood of the car. Hearing him scream out in pain, the officers looked at Vonda then to Garrett, shook their heads, and walked back to their vehicle. Now Jay-Boy may need to go to the hospital. Garrett was sure his nose was broken.

They arrived back at the station to begin their report. They were met by Lieutenant Manning, and he didn't look too happy.

"Hart, Bradley get in my office now!" Garrett looked at Vonda, and they both followed him. Before he could close the door, the Lieutenant was all over them. "Detective Hart what the hell happened today! I sent you on a routine ride-along, and now I have a suspect with the side of his face looking like it's been rubbed over a cheese grater, and a broken nose!" The Lieutenant opened his desk drawer, took out a bottle of aspirin, and downed two of the white tablets without water.

"Lieutenant let me explain..." Garrett said.

"No, you went into a drug hole, and jeopardized another detective's life with your bullshit heroics!" He screamed.

"Lieutenant." Vonda tried to interrupt.

"No Bradley. I knew it was a bad idea to send anyone out with this wild man."

"Lieutenant it wasn't all Detective Hart's fault. I was the one that ran down Jay-Boy and cuffed him. And...I may have injured his nose putting him in the cruiser." Vonda explained. Manning couldn't believe what he was hearing and looked from Vonda to Garrett. He threw his hands up in the air saying.

"Hell, now I have two gung-ho Rambo's on my hands!" He shouted. "Get out of my office the both of you. I want that report on my desk before you leave!" Both stood, exiting the room, as fast as they could. On the safe side of the door, Garrett looked at Vonda and said, "Welcome to the Sunshine State."

Chapter

Five

Calisa Hart moaned from the tight grip Lamar held on her arm. She hoped their conversation wouldn't come to this, but there was no getting passed it. She went to break off their year plus relationship face to face, but now she thought that it was a bad idea. She thought if he saw how serious she was, it may shake him enough into coming to grips, that he had a serious problem. That he would need to change his ways if they were going to continue their relationship. No way could she keep hiding the bruises from her parents, and her brother. Garrett would kill him for sure if he knew what was going on. Hell, he'll kill her for not telling him about it.

She loved Lamar, and if he loved her, as much as he said, why was he abusing her like this. He was smart enough to never hit her in the face. His punches usually were to her thighs and arms. It all came to ahead with the latest incident, it terrified her the most. He grabbed her around her neck, choking her enough to leave his fingers imprints on her skin.

"What do you mean it's over?" He yelled, as he forcefully gripped her around the back of her neck. "I'm the one who decides when it's over, and I'm not finished with you yet." He tried to run his free hand between her legs to claim what he said was his.

She pushed his hand away in an attempt to break his hold on her.

"Lamar let me go. I'll tell Garrett!" She screamed her warning. Her brother was known in the neighborhood for his, as they put it, John Wayne attitude, when you were on the wrong side of the law or him.

Lamar paused, "Garrett! Garrett! I'm not scared of your badass pig brother. You can tell him that I said it." He released his grip on her neck, pushing her to the ground. Lamar was lying. He was afraid of Garrett, as were most of the thugs in the neighborhood. They knew Garrett had a temper, and when it came to his baby sister, he would snap on a nigga in a heartbeat. Lamar had to think of something fast and pray she didn't keep her promise and go snitch to Garrett. "Look Calisa, see what you made me do," He said looking down at her. "You know just how to push my buttons, and make me do this kind of shit to you!" He held out his hand, to help her up from the ground. "You got to stop doing this to us baby," She took his hand and pulled herself up. "You know you'll all I got. I love you. I can't even think about what I'll do if I lose you." He leaned over, placing a gentle kiss on her cheek.

She looked into his eyes and knew he was lying to save face. And an ass whipping from her brother.

"Lamar, I can't take this anymore. You say you love me, but your actions say otherwise. It's over." She turned, walking away from him. She kept on guard, expecting him to retaliate.

Lamar's mind raced as to whether he should leave town, or just lay low. If she did go to Garrett, he was a dead man for sure.

"Calisa baby, let's talk about it! We can work this out! Come on!" He pleaded. Turning in circles, he rubbed his hands over his face when she didn't stop walking. "I'm a dead man," He said under his breath. He thought back on the warnings a few of his friends had given him when he first started messing with Calisa, now he wished he had listened.

Scared, Lamar returned to the abandoned factory where he and his crew hung out and waited. He knew it was only a matter of time before Garrett found him. He just hoped he wouldn't cause a scene in front of his boys, by beating him within an inch of his life. Maybe he could talk his way out of an ass whipping without looking like the coward that he was. He knew better than that. And from what he heard, when Garrett wanted you, he would move heaven and earth to find you, and wouldn't care who was around when he took you down. He looked around at his crew that had gathered tonight and knew they wouldn't help him.

Most were juvenile's, ages ranging from thirteen to sixteen. They acted like badasses, but the truth, most were just scared kids running from something or someone. They just wanted to belong to something or somebody.

Garrett didn't listen to many people other than his mother. If Garrett was looking for him, that meant he had seen those marks on Calisa's neck by now. Concerned, Lamar removed another beer from the cooler, this was his fourth and took a big swig to try to calm his nerves. He looked over his shoulder and thought better because Garret wouldn't sneak up on him. He would come at him head-on. He even thought of calling Calisa to try to talk her into calling off her brother.

"F him," He thought, pulling a baggie from his back pocket, removing one of the ten joints that he had rolled earlier. Lighting it, he drew in a deep breath and coughed from the smoke, which made a few members laugh. He gave them a stern look, and the laughter stopped, as fast as it started. Between the beers, and the joint, Lamar was beginning to feel mellow, and soon let his guard down, which would prove to be a mistake.

Chapter

Six

Calisa cautiously unlocked the door to her parent's house. She peered in, listening for any sounds that they may be still awake. The only sound that she could hear was the faint hum of the icemaker in the freezer. Quietly closing the door behind her, she stepped in the hallway leading to the stairs.

"Calisa, you're home early. Is everything all right? She asked as she stepped into view.

Calisa froze, surprised that anyone was still awake. She answered with her back to her mother, "Yes ma'am. Everything is fine; now go on back to bed. Goodnight."

Since her dad became sick, he was unable to climb up and down the stairs. They had temporarily converted the den into their bedroom. Which made it harder for her to sneak out of the house after hours. She was grown, and she shouldn't have to sneak around.

"Okay baby girl, I'll see you in the morning," Carol replied but could feel something was wrong. She moved from the foyer out of Calisa's sight, waited for her to round the corner, and turned on the light.

"Oh my God! Calisa what happened to your neck?" Carol didn't need an answer. Calisa's neck showed ominous signs of bruises, and her skirt was stained with dirt. It didn't take much for the bruises to show on her fair complexion. She knew Lamar had done this, and she expected he had been for some time now. She had seen the signs and tried to talk to her daughter about this before. But Calisa assured her that nothing was going on and, in other words, told her to butt out, plain and simple. "Baby did Lamar do this to you?" she asked in a whisper.

"What's wrong Carol? Is Lisa okay?" Charles called from the other room.

"Nothing honey. Everything is fine, go back to sleep," Carol said, and closed the French doors behind her. "Lisa, you talk to me right now. I want answers!" She demanded in a low tone.

"Momma, leave me alone. I'm tired and want to go to bed," were her last words, as she ran up the stairs to her bedroom. Carol didn't want to involve Garrett, but she didn't have a choice. She rushed to the kitchen to the phone mounted on the wall and punched in Garrett's number.

Garrett was glad to be home; it had been a long rough day. He opened the door and bent down to pick up his mail from the floor. Looking through it, he determined it was mostly junk as he walked to the kitchen, and placed it on the table. He took a carton of juice from the refrigerator, and took a swig, then put it back on the shelf when the phone rang.

"Garrett," he said into the receiver.

"Garrett, it's Mom. I need you. This has got to stop. Please hurry!" Carol said. He didn't ask any questions and hung up the receiver. He didn't need to when his family needed him. He rushed from the house, only stopping long enough to lock the door behind him.

Calisa cracked her bedroom door, listening to her mother talk with Garrett on the phone. The conversation was brief, which alerted her that he was on his way. She closed the door, cursed and sat on her bed thinking of a way to stop him from killing Lamar. Although she had threatened Lamar with telling Garrett about the abuse, she wouldn't have done it, she loved him. Garrett had a short fuse when it came to her. She thought back to how it was almost impossible for her to get a boyfriend, let alone a date. He managed in one way, or another to scare off every boy that showed interest in her. A few guys did try to hang in there for a while, but soon became tired of his intimidations and called it quits.

If it weren't for her best friend Glenda, she would have led a lonely life. She knew Glenda had a major crush on Garrett. That's why she hung around so much. But, it was all good because she and Glenda were much alike and enjoyed the same things. With the exception of her brother. At times, she couldn't stand Garrett and wished she was an only child. But, there were other times when she loved him to death for the same reason she hated him. Yes, he was overprotected, but he also loved her unconditionally. For example, when she wanted something, that was too expensive for her parents to afford, or thought wasn't worth the money. He would give her his allowance, or do odd jobs to buy it for her. Or how he took the blame for something she had done, just to keep her out of trouble, which she seemed to always involved. Nevertheless, she was grown now, and he needed to let her handle her own business. She had to warn Lamar that Garrett was looking for him, and convince him she hadn't told him anything.

Chapter

Seven

Garrett drove like a lunatic to his parents' home. The urgency in his mother's voice alarmed him, so he wasted no time getting there. His mind raced with questions about what was wrong. Could it be his father, had his health taken a turn for the worse, or maybe he had fallen? Then he remembered her saying that it had to stop, which meant it had to be Calisa. What had she gotten herself into now? Lis, which was how he referred to her, was twenty-five years old and needed to start making better decisions for herself. He knew much of how she acted was his fault. He had been overly protective of her, ever since he could remember. He should have let her fight her own battles, and get a taste of life without the sugar coating.

He reached for his phone and realized in his rush he forgotten it on the table. He couldn't call her to get more information. He would just have to wait until he got there to get the entire story. He just hoped his mother was being overly dramatic. He knew she wasn't that type of person. She was the coolest, calmest person he knew.

However, after the day he had with his new partner, things couldn't get any worse, he hoped. He had a partner, and of all things, a woman partner at that. What did Manning mean by no other Detective wanted to work with him? He couldn't help that they couldn't keep up, or have the balls to take the risk as he did. Taking risk was part of the job. That's why he loved it so much. Detective Bradley showed a little spunk today, and it surprised him how she tackled Jay-Boy like that. Now that impressed him, but he still didn't need a partner. Not even if she was, hot.

Calisa was pulling on her jacket to leave, when he abruptly opened the door, startling everyone. He looked at his mother for answers, and she nodded towards Calisa. His eyes followed her glance and saw what the problem was, and immediately his blood boiled.

"What the hell happened to your neck, Lis?" Garrett bellowed forgetting his mother was standing there.

"Granite, it's none of your business. Stay out of it. I can take care of this myself." Calisa stared directly at him. She knew how much he hated it when she called him that.

"No, no Garrett, she can't take care of this herself. You got to make this stop!" Carol cried, waving her hand towards Calisa.

"Who did this to you Calisa?" He asked as he stepped in front of his sister to block her from leaving. Carol interrupted and answered for her.

"You know who! That no good Lamar! He's hit my daughter for the last time!"

"You mean he's done this before?" He questioned, as he glanced from his mother to his sister. "Why the hell hadn't anyone let me know?" His temper had reached another notch higher. Not caring what he said at that point. All he wanted to do was get his hands around Lamar's neck.

"Because, Granite like I said, it's none of your business. It's not anybody's business! So go back to playing cop and leave me alone!" She demanded, pulling the collar of the jacket close to her neck. She knew her mother was right. Nevertheless, she had to do it her own way.

He threw his hand in the air repeating, "Playing Cop! Playing Cop! Oh, so you think I'm playing cop?" Garrett pounded his finger on his chest with rage, "Well I'll show you who's playing when I rip Lamar a new one!" He turned to leave the house and heard the warning his mother gave him.

"Garrett stop! Don't jeopardize your job over him. Just have a talk with him, and make sure he doesn't do this again." Seeing his rage, Carol was having second thoughts about getting Garrett involved. At the time, she didn't know what else to do, since her daughter refused to leave Lamar. She had seen and heard about too many women staying in a relationship, for one reason or another and ending up dead. Carol would die and go to hell before she let her daughter be subjected to such treatment. However, once Garrett is worked up about something, there was no stopping him. "Now, you promise me you won't do anything foolish."

"What! Look what he did to my sister. No man, and I mean no man, will ever put his hands on her or any other woman I know. He disrespected her and me!" He clenched his fists at his side.

"Carol, what's going on out there? Is Lis okay? Is that Garrett I'm hearing?" Carol looked to both of her children with tears in her eyes. She cleared her throat and answered her husband. "Yes, Charles. Calisa is alright, and Garrett just stopped by to check on things. Now go back to sleep. I'll be there in a moment." Carol motioned for them to move the conversation to the kitchen. She didn't want to worry him at this point. He was just starting to show signs of improvement from the new medication. She didn't want anything to set his recovery back.

Carol sat at the kitchen table, but her two stubborn children chose to stand. She could see Garrett getting angrier by the second, and Calisa was clamming up tighter than a clam in its shell. Which was the norm for them since children? Her two children were very different but more alike than they knew. Garret, on the other hand, would plead his case to the very end, when he got into trouble, which was often. When he was angry, his jaw would twitch, he balled his fists and held them close to his side, like now. There was no talking to neither of them when they were like this, and tonight was no exception.

"Lis, go to your room. I'll deal with you in the morning." Carol demanded in the calmest voice she could. "Garrett sit down. I need to talk to you." He opened his mouth to object, but saw the set expression on her face, and knew she didn't want to hear any backtalk. He pulled out a chair, sat down and watched Calisa storm out of the kitchen towards her room, without even a goodnight. Carol placed her hands on top of the table palms down, taking a deep breath, and watched her son fume.

"Garrett baby. I know I was the one that called you. And I should have dealt with this myself. But what you're thinking about doing will get you put in jail, lose your job or both." She paused and noticed the tension in his shoulder relax just a fraction.

"Mom I don't know what you're talking about. I'm not going to hurt him - much." With a straight face, Garrett placed his clenched fists on the table.

"Child don't lie to me!" She raised her voice, then remembered Charles was in the other room and lowered it a bit. "I know how you feel about your sister, your family, but what you're thinking of doing to him isn't right. Not even for him. Now I suggest you go home, cool off, and tackle this in the morning." She took his clenched fists in her gentle hands and opened them. She brought them to her lips and kissed the palms. He loved his mother and would do anything she asked, but Lamar had it coming to him, tonight.

"Yes, ma'am. I'll go home, but I won't forget this." He stood and leaned over and kissed her on the cheek and left the house.

Chapter

Eight

Garrett combed the neighborhood looking for Lamar. Yeah, he promised his mother that he would go home, and he would, but not before, he beat Lamar within an inch of his life. He knew these streets like the back of his hands and had a good idea where Lamar's slimy butt may be hiding. Lamar had put his hands on his baby sister, or anyone else for the last time. He thought he would first break his fingers, then maybe an arm or both. Decisions. Decisions. He'll just have to play it by ear, once he catches him.

Garrett's years as a street cop had taught him well. However, as a Detective, when needed, he lived by a code of his own, and it was definitely needed now. Calisa had grown into a lovely young woman, but in his opinion, she has been choosing the wrong men. Recently, he tried to stay out of her personal life, but when it came to this, he had to draw the line. Her life was his to protect as a man, a detective and as her big brother.

Since high school, Garrett Hart was also known as Granite, depending on who you were. The women might say it was because of his rock-hard body, which he worked on religiously. However, if you asked some of his fellow detectives or anyone on the opposite side of the law, they would say it was because he was hardcore when it came to justice. Calisa was the only person in his family that called him Granite, just to get on his last nerves. Carol Hart in his eyes was the greatest mother of all mothers and his angel here on earth. He loved her more than life itself and would move heaven and earth to do anything that she asked. Garrett always looked up to his father as long as he could remember. Charles Hart worked two jobs to make sure his family had everything they needed. His parents made sure their children stayed on the right side of the law and received a paid college education. In their house, there were no other options than college, and now he thanked them for it. They raised their children to be respectable, honest, leaders and to think for themselves. Right now, Garrett was thinking how he was going to break every bone in Lamar's body.

Turning off the headlights of his Mustang GT, he pulled off the highway onto a gravel road. He stopped near the old abandoned factory on the south side of the city. When the plant closed, hundreds of people, men, and women lost their jobs and had to relocate to other cities just to provide for their families. The city never seemed to recover after that. With the prospect of a new automobile factory moving their overseas branch back to the states; Florida was in the top five states bidding for the contract.

This building was used as a hangout for delinquent teens, as well as a shelter for some homeless people in the city. Before his father became ill, he would bring hot meals on Sunday to whomever he could find out here. Garrett accompanied him a few times but lately hadn't found the time.

He shifted the car into park, quietly opened the driver's side door, and slightly closed it behind him. Walking closer to the building, he stopped behind some old empty steel oil drums, to get a better look at who was inside. He could see Lamar's old beat-up Ford through the opened rusted tin doors to the building. He spotted him in the middle of a group of people, with a beer bottle in one hand and a joint in the other. Garrett jaws tighten at the sight of him standing there so cocky as if he didn't have a care in the world.

Lamar liked hanging with the teen crowd. It made him feel like a big shot, and that he was in charge of everything, but in actuality, he wasn't in charge of nothing, including himself. He was a negative influence on them in the worst way. Lamar came from an abusive home. He heard he had taken care of himself from an early age. His father was doing ten years to life, in the Florida Correctional system for armed robbery, under the third strike law. His mother moved to Georgia with his sister, but he refused to go with them. It was ironic that he also had a younger sister. How would he feel, if some dude treated her the way he did Calisa? He would just have to remind him of that while he was whipping his ass. Garrett noticed him hugged up with a girl that couldn't be any older than seventeen or eighteen. In Garrett's eyes that made him a child molester. He sized up the group and knew once he took out Lamar; the others would scatter like rats. He had been after the city to tear down this section of the abandoned factory for safety reasons alone, but with all the bureaucratic bull, it may take years before that happens. He made his way back to his car, and slipped behind the wheel, closed the door and secured his seat belt.

Tightening his grip on the steering wheel, he contemplated whether to take his mother's advice, go home, and cool off before he confronted Lamar. He was never one to take good advice. He floored the gas pedal, and the GT's engine roared to life, taking off in the direction of the entrance of the building. He wanted to catch Lamar off guard and waited to turn on the head lights high beams at the precise moment. The lights flooded the area, blinding Lamar for a second, giving Garrett the advantage he needed. He swerved the car a few feet from where Lamar stood frozen. As he jerked the car into park, he opened his door, jumped out, and grabbed Lamar by the back of his coat as he tried to run. Everyone ran terrified, seeing Granite collar their leader. Blinded by rage, Garrett had the urge to kill him on the spot.

Slamming Lamar to the ground, Garrett stood over him and yelled. "Lamar, you must have lost your ever-loving mind putting your hands on my sister!"

"Granite man, I didn't touch her! I swear!" He tried to explain while fending off the blows from Garrett's pounding fist.

"Are you calling my sister a liar?" Landing another blow to his already bleeding face, he asked.

"No! I mean yes! It wasn't me Granite I swear!" Confused, Lamar wasn't sure what to say. He just wanted him to stop hitting him.

Grabbing him by the front of his coat, Garrett yanked him to his feet. Lamar was dazed, and could hardly stand, but Garrett held him up with one hand.

"You're doing a little too much swearing if you ask me!" He delivered a solid blow to his midsection lifting him off the ground. The punch to his stomach caused Lamar to vomit the beer he had drunk, then he let out an excruciating scream, followed by more vomiting. Garrett stepped to the side, to avoid getting any on him. He dragged Lamar over to his car and slammed him against the hood. Garrett looked at his car hood, noticed the dent, and got madder if it was possible. The muscles in his arms strained against the fabric of his shirt, stretching the material to its fullest. A few teens hung around but looked on from a distance. They didn't dare try to stop him or get involved in fear that he would do the same to them. He angrily stared down into Lamar's bruised face, promising through clenched teeth. "After I'm finished with you, you'll never lay another hand on my sister or any other woman again."

"Man stop! You're a cop! You can't do this! I'll report your ass to your captain!" Lamar threatened.

"Well, let me give you something to tell him. But I don't think he will believe you, with me being an upstanding member of law enforcement and all." Garrett assured him and landed another punch to his ribs. "Now I strongly suggest that you keep this little conflict between us or ..."

Terrified, Lamar screamed for his life, "HELP! HELP! Somebody, please help me!"

"Was that how my sister screamed for help? Was that how she begged for you to stop hitting her those other times?" Garrett stretched out Lamar's hand and held him secure around his neck with his other and asked. "Is this the hand you hit Calisa with?"

"Granite man, I'm sorry!" Lamar cried, "It'll never happen again!"

"You damn right it will never happen again," Garrett slammed Lamar's hand in the door of his Mustang. Lamar's screams could be heard throughout the abandoned factory, echoing out into the night. Silence followed as he fell to the ground. Garrett stood over his lifeless body. No, he wasn't dead, he just fainted. He wanted to beat him some more, but remembered his mother's warning, and left him where he laid. He got into his car and drove away.

Garrett returned to his parent's home a few hours later after he had cooled down. He advised her and Calisa that Lamar would never hit her again. Calisa was outraged that once again, he took matters into his own hands. She stormed off, vowing never to speak to him again. She ran up the stairs to her room and slammed the door. Carol looked at him upset, that he had disobeyed her and went after Lamar. She only had one question, if Lamar was dead or alive. Garrett assured her he was alive, barely, but he was alive. He left them a little after midnight and headed home. He didn't realize how tense he was until his body ached, as he climbed the steps to his South Tampa Brownstone apartment. Once inside, he dropped his jacket to the foyer floor and went to the downstairs bathroom. Washing the blood stains off his hands, he applied some antibiotic cream to his knuckles, then wrapped a bandage around it. With his scrapes tended to, he had calmed down enough to realize he hadn't eaten since lunch. Not sure if he was hungrier, than he was tired, but went to the kitchen. He opened the refrigerator he saw several Styrofoam containers of leftover from the past weeks. He decided he wasn't hungry, but grabbed an apple from the bowl, then went upstairs to his bedroom.

He purchased the brownstone over a year ago but hadn't done much to furnish it. He took the old dining table and chairs from his parents' storage unit outside in the back yard of their house. His mother kept it with an assortment of furniture to use for holidays, and other occasions. He promised to return it to them, as soon as he got around to buying one of his own, which was six months ago. He liked his privacy, and solitude most of the time after a long day at work. He did manage to buy two oversized chairs for the living room, for the occasional guest that he did invite. However, in his bedroom, you would have thought you stepped into the showroom of an interior designer store.

74

His wooden dark four-post California, king size bed, was positioned in front of an accented wall, painted in dark purple with light specks of gold blended throughout. The chocolate brown comforter with purple linen adorned the bed, and accessories pillows flanked the head of the board and carried throughout the room. Across from the bed, was a gas fireplace with a 54" HD-3D TV mounted over it. This place definitely oozed sensuality at its best. He loved women and was a romantic at heart. Moreover, he enjoyed pleasing them in the bed, and he was good at it. When he had the time for female companionship or deemed her special enough to bring to his home, he knew the right atmosphere, added up to a night of pleasure. A roaring fire, scented candles, the perfect music, a great bottle of wine, and him, was the perfect combination for romance. However, tonight it was only himself, an empty bed, and hopefully a good night's sleep.

He showered, put on his pajamas pants, and re-wrapped his injured hand then left the bathroom. He looked at the clock, "Damn," he cursed, one o'clock, four hours until he had to be up for work. Well, he had worked on less sleep. He turned on the stereo, lowered the volume, climbing into bed. He laid on his back, looking up at the ceiling and waited for sleep to come. He thought of his sister and had a gut feeling this wasn't over. Sleep took over his weary body, as his mind wandered to Vonda Bradley. He liked her. She had spunk and heart; something he hadn't anticipated. She was a very attractive woman, if only she got rid of that chip on her shoulder. She was a perfect size, as far as women went, not too thick, but plenty in the right places. Her firm body, down to her small waist, and from what he could see, she had a nice butt. And the D's on her chest was perfect. He was getting a hard-on thinking about her. His hand automatically reached down to adjust his shaft pressing against his silk pajamas pants. His eyes slowly drifted closed, his breathing slowed, and within minutes, he was fast asleep.

Chapter

Nine

Garrett awakened bone tired, and a hell of a hard-on. He hadn't gotten much sleep and what he did get, was restless. He still wanted to kill Lamar and shake some sense into his sister for allowing this to go on for so long. He couldn't figure people out sometimes but thought he knew his sister better. He wondered how they would let someone abuse them physically, or mentally and justify it as love. That's one reason why he never got into a serious relationship. He didn't have time to devote into one, and he wouldn't want to put someone he loved through wondering if he would come home at night. He watched how it worried his mother when his father left for work every day. Or when the phone rang, and she would be too scared to answer, thinking it was the hospital or someone calling to give her the bad news. Nevertheless, that was the career he chose long before he married. She understood what she was getting herself into when she married him. She had to accept him, as well as the badge, and she understood. That wasn't the life he wanted for his family. He decided a life of love from his family was all he needed, and the occasional sex from a woman of his choosing when he needed it.

He showered to cool down the hard-on he woken with. His thoughts returned to Vonda, how she handled him, and the situation with Jay-Boy. He rubbed his palm across his shaft, releasing a muffled moan from his throat. He jerked his hand away, turning off the hot water, letting the cold-water spray over him, bringing him back to his senses. He finished his shower, then wrapped a towel around his waist and draped another over his shoulders to dry his body. He padded barefoot down the stairs to the kitchen. He blended up an energy smoothie from freshly washed strawberries, blueberries, banana, and a scoop of energy powder and milk. He watched the mixture blend then poured it into a tall glass, and took it back upstairs to drink while he dressed.

Dressed, he left for the garage behind his house, opened the automatic door, got into his car and headed for the office.

He temporarily forgot about Vonda Bradley until he spotted her sitting across from his desk. She dressed similar as yesterday, but it didn't diminish the beauty he saw in her. He thought if she wore her hair loose around her face, she would be quite sexy. She also needed to remove that scowl, it wasn't becoming at all. In fact, the only time yesterday she showed a slight hint of a smile, was when she tackled Jay-Boy and handcuffed him. He wondered what her story was, and why she transferred to Tampa. Don't get him wrong Tampa was a great city but wasn't one of the top locations to work right now. Companies were closing down all over the city, and if you were lucky to find a job, the pay was lousy. Because of the lack of jobs, crime was on the rise. He was hoping the city's situation would turn around for the best, with the proposal for a new transit rail system. With this new Governor-elected, the word was he didn't want the transportation system, and would reject the money the government offered.

"Good morning, Detective Bradley," Garrett said, as he pulled out his chair and sat.

"Morning," Vonda replied, without looking up, and continued looking through the apps on her phone. He looked over at her and thought it was too early to be acting like a butthole. His desk phone rang, and he answered it. The voice on the other end was the Lieutenant advising him of a shootout and needed him and Detective Bradley to go lend a hand to the crime scene.

After a moment on the phone, he looked over at her and said, "Let's go. I'll fill you in on the case in the car." He stood, and headed for the door, not taking the time to look back to see if she was following.

Vonda followed behind him, and couldn't help noticing how firm his pants fit his smack um'licious ass. Her thoughts went to his high school photo, and she unconsciously licked her lips. She averted her eyes, to see if anyone caught her, then picked up her pace to walk beside him.

He filled her in on the case in the car. A couple of drug dealers had a shootout over territory, leaving two of their members' dead. Jobs may have been on the decline, but the drug trade business was on the rise more every day. Though it was two drug dealers killed, the case still had to be investigated, because they were someone's family member, a son, or brother, it didn't

80

matter. It was a life cut short, and they needed to find out the whys, and who's, like any other case. After the photos had been taken, and the evidence bagged, sheets had been placed over the bodies in respect of the family at the scene. Word spread fast and, at least, two dozen or more people gathered around to watch. One of the bodies was of a 16-year-old boy. Garrett thought it was sad, that a life so young was lost to the streets. He scanned the crowd and thought, where was this young boy's mother and dreaded having to be the one to deliver the bad news of her son's death. Garrett spoke with one the officers and got as much information as he could before he talked to a few onlookers.

Vonda watched the crowd and noticed one young boy standing in the back, nervously pacing back and forth. She walked in his direction, and before she reached him, he took off running. She yelled to Garrett and took off after him. Garrett turned in the direction Vonda's voice came from and caught a glimpse of her running after someone. He didn't give it a second thought and took off through the crowd after her. Vonda was surprised to see the boy stop and turn to face her after they were some distance from the group. She pulled her gun from her holster and thought he was going to pull a gun on her. Instead, he put his hands in the air and fell to his knees. She kept her gun pointed at him demanding he lay on the ground with his hands behind his head. She holstered her weapon and cuffed him. Garrett arrived as she proceeded to pat him down then pulled him to his feet.

"Now, why did you run boy?" She asked catching her breath.

"That is my cousin lying on the ground. I saw who did it," He whispered looking around to see if anyone was listening.

Garrett slowed as he approached them, "Speed, what's the matter with you? Detective Bradley could have shot you boy," Garrett asked, pulling him off to the side. Speed lived in the area and had been living on and off these streets since he was 9 years old, but now lived back with his mother, brothers, and sisters. Vonda watched the two and wondered what the deal was with them. Garrett reached in his pocket for his handcuff key and unlocked the cuffs.

"Hey what the hell are you doing?" She protested.

"I'm letting him go. What does it look like?" He replied. "Now you go on and call me later and tell me what you know. You still have my number?" He asked.

"Yes sir," Speed answered. The wide-eyed kid looked around to make sure no one was looking. Garrett reached in his back pocket, removed two twenty-dollar bills from his wallet, and handed it to him.

"Now take this and get you and your family something to eat," Garrett said. "And go home after you leave the store," Garrett added as Vonda watched confused.

"Okay, Okay Granite," He said as he ran off. Vonda followed Garrett back to the crime scene.

"I'm sure at some point you will explain what is going on?" She asked.

"Yes, but for now, make it look like the kid out ran you," He asked. Vonda stood with her hands on her hips and said loud enough for a few people to hear.

"Man, that kid is fast. I didn't even get a good look at him." Then she turned to the crowd and asked, "Does anyone know who that kid was?" The only response she got was a few outbursts of laughter. They went back to work and obtained as much information as they could, but it looked like if Speed didn't have any substantial information this was going to be just another cold case.

They left the crime scene and returned to the office, but before they could start on the paperwork, they were sent out on another homicide case. Was there a full moon tonight? Two homicides and it wasn't one o'clock yet. There were other officers at the scene handling the case. They were mainly there to get her familiar with how things worked. They hadn't slowed down, not even for lunch and her stomach was complaining. Garrett must have read her mind, suggesting they stop and grab a bite on the way back.

Vonda looked at her bowl of chili and thought it looked a lot like the last crime scene. She pushed it aside and opted to eat her fries instead. Garrett noticed what she did and commented.

"Stomach not up for this?"

"There's nothing wrong with my stomach. Thank you very much." She sarcastically replied.

He held up his hand in defenses, "Hey no offense. I know some men that can't handle this stuff."

"What are you saying Hart, that because I'm a woman, I can't stomach this?" She was getting angrier by the minute.

"No, what I'm saying is you have to be a special kind of person to work homicide. It takes a lot to see what we see every day and not go crazy. That's all I'm saying." He commented. He studied Vonda for a moment and asked. "What division did you work in New York?"

"Mostly missing person cases for the first year, and then some drug-related cases," She replied.

"Well, to let you in on a little secret." He looked from side to side then added, "It still gets to me sometimes," He said with a smile, which for some reason mellowed her mood. For the first time, she noticed the gauze bandage on his hand and a few scrapes on his knuckles on the other.

"What happened to your fist?" She asked as she placed his bandaged hand in hers. Surprised by her concern, but he didn't want to involve her in his personal business.

"I had a run-in with a punching bag, and it won." He smiled a smiled that sent chills through her body. She shook slightly then released his hand, and went back to eating her fries then asked.

"You box?"

"Only in the gym. It helps keep me in shape," Garrett replied doing a one-two punch in the air. "How about you?"

"No, I don't box. I used to go to my gym on the regular to work out. But I haven't had time to find a gym I like here." His eyes rolled over her upper body and thought he would like to work her out, but said.

"The department has a gym located near the station. You can use it anytime you like. It's available 24-hours, but I go late at night when it's not crowded. That way I can use all the machines without having to wait."

"Thanks for the info. I may do just that." She replied and added a small smile as thanks.

****

The remainder of the day went quickly, and Vonda thanked the heavens above to be home. This was only her second day, and it felt like she had been there for months. She opened her apartment door and was greeted with more unpacked boxes. She closed the door in disgust, then dropped her key on top of the nearest crate. Her shoes felt like led on her feet. She couldn't wait to kick them off and jump into the shower. She wasn't sure if it was the Florida heat that was getting to her, or working so close to Garrett. Either way, her hormones were racing, and if she didn't get this monkey off her back, she might just have to get stronger batteries for her friend. Just thinking about him, caused the heat to rise. It has been too long since she had sex. That's one thing she missed about Jerrod. The sex was out of this world.

Entering her bedroom, she walked to the closet to lock away her guns after she removed the clip. She removed her clothes, and headed for the shower to wash away today's grime, and calm the sexual need rising within her.

Another night sitting in front of the TV, trying to clear her head of the gruesome sights she witnessed at the last crime scenes. Lord, she couldn't wait for a spot to come open in another city. Maybe she should give them a call to let them know, that she was interested in a position in their Missing Person Unit. Anything except homicide, at this point. Garrett was right; she wasn't cut out for this kind of work, and it pissed her off. She opened her laptop, and composed a short email to each HR department and prayed for a quick answer.

Afterward, she browsed through her emails and deleted the junk mail. She then checked her bank balance out of habit. She had more than enough money to cover her expenses. A bing tone alerted her that she had a new email. It had to be a mistake or some prank. She had received several emails from her ex-husband. She hadn't seen or spoken to him for over a year. Her first thought was f-him, and delete them. But being the detective that she was, her curiosity got the best of her. She clicked the date order button to read the oldest first.

"Vonda, I know I'm the last person you want to hear from, but I really need to talk to you. Please call me. My number is still the same." Fat chance, she thought and deleted it. The second message was much like the first, and she deleted it. However, the third email caught her off guard.

"Vonda, I know I was wrong for what I did to you, and I'm terribly sorry. I really miss you. I really miss us. I made a mistake, and for the record, that was the first time, I had ever cheated on you. Please call me. I really want to talk to you. Still loving you as much as I did the day, we married. Love Jerrod,"

She sat back, looking out into space. After a moment, she bursts out into laughter. Tears formed in her eyes and rolled down her cheeks. The laughter soon turned to a hurtful heartfelt cry. She composed herself, and read the email once more to make sure she hadn't read it wrong. She took a deep breath, hit the reply icon. Pausing, she placed her fingers on the keys, typing in big bold letters. FUCK YOU! Then clicked the send button. Powering down her laptop she went to bed feeling a little better.

88

Chapter

Ten

Vonda thought she really needed this workout as she entered the gym. She was getting a little flabby around the middle. Their gym was nice, but she didn't feel comfortable working out with a room full of testosterone. Her New York gym was for women only, and she missed that. All the equipment and exercise programs were geared for a woman. Even the instructors were all woman, which made it easier to convey what your body was going through. The first time she went to work out, the gym was packed. When she walked in, all eyes turned their attention to her, which made her very uncomfortable. She ignored their prying eyes while finding an available treadmill. She put her earplugs in and then started the machine. She was up to a good speed when out of nowhere appeared a well-built man. She removed one earpiece but didn't stop her run saying, "Yes."

He smiled and introduced himself, but for the life of her, she couldn't remember his name. He proceeded to make small talk until she finally had to point out that she was trying to work out. Asking if this conversation could wait until another time. That seemed to put him off that she wouldn't stop what she was doing to talk to him. She watched his reflection in the mirror as he walked away. By the expression on his face, she guessed a woman had never put him off before. He didn't take the rejection very well. She must have looked desperate, or helpless because more than a few men asked if she needed help. She wasn't sure, if they were being nice, or if this was another come-on. After about an hour of interruptions, she gave up on her workout and went home.

She returned to the gym the following week. This time, she waited until later in the evening to avoid everyone. She liked working out alone, just her and her music. She was nearly out of breath after completing her six-mile jog on the treadmill. She wiped the sweat off her face, then threw the towel over her shoulder. She did another twenty minutes on the elliptical trainer and was ready to hit the dumbbells and weights. She grabbed her bottle of water, heading to the weight room. She wasn't surprised to see it empty on a Friday night. She suspected many of the off-duty officers were spending time with their families, or that special person. Which she had neither. Vonda removed two ten pound dumbbells from the rack and stood in front of the wall to wall mirrors. Studying her reflection, she began five sets of twelve repetitions of arm curls. The burning of her muscles reminded her that she had neglected them for far too long. It was vital that she maintain her upper body strength in her job. Most of the criminals she encountered had the upper hand, just being a man. So, strengthening her upper body helped in subduing them. In the middle of her final stretching routine, she heard the door buzzer sound, alerting her that someone had come in.

Garrett was glad there was only one car in the lot. He would practically have the gym to himself. He looked forward to getting a good workout in the weight room. He needed to release the added tension that had built up over the week. Afterward, he hoped to get a good night's sleep. He had converted a section of his garage into a small gym. Nevertheless, he loved to use the big weights and equipment at the gym to keep his body in shape, and arms tight.

He entered the weight room, and almost dropped his gym bag. He got the full view of Vonda with her head down, legs spread; butt high in the air and holding her ankles. He instantly became aware of the erection growing beneath his sweatpants. He bit down on his trigger finger to stifle the curse word that almost escapes his mouth, '*Damn!*' He averted his gaze, clearing his throat, to alert her that he was behind her.

From Vonda's position, she could see every muscular inch of him. Granite. Man did that nickname fit. He was a sight to behold. Standing there in a white undershirt that stretched from the size of his chest, gray sweatpants that showed the print of a semi-arousal. She straightened, looked over her shoulder, and managed to say, "Hey."

Garrett found his voice, replying, "Evening - I didn't mean to disturb your -stretching. I won't bother you. I'm just here to work out," He strode towards the weight racks, trying to get her bent over image out of his head. He removed two thirty-pound dumbbells from the rack, and position himself in front of the mirrors.

She watched as he easily raised them to his chest repeatedly. She gazed as the muscles in his arms expanded to their fullest under the strain, then relaxed, as he lowered his arms. She noticed his tattoo on his right arm, 'Hard as Granite.' She blew out a shaky breath, thinking *"Ain't that the truth."*

He noticed her watching him, and smiled when they made eye contact. She saw the smirk on his face and knew he had caught her staring. To avert her thoughts elsewhere, she asked.

"How long have you been lifting?" She asked glancing up in his direction.

"Since high school, I guess," He answered without missing a rep.

"I started about five years ago but stopped. This is the first time I've been back at it in over a year." She felt the need to explain.

"Don't look like you took a break at all. You look good."

"Thanks, but I'm having a hard time getting my abs back tight." She lifted her shirt a little without thinking to show him. Then realized what she had done when she saw the heat ignite in his eyes. He held her gaze in the mirror and stopped his set.

"Your abs look good to me. Besides, I – I mean," He couldn't get his words straight. "Most men don't want their woman as hard as them. I prefer my women soft and cuddly." *'TMI'* He thought and decided to be quiet.

"Well, I like my body a certain way, and I'm going to keep at it until I achieve just that."

Garrett returned the dumbbells to the rack, then walked up behind her and gently lifted her arm.

"See, look at your upper arms," He said, running a lingering finger across her skin. "You have just the right amount of definition for a woman." Her knees weaken from the heat of his touched. Their eyes locked, and the sexual charge couldn't be denied. They both felt it. He studied her face. Her lips were full, and her eyes burned with passion. Garrett took a step back before he did the unthinkable. Kissed his partner. A faint scent of vanilla lingered on her, arousing him even more.

She watched a drop of perspiration rolled down the side of his face, landing on his chest. His lips moved, but she didn't hear a word he said. Her mouth slightly parted, slowly licking her lips, tempted to taste his mouth on hers.

"Detective, you feel like spotting me?" He asked, and waited for her reply then continued, "It won't take long. I promise." He added with a smile. That smile probably had gotten him his way all his life, and tonight was no exception.

She cleared her throat, managing to ask, "Okay, where do you want me?"

For a moment, Garrett mind flashed to the image of her bending over, touching her toes, while he drove his shaft deep into her from behind. Instead, he directed her over to the bench to the far left. He placed two one-hundred-pound weights on the bar and locked them in place. He laid on the bench beneath the bar, and she took her position at his head. He had a bird's eye view of her breasts looming over his face. It took all he had, not to lean up, take the cloth covered nipple in his mouth, and sucked it to ripeness. He exhaled, closed his eyes, gripped the bar tightly, then lifted it from the stand. Lowering it to his chest and back up again several times. He opened his eyes and lost his concentration when he looked up between Vonda's legs spread apart. Her spandex short clung to her, showing her shapely body. The thought of her hips straddled across his face, tasting her made him lose his grip, and practically drop the weights.

Vonda quickly grabbed the bar and helped him lift it back in place. He sat up and thanked her as he worked his arms from side to side.

"It's a good thing I was here. You could have seriously injured yourself." Making light of the situation, she teased, "I wouldn't want to train a new partner. You know how hard it was getting you to work with me." She laughed. He laughed at her attempt at humor. It was the first time she had laughed, or attempted to make a joke since they started working together. She had a beautiful smile, and he hoped to see it more often.

"Hey, that would have been a task. I don't think none of the other detectives could handle you." Garrett jokingly replied.

"Who said you can handle me, Mr. Hard as Granite?" She said referring to his tattoo. He looked at his arm and laughed.

"Yeah, I thought it was a good idea at the time."

"Well, I think it's cool. It fits." Vonda wasn't sure why she said that, but it was too late to take it back. His demeanor changed as he looked up at her.

"You think I'm hard?" He asked.

"Sure, look at your body. It couldn't get any harder or fit." She answered, but she knew the real meaning of the tattoo.

"Yeah, I guess you're right." He smiled, and flexed his muscles, making them both laugh again. Vonda was beginning to feel uncomfortable. She looked at her watch, announcing that she should be getting home.

"I'll walk you to your car." Garrett volunteered without a second thought.

"No that's okay. I can make it by myself." She protested, needing to put some space between them.

"Now what would my mother think, if she heard that I let a lady walk to her car by herself at this hour of the night." He stood twisting at the waist from side to side.

"She would think, that you finally met a woman that can take care of herself." Vonda gave him the stare.

"I'm sure you can." His gaze scanned down her body. "But I wasn't raised that way. So, after you detective," He motioned for her to lead the way.

Standing between their cars, he asked if she needed him to follow her home and, of course, she declined. He noticed she was still driving a rental car.

"This car has to be costing you a bundle." He asked.

"You got that right, but I don't want to invest in a car right now. I'll be relocating again, hopefully soon, and I don't want to have to take the car with me, or go through the trouble of selling it." Garrett was a little surprised to hear that, and it showed on his face.

"You didn't know that this is a temporary assignment. Until one of the stations I requested comes through." Vonda thought she saw a glimpse of disappointment on his face but pushed it aside.

"Well, if you like, I can recommend a place where you can get a good reasonable priced car - until your new assignment comes through."

"Thanks. I'll think it over and let you know." The air became thick with silence until she spoke, "Well, thanks again and I'll see you Monday."

"Maybe we can work out again soon. You can come over to my place. I have a small gym in my garage, but it does the job." Garrett offered.

"Look, Hart, I'm not sure it's a good idea and -," She was trying to find the right words.

"Hey, I'm not trying to seduce you or anything. I just knew you don't have any family here." Garrett took a deep breath, "I was attempting to be nice." He straightened, tapped the hood of the car, then walked away. He opened his car door, but before he could get in, Vonda blew her horn to get his attention. He looked over his hood in her direction but didn't speak.

"What are you doing tomorrow?"

"Not much just hanging with my folks. Why?"

"How about we go jogging in the morning?" She asked. She'd been in Tampa for six months. She was getting a little tired of sitting at home and doing things by herself.

"I can pick you up." He offered.

"How about I meet you at the station? And we can go from there." She replied. He smiled and drove off.

Garrett stopped by his parents' house to check on his dad. His recovery was going well, and they had moved back to their bedroom upstairs. When his dad had his heart attack, Garrett was devastated. He couldn't imagine living without him. Charles Hart raised Garrett to be the man he was today. He taught him to be respectful, honorable, and have self-worth. He emphasized those were the key things to life, and he stood by them.

Garrett dreaded going to the house. Lis was still mad at him for beating up on Lamar and wasn't speaking to him. She even refused to be in the same room with him. Which hurt, he loved his sister, and they were close growing up. His mother assured him that she would eventually come around. That was six months ago.

He opened the front door, calling out, announcing his entrance. His mother answered, directing him to the kitchen. He passed Calisa in the hall. He spoke to her, but she gave him the evil eye and continued on her way.

"Hey, my peoples," He greeted. "I see Lis is still not talking to me," He said as he gave his mother a kiss on the cheek, and hugged his father playfully.

"You know how stubborn she can be, baby. She'll soon come around." Carol replied.

"What are you two still doing up? It's almost eleven o'clock." Garrett asked.

"I should be asking you the same thing. Why are you here and not out on a date? I'm sure there's some lucky lady that would enjoy your company." Charles asked, taking a bite of his pie from his fork. Garrett laughed, at his parents for assuming he was some type of player.

"Whew! Carol teased as she fanned her hand in front of her face. "I think you better go home and take a bath first."

"Hey, I just came from working out at the gym, for your information."

"Baby, I have told you about going to that gym by yourself. You could get hurt." Carol complained.

"I wasn't by myself, mother dear, my new partner was there too," He leaned against the counter.

"How is that working out having a partner?" Charles asked, continuing eating his pie.

"It's okay, just taking some getting used to." Shrugging his shoulders, "So far, no problems." Garrett hadn't told them his partner was a woman and planned to keep it that way for as long as he could. "Enough questions, can a brother get a slice of that apple pie? If it's not too much trouble, and a scoop of ice cream, too?" He pulled out a chair and sat at the table.

Calisa nearly slammed her bedroom door. She refused to be in the same room with Granite for what he did to Lamar. Lamar was wrong, there was no doubt about it, but Garrett went a little too far. He broke Lamar's nose, two of his fingers, and that cut over his eye may never heal completely. She laid on her bed when her cell phone rang. It was her girl, Glenda.

"Hey Glenda," she answered cheerfully. "Where have you been?"

"Hi Calisa," she replied, "I don't have long to talk, just want to hear a friendly voice before I called it a night." Calisa could hear the strained tone in her voice. That worried her. They had been friends for what seemed like forever. She felt something was wrong, she sat up giving Glenda her full attention.

"What's wrong Sis?" They referred to each other as Sis, from time to time as a show of affection and love. "Is there something wrong with the kids; where are they?"

"No, the kids are great. I put them to bed an hour ago. I'm just tired, that's all." Glenda was tired, also hurting from the black eye Derek had given her, for not having washed his favorite shirt he wanted to wear out. "Just got a lot on my plate right now with the house, the kids, Derek and keeping my travel agency from going under. I'm just beat." Glenda sighed.

"Well, Sis if anyone can make it work, you can. If you need help with those kids, let me know. I'm more than willing to take them off your hands for a few hours. Maybe when your business picks back up, a girl can get a discount." Calisa replied, trying to offer her support.

"Thanks, girl I may just take you up on that." There was a moment of silence on the line when she asked. "How's that brother of yours; he still on the force?"

"I guess he's okay. I'm not talking to him right now." Calisa answered.

"What did he do now?" Glenda asked, with a slight humor in her voice.

"Just being Granite. Putting his nose where it doesn't belong - again."

"I remember how that was. Just be glad you have someone to look after you like he does."

"You are just saying that because you still have a big crush on him." She laughed, remembering how Glenda used to look dreamy-eyed at him.

"That may be true then. I love my Derek. Thank- you- very-much." She teased, feeling a little better after talking to her friend. "Girl, let me go. I have so much to do tonight. Hey, when you're back talking to Garrett, tell him I said hey."

"Well, you may be waiting a long time on that one." She huffed. "Take it easy, and I meant what I said. Call me if you need me." Calisa replied with sincerity.

"I sure will Lis. Love you. Goodnight."

Glenda hung up the phone, then walked to the mirror in her bedroom. Examining the black and blue bruise on her face. She wished she had never married Derek. In spite of his nickname, Garrett would have never laid a hand on her. Other than to show her love. He always treated her nice back then. She examined her reflection in the mirror, she wasn't a girl anymore. She thought maybe it was time that she showed him how she really felt about him. She would have to be smart going about it. She couldn't dare let Derek find out. He would kill her for sure.

It was settled, she would plan to work her way back into Garrett's life, and have him get Derek out of hers. A smile creased her lips. She flinched at the pain. Looking at her reflection again, she gently touched her face, signing then left the room to clean up the mess Derek had made before he left to party with his boys.

Chapter

Eleven

Vonda and Garrett met as planned. They jogged through the downtown area, along the Hillsborough River, the Starz Center, and back to the station where they began. She hadn't jogged in a while and was feeling the pain in her legs. She refused to stop if Garrett didn't.

Garrett, on the other hand, kept a steady pace by her side. He couldn't resist from occasionally averted his eyes to glance at her breast bouncing as she ran. Her breathing came faster thinking how soft they would feel in his hands before he sucked the nipples into his mouth. He closed his eyes for a moment to get that glorious image out of his head.

They didn't talk, other than him giving her directions on where to turn. She was thankful for that. No way could she talk, jog and control her breathing. The earphone in her ears made that possible. By the time they reached the station their clothes clung to their bodies, they had worked up a good sweat. They sat on a bench near the grassy area outside of the station. Garrett removed his shirt, wiping the sweat from his face and upper body. Her pulse quicken watching him. Time seemed to move in slow motion, as the white cotton shirt glided over his skin like silk.

As they cooled down, their conversation steered towards safer subjects. Weight lifting, strength training; also her biggest concern, toning her abs. She realized Garrett was easy for her to talk with. He hadn't made one single pass at her. Though, she likely wasn't the type of woman that interested him. Most men avoided strong independent women. They preferred the passive, mindless model types. All legs, and no brains. Maybe she wasn't fair to assume models were stupid. She personally didn't know any. She was sure most of them didn't get their fame without having some knowledge of the business in their lovely heads. Take Tyra Banks for example. She has a successful modeling career, her own reality, and talk show and is a smart businesswoman. And she had a hard time finding a good man; come to think of it. So, what chance did she have at finding one? If she was looking?

Standing she propped one leg on the bench to stretch it out, then did the same to the other. Vonda looked at Garrett, noticing his chatter had stopped.

Garrett stopped talking to watch Vonda. He hadn't actually remembered what she said. He focused his attention on the pink strip on her black knee length shorts hugging her butt and firm thighs. She looked so cute, how she tilted her head. He realized she was waiting for his response. He averted his eyes up towards her face, smiling and said. "I'm sorry, what did you say?"

"You would have heard me the first time if you weren't gawking at my ass," She stated.

"I'm sorry, but I couldn't help it. It was directly in my face." He replied with a strained laugh.

"Yeah right," she blew out an exasperating breath, storming off towards the area where they parked their cars. Garrett caught up with her. He had messed up what started out being a perfect morning.

"I'm sorry, but it was right there. Don't be mad. If it's any consolation, it's a nice ass." He said, trying to make her laugh.

She stopped, turning to face him and rolled her eyes. "Look, I should have known this was a bad idea. We are partners, and that's all. So, don't get any funny ideas, okay?"

"Hey, it's a man's thing to look at women. And if I have offended you by looking at your butt - that was right in my face, then I apologize," He said with a serious face.

She looked at him, grunted, turned her back to him, and continued to her car. He bit his bottom lip, watching her hips sway, thinking, *"Damn, what a nice ass!"*

Nine months as partners, and they still didn't know much about one another. Other than they both liked to work out and had a slight temper. Well, maybe a little more than slight. Garrett's mother was having a cookout and invited a few friends to celebrate Charles's recovery. She asked Garrett, to ask his partner to come. Lately, his mother had been curious about his partner and asked a lot of questions. He still hadn't mentioned that Detective Bradley was a woman. So, the question was, should he break the news now, or wait to see if Vonda accepts his invitation. They worked well together, but once off the clock, they went their separate ways. The last time, they tried to do something after work it didn't go well. Neither one talked much about their personal life. As if they had one. In fact, he heard more about her past through the rumor mill at the office, but he didn't believe half of what was said.

He opted to wait and see if she showed up before letting the cat out of the bag. Because his mother was known for her meddlesome matchmaking talents, once she got it into her head that she needed to find you a companion, she kicked into high gear, and there was no stopping her. His mother in the past had tried to hook him up with almost every single woman she ran across. She complained that she wanted grandchildren before she and his father were too old to enjoy them. He told her she was barking up the wrong tree, and she may have better luck matching Calisa up.

His thoughts came back to the moment when Vonda opened the car door, got in, and fastened her seatbelt. She waited for Garrett to start the car so they could begin their day.

"Let's go, partner." She impatiently said.

"Vonda," He paused turning to face her, "Um…Vonda, my family, is having a cookout this weekend, and my mother wanted me to invite you. I know it's last minute and all, but they really would like to meet you, my partner."

There was an uncomfortable silence in the car before she answered. "Look, Garrett, I'm not up to it. Maybe next time?" She had already broken one promise not to get too friendly with him or anyone else. Now he's asking her to attend a family cookout, *no way*, she thought.

"Okay, I'm sure you have other plans, but I'll give you my address, just in case you change your mind." He had written it on the back of his business card, then handed it to her. She looked at him as if he was speaking another language, but finally took the card, and placed it in her coat pocket. He gave her one last glance, started the car, and pulled out of the lot. Their day started like any other day. They followed up on an assault case that had occurred a week ago. They had received a tip on a possible suspect and wanted to show her a few mug shots. After following up on more leads, they returned to the precinct and completed more paperwork. There were only a few other detectives that Garrett was friends except Manning, that was invited to a cookout. Manning stopped at his desk before leaving for the day, and told him he and his family would be there, and asked if they could bring anything. To Vonda surprise, she watched the friendly exchange of conversation between the two men and wondered how long they knew each other outside of work.

"I didn't know you knew Lieutenant Manning like that?" She questioned.

"I've known him for most of my life. He and my father were partners at one time."

"Your father was a cop?"

"Yeah, twenty-five years on the force, but he took an early retirement because of his heart condition," He said with pride, "But they remained close friends to this day."

"I guess it's good to have a Lieutenant in your corner."

"What do you mean by that?" he asked in offense.

"I'm just saying it's good to have a Lieutenant on your side."

"Well, I'm not sure I like what you are implying. The Lieutenant doesn't show me any special treatment. In fact, I think he expects more from me because of my father. So, don't go getting any ideas that I'm treated differently around here." He didn't like where this conversation was headed, so he stood, picked up some case folders, and walked towards the records room.

She knew it came out wrong and was sorry she implied such a thing. "Hey, look, Hart, I didn't mean anything by that," She said as he walked away. Lately, she had been on edge, and she knew why. This weekend would have been her and Jerrod's anniversary. And the thought of it, made her just want to crawl into bed, watch a little TV, sleep the weekend away, and try to forget what happened. She dropped her pen to the desk, and sat back in her chair, wishing she could take the comment back. Damn, she wished that transfer would hurry up and come through. She needed to get out of this City. Deep down she knew she couldn't keep running from the past. Because the pain she still carried in her heart would follow her anywhere. This city was no different from the next. It was she that needed to change and come to grips that what happened was not her fault.

Chapter

Twelve

"Yes, mommy I said I'm okay. Now stop worrying about me." Vonda said to her mother as she rolled her eyes. Gina Bradley knew her daughter and didn't want her sitting at home moping around all weekend feeling sorry for herself. She wished Vonda had moved closer to home, that way she could be there as moral support for her, and check on her from time to time.

"Okay baby, but it's my job to worry about you. Have you made any new friends yet?" Gina asked.

"No, I'm not looking to be here long enough to make friends. Besides, the last friend I had, slept with my husband." Vonda regretted her smart remark as soon as she said it. Her parents had been her rock through the entire ordeal, and she had no right to take her frustration out on them.

"Honey, you can't let that stop you from living your life. That's old news now, and I know it's going to be hard, but you got to move on." Gina advised her daughter.

"Mommy, I got to go. I have a cookout to go to." She lied just to get off the phone, but she didn't want her to worry about her.

"So you have made friends. Who is it?"

"Well, it's not exactly a friend. It's my partner and his family; they invited me, and I sort of accepted."

"That's excellent news. Well, you have yourself a good time, and call me and tell me all about it tonight."

"I sure will mommy, and I'm sorry for what I said. I love you."

"I love you too pumpkin." Gina just hoped her daughter wasn't lying to her to get her off the phone because she did that at times. She just wanted her to be happy again, and maybe find a man to be faithful to her and love her forever.

Gina and her husband, Aaron, were married for 50 years. They have had their share of difficulties, but they held true to their vows and toughened out their problems. Aaron was out collecting the rent from a tenant that was late paying again. She just hoped he came back with the money, and not let them slide with another lame excuse because they were already two months behind. Gina wasn't a greedy hard-hearted person by any means, but if they could party all night drinking, they should be able to get their butts up, and go to work and pay their bills. Out of ten units, they were the only tenants they were having trouble collecting from. As much as she hated to, she would evict them if she had to. They had invested in this property years ago when they were thinking about retiring, and so far, it has paid off. They had always had good tenants, some have lived there since the beginning, but this last tenant has been nothing but trouble, and this was the last straw.

After Vonda had ended the call, she picked up Garrett's card off the nightstand that he scribbled his address on and looked at it. Things didn't end very well for them at the office, and maybe his invite didn't stand now. She looked around her bedroom, and the silence and feel of loneliness were scary. She looked at the clock, two-fifteen, and thought by the time she dressed, and got there it would be around four o'clock. So if she didn't like the way things were going, she could leave without looking like a fool if he treated her coldly. She still didn't have a car of her own, and she had turned in the rental. It cost too much to keep, and besides, it wasn't as if she couldn't afford a new car. She found the phone book, and located the cab company's phone number then called. The friendly voice on the other end greeted her, asked for her address, and told her the approximate time of arrival. She had showered and dressed by the time the taxi arrived. She settled into the back seat, read the address, and was surprised to discover that Garrett lived about forty-five minutes from her apartment.

As the cab slowed to a stop, she was a little speechless at the sight of his townhouse. It reminded her of the Brownstone apartments in New York. She paid the driver, asked for his card, and asked if she could call him to pick her up in about an hour. He told her he may be off duty, but she still could ask for him if she liked. She climbed the few steps to the door, then rang the bell, and waited for someone to answer. She nervously gripped the strap of her oversized purse, then impatiently rang the bell again. She could hear a woman's voice yelling to hold on, and then the door opened abruptly. To her surprise, she stood facing a younger version of Garrett that asked, "Yes?" with an edge to her voice.

Vonda could see where the bad attitude came from and hoped it wasn't genetic, hoping it skipped their parents. Vonda guessed this was Calisa, his younger sister. She overheard him talking to her several times on the phone. From what she could hear, there was a problem with her boyfriend, and she was mad at how Garrett handled it. Vonda wasn't sure if she should turn around, and leave while she was ahead, but decided what the hell since she was there.

"Hello is Detective Hart's home? He invited me to a cookout." She asked. The young woman looked her up and down, then stepped aside for her to enter.

"Come on, he's somewhere in the back." Then she led her towards the cheerful commotion in the back yard. She looked around and wondered how he could afford such a luxurious house on his salary. It was large, three maybe four bedrooms and *"Wow,"* look at that kitchen, she thought as they walked through it. The cherry oak cabinets with granite counter tops had to cost him a grip in itself, not to mention all the new stainless appliances. At the outburst of laughter, she turned her attention back to the gathering and could see Garrett out on the terrace, through the opened French double doors standing next to the grill.

"Granite! You got company!" Calisa yelled, then turned and walked away. Even though it had been several months since the Lamar incidence, it was obvious she was still mad at him. He lowered the lid on the grill, turned and was pleasantly surprised to see Vonda, as was everyone else. Vonda felt a little uneasy when all eyes turned and fixed on her. She gripped her purse strap tighter and put on a fake smile as Garrett walked in her direction.

"Hey, I'm glad you could make it." He greeted with a big smile.

"Well, I wasn't sure I was still invited after yesterday," She said with regret in her voice. "I'm really sorry about that."

"Don't worry about it. I'm glad you decided to come." He turned to everyone, "Hey everyone this is my partner, Detective Vonda Bradley. Vonda, this is my family." He announced, with his arms stretched out in front of him with pride. She gave a nod of her head, smiled and gave a small wave. He turned to face her and whispered, "One thing, I hadn't told my family that my partner was a woman. So. don't be surprised at the shocked expressions." He took her by the hand and led her towards his waiting guests.

"You got something against women partners," She asked a little upset.

"No, but my mother fancies herself as a matchmaker if you know what I mean. And I'm not trying to get hitched to anyone at the moment." Introductions and warm greetings were made to every one of his guests, but he saved his parents for last. He knew his mother would have many questions for both him and Vonda.

"Mom, Dad, I would like you to meet my partner, Detective Vonda Bradley. Detective Bradley, these are my parents, Charles and Carol Hart." Carol extended her hand to Vonda, who took it willingly.

"Son, why have you been keeping this lovely lady a secret?" Carol asked, still holding on to Vonda's hand. "Dear would it be okay to call you Vonda? You are among family and friends here, and Detective Bradley sounds so formal." Carol asked with a warm smile. Garrett could see the matchmaking wheels turning in his mother's mind plotting the setup.

"Yes, Mrs. Hart that will be okay," Vonda answered, as she slid her hand from Carol.

Garrett turns his attention to his father, "And this is the man of the hour, my Dad." He said proudly, as he went to stand next to Charles, placing a caring hand on his shoulder.

"Pleased to meet you, Mr. Hart," She greeted with a smile.

"All this is for him," Garrett explained. "We're celebrating his belated birthday, and to his good health."

"Yes, we are. And I'm eating whatever I want, and a big slice of my birthday cake." As Charles eyed his chocolate sheet cake. Carol has been keeping a tight ring of his eating habits since he returned home, but today the rings were off, and he was going to get his fill. BBQ chicken with extra sauce, homemade potato salad, macaroni and cheese and the Harts' famous baked beans. His mouth salivated just thinking about it all.

"Whatever you want Dad," Garrett agreed and received a warning look from Carol. "I mean within moderation." Charles

Hart had spent his birthday in the hospital, recovering from heart surgery. It was tough on everyone because he had to stay in ICU for over a month. Garrett wasn't much help due to he was recovering from his own injuries. When he finally was able to come home, Carol didn't want him to climb the stairs to their bedroom. So they converted the den into a temporary bedroom until she felt he was healthy enough to go upstairs. Nevertheless, he was better now and had made a full recovery.

Among the guests were Lieutenant Manning, and his wife, Nora, with their two children, Dan Jr., and Danielle. The Lieutenant and Nora were playing cards, and by the looks of it, they were losing. Vonda inwardly laughed at the display of the couple trying to prove their point, as to why the other was at fault, that they were losing. After all the introductions, she was led to the buffet table, given a plate, and instructed by Garrett not to be shy, and take as much as she liked. He left her at the table and went back to the grill to check on the last of the grilling meat. He noticed Vonda had made her plate, and taken a chair at the far side of the patio by herself. With her fork, she picked at the plate of food she held in her hand. She seemed to be deep in thought by the frown on her face. He quickly removed the last of the meat on the grill, then placed the platter on the table. He made himself a plate; then grabbed a chair and took it over to where she sat and joined her.

"Is my cooking that bad?" He joked, as she pulled her attention back and looked up at his handsome face.

"No, no it's fine I was just thinking," She answered with a strained smiled.

"You could have fooled me, by the way, you were picking at it," He stated as he bit down on a piece of BBQ rib.

She looked at the food on her plate and laughed. The beans were mixed in with the potato salad; her chicken looked like it had been put through a grinder. "I'm sorry. To be honest, I haven't taken a bite of it, but I'm sure it's good." She said as she placed her plate on the table next to her. "I think I better go." She attempted to stand when he said.

"Hey wait, what's the hurry, you just got here? Besides, I can't let you leave on an empty stomach. Now take a taste of this." He took his fork, scooped up a fork full of his beans, lifting the fork to her lips. Surprised she gave him a *"You got to be kidding me look,"* but he held the fork steady. "Come on, just one taste. Please." He added. She gazed into his brown eyes as she leaned towards him, slowly opened her mouth, and allowed him to feed her. He watched as her lips closed around the fork, drawing the food into her mouth. All sorts of thoughts ran through his mind at that moment, like kissing her full lips until she melted in his arms. Pleased, he smiled and asked, "Good, right?" She licked her lips, savoring the sweet, tangy taste exploding in her mouth. She eyed his slightly opened lips, and secretly wished to taste his lips on hers. She blinked and said, "Very," and smiled a real smile for the first time that day. That was the first time she had smiled a genuine smile for a long time, and if felt like a breath of fresh air. She leaned back in her chair and looked around noticing everyone looking at them. He followed her gaze, lowering his arm, and placing the fork back on his plate. His parents, as well as the other guests, were surprised to see Garrett openly showing such affection to anyone other than his family. Carol smiled to think that her son might have found someone to share his life, and with a little encouragement maybe love. Only time and a little push in the right direction from her would tell.

"Now, what were you saying about leaving?" He asked. She shrugged her shoulders and answered.

"Nothing, I was just feeling a little out of place," She said.

"Why?"

"I'm the outsider here," She answered, as she scanned the people around them. "Everyone else is either your family or friends."

He realized what she meant, and felt he should have introduced her to his family a long time ago. "Hey, I think of you not only as my partner but a friend. Look, I'm not sure what happened back in New York, or how things worked there, but this is Tampa, and it's a fresh start if you want it to be." The thought of him mentioning New York made her angry. She knew there had been gossip around the station about the circumstances in which she came to Florida, but she never thought that Garrett would be the one to bring it up. She thought better of him.

"Hart, you don't know anything about New York or me." She stood, grabbed her purse and headed towards the house. Garrett wasn't sure what had set her off, but he couldn't let her leave like this. He placed his plate on the chair and started after her. She had reached the front door when he caught up with her.

"Vonda, what did I say?" He asked as he grabbed her arm.

"Don't touch me, Hart! You don't know anything!" She said through clench teeth. Garrett looked around and noticed Calisa standing in the hall looking at them. Whatever was going on, they needed to discuss this in private? He grabbed Vonda's arm, pulled her upstairs to his bedroom, and slammed the door behind them, asking.

"Woman, what is your problem?" He wasn't sure if he could take her sudden mood swings any longer.

"My problem is people talking behind my back, that's all. Of all people, I would have thought better of you. Partner!" She spat. Garrett didn't know what to say. Yes, there had been gossip around the office about her bitter divorce, but no one would dare ask him if he knew anything about it. He didn't like gossiping or gossipers, and everyone knew that about him. Besides, he felt it was his personal duty, as her partner, to protect her privacy. He placed a comforting hand on her shoulder to calm her down, which was a big mistake. Vonda had held in her anger for so long, this simple show of affection set her off. She knocked his hand off her shoulder and slapped him in the face with her other hand. The slap caught him off guard, and if it had been any other person, they would have been looking up at him from the floor. Instead, the over-powering urge struck him to kiss her. He grabbed her by the shoulders; pulling her into his arms, and kissed her with such intensity, it rocked both deeply. He wasn't the only one caught off guard and shaken by his actions. Vonda wrapped her arms around his neck and held on to him as she deepened the kiss. Their hands were all over each other, searching for something they both had lost somewhere in life, passion. The kiss deepened as their tongues fought to overpower the other for control. All their pent-up emotions were released in a ball of fury. Garrett released her mouth and directed his attention to her neck, then to the valley between her breasts. Cupping her ample breast in his palmed hand through her blouse, he could feel her nipple harden in response. Vonda's anger rose, as did her passion. He reminded her that she was more woman than, a detective hiding behind her badge. Her mind reeled from a desire to feel him deep inside her, stroking away her pain. The deep pain she felt from Jerrod's betrayal was much stronger, and took over her desire, and she pushed back withdrawing into her protective shell.

"Jerrod stop!" She shouted through labored breath then placed her hands over her mouth, but it was too late. Confused, he looked at her and thought. *"What had this man done to her to hurt her this badly?"* "Vonda, who is Jerrod?" he asked. Vonda couldn't believe what she had said and stared at him in disbelief. She pushed past him and then ran towards the door, away from the horrible nightmare, she had created for herself. He couldn't let her leave, not until he got some answers. He stopped her by placing his hand against the door.

She couldn't face him as the tears rolled down her face. She was unable to keep up this pretense any longer, her legs weakened, and she sank to the floor in a heap at his feet. Her body shook as all the hurt rose, and she cried hard for the first time since she left, New York. Garrett lowered his body to sit next to her and cuddled her as she cried as if he had seen another woman cry. His muscular arms embraced her tenderly to his chest, and he would hold her for as long as she needed him. He gently stroked her hair with the palm of his hand in hopes to ease her pain.

"Why can't I stop crying?" She thought as she lay nestled in his arms against his chest. It felt good being held this way. Who would have thought a man nicknamed Granite would comfort her so tenderly? Vonda sat up, wiped away the tears with the back of her hands. He looked into her red-stained eyes and asked, "Vonda, who is Jerrod?" He wanted to know who the man was, that caused her so much pain. He wanted to break every bone in his body and make sure he never did again. He patiently waited for her to answer. She sniffed and replied as he ran his thumb along her cheek.

"He's my ex-husband," She answered. He thought, *"So that explained the hurt she had been carrying since she arrived."*

"Wow, he must have been some piece of work?" He added.

"Yes, I guess you could say that." She exhaled and continued, "He cheated on me in the worst way." He waited for her to find the words, "He cheated with my best friend in our home."

His facial expression hardens as he said, "Bastard! What man would do such a thing to his wife?" He wanted to find her ex, and teach him a lesson he would never forget.

"Yeah, that's what I said. And to think I came this close to throwing my career and life away by shooting them both." She measures out with her fingers. Garrett leaned up and looked her in the face.

"Wow, what stopped you?" he asked. Vonda shrugged her shoulders then answered.

"I'm not sure. I guess it wasn't worth the bullets, or spending the rest of my life behind bars." He pulled her back into his arms, and stroked her shoulder for a moment longer, finding her body tensed. The warmth of her hips across his lap caused his shaft to twitch against her butt. He didn't want to let her go but knew if he didn't soon he would try his hardest to have her in his bed. The thought of having her legs wrapped around his waist, as he drove his cock deep inside her made him crazy. She felt his shaft twitch against her butt. He was large, and it aroused her more than she wanted him to know. She had let her guard down once but never again. She eased from his lap to sit next to him on the floor.

He needed to think of a way to release some of her anger, and his arousal, he suggested.

"How about a workout?"

"What kind?" she looked at him skeptically, knowing they came very close to having the workout of their life.

He smiled, catching her meaning. "No, not that, but I bet it would have been nice." He ran his thumb along her jawline, wiping at a wet spot. "I'm talking about working out on the punching bags. I find it helps me to release the tension after a long day.

"Sounds good, but I don't feel like going to the gym."

"We don't have to, I have one in my gym in the garage," He jumped to his feet, and then pulled her up by her hands. "I have a pair of sweats, that you can wear, so you won't get that cute top dirty." She scrunched up her nose at the thought of wearing one of his woman's clothes, and he caught the look. "They belong to my sister. She leaves a change of clothes here. If you don't believe me, you can ask her." He said with a smile, that would pale the sun. She agreed, then waited for him to return. While he was gone, she got a good look at his bedroom. It was nothing like she would have expected from him. It was cozy and romantic. The big bed was the only thing that she felt was suited to him. The fireplace surrounded by beautiful candles, and big pillows scattered around was a big surprise. This would be something she would select for her bedroom if it weren't so small. She felt a hint of jealousy for a second, thinking of how many women he may have had sex with in this room, but quickly pushed it aside. She could still feel the heat of his hand on her breast. Just thinking about it made her nipples harden again. She closed her eyes and thought what it would be like to have made love to him here in his domain. The tip of her tongue licked her upper lip. Imagining, her brown legs, wrapped around his waist, as she drove his shaft deep inside her until their bodies perspired from the heat they generated. Anticipating the final climax, as they breathless called each other's name. The door flew open interrupting the moment. Garrett entered with the sweats folded in his arms. He gave her a puzzled look, handed her the clothes, and pointed her in the direction of the bathroom. She quickly took the items and hurried in the direction he pointed, hoping he didn't see the blush on her cheeks.

He headed towards his walk-in closet doors to change and found a pair of gray sweatpants and a white undershirt. He proceeded to removed his clothes and placed them on the chair in the corner. Vonda returned to the bedroom, and from where she stood, she could see Garrett in all his naked glory from behind. She was speechless, and couldn't bring herself to look away. He had the finest body she had seen on any man, including her ex-husband, what's his name. She imagined the right thing to do was turn her head, or back out of the room, but at that moment, she was enjoying the view. She watched until he was fully dressed, then cleared her throat. He turned to see her standing in the middle of the room, and wondered just how long she had been standing there.

"Hey, you're ready?" He asked walking up to her.

"Yeah, I'm ready," She replied, and they headed out of the room.

He crossed the patio to where his parents sat, and received a mean look from Calisa as they passed her, "Are those my clothes?" She asked. He ignored her question the same way she had been ignoring him. Garrett directed his statement to his parents telling them they would be in the garage working out if anyone needed them. Calisa huffed and warned him that had better be all they were doing. She also reminded him of the time he was seventeen, and she caught him in their garage with that fast girl, that lived down the street from them. Vonda looked at his sister and laughed at her remark. He looked around, still embarrassed about the incident, to see if anyone had heard her, and reminded her that was a long time ago, and he was a reformed gentleman. Charles laughed at the memory of that day, and he received a stern look from Carol. She looked around him at Vonda, who stood a few feet from them, and noticed she had changed clothes also. Carol gave him one last unapprovingly grunt and then turned her focus back to her card game.

Garrett took Vonda by the arm and led her to the garage before his sister brought up another embarrassing memory from his past. He unlocked the side door, and stepped aside allowing her to enter first, then turned on the lights. The three-car garage and utility space were spacious, and to her surprise, was very organized. Everything was in its place; several tools were mounted on the far wall above the work table arranged, by size and type. Which surprised her because Garrett usually couldn't find a pen on his desk for all the clutter. His classic Mustang GT parked nested in its spot, as well as a few spare tires with those custom rims.

He opened a locker and took out a pair of boxing gloves, and tossed them to her. As she put them on, he pulled out a punching bag, hanging from a chain suspended from a railing, that was mounted on the ceiling. He helped her put on her gloves, then he gave her some basic instructions on techniques and let her go for it. He told her to start out slow to ensure she wouldn't hurt herself, and she should stop from time to time to give her arms a rest. She wasn't sure if this was going to work for her, but at this point, she would try it. As she pounded the bag, he talked to her, asking her about New York, her family. Once he felt she was concentrating on the bag, he would slip in a question about Jerrod, or Tierra to keep that anger coming. The more she talked about them, the harder she hit that bag, and the more anger she released, the better she felt.

She couldn't hit that bag one more time. Her arms burned like fire and felt as solid as bricks, but her heart and mind felt clearer and lighter. Both were drenched in sweat from the workout and hot garage. She sat on the weight bench and let her arms hang at her side as Garrett pushed the bag back into its space. She lifted her head to catch a warm breeze, from the rotating fan above.

"Arms burning?" he asked as he looked down at her.

"Yeah, like fire," She answered. Garrett straddled the bench next to her and removed her gloves to examined her hands. As he slid them off her hands, she sucked in air through clenched teeth from the pain. She had slightly broken the skin on a few of her knuckles, from pounding the bag so hard.

"I warned you to take it easy, now look at that," He scorned, then walked to the locker, bringing back the first aid kit. Pouring some peroxide onto a piece of gauze, he gently wiped at the red spots. As he dabbed her scars, he glanced up at her, thought how beautiful she was, and wished they had met under better circumstances. She was too vulnerable to her emotions right now. His mind was telling him not to take advantage of her, but his dick was saying something else and was winning the battle. She could feel his burning eyes on her, igniting the fire in her again. This time, the fire wasn't from anger, but from lust. She slowly removed her hand from his and balled them into fists at her side. He noticed her reaction, placed the kit on the floor, and slid closer to her. She straightened her back, and braced herself for what she hoped was to come. He took her fists in his hands, brought them to his chest, and said.

"Vonda, you got to let them go, and get on with your life."
She didn't respond. She gazed into his caring brown eyes, pleading
for him to show her how. "You have so much to offer the right
man. Let it go, please.

"I can't Garrett. I don't know how." She confessed, as tears
formed in her eyes and rolled down her face. He wiped a single
teardrop from her cheek with his thumb, and then placed a tender
kiss there. She closed her eyes to relish the simple show of
affection. She had denied herself to feel anything in over a year. He
stood, and placed one of her legs across the bench allowing her to
face him. Placing his hands on her hips, he scooted her closer to
him, so her legs covered his thighs. She wasn't sure if this was
what they should be doing, but it sure felt right. She lowered her
eyes lids, she couldn't hold his gaze; it was too powerful, too
intense. Lifting her chin so their eyes could meet, he leaned
forward, then paused before placing tender kisses on her lips, until
they parted to welcome his gentle probing tongue. She shivered
from the electrified charged when their tongues connected. He
released a deep moan that stirred his soul. He pulled her closer, to
feel his hard shaft pressing against his pants. The pulsating
sensation deep within her, caused her juices to flow, wetting her
silk panties. His hand explored her back, and ass, getting her
familiar with his touch, as the other ventured to her breast. Sliding
his hand under her shirt, he rubbed the soft skin at her waist, up to
her bra. He taunted her nipple through the sheer fabric.

She softly moaned, when his thumb rubbed across her nipple. His hand at her back kept her steady against him. She could feel his shaft twitch against her, and she wrapped her legs around his back. Reaching for the hem of his shirt, she ripped it over his head leaving no doubt of what she wanted. He lifted her shirt pushing the bra up with it, giving him free access to her breasts. His need to taste her was great. Breaking the kiss, he glanced into her eyes before he lowered his head to run his tongue over her nipple. Repeatedly, he taunted her with his tongue, until he wanted more. His mouth engulfed as much of the soft, sweet flesh as he could take in.

Vonda body burned to feel him inside her, as his mouth ignited every sensation in her. She held his shoulders as he sucked her deep into his mouth. She couldn't control her hips from grinding against his shaft resting between her thighs. With every thrust, it rubbed the sensitive bud bringing her closer to climaxing. His mind told him to stop. She was his partner, and they shouldn't do this. But the bulge between his legs wanted to feel her heat rubbing his shaft. He never felt so aroused, so ready in his entire life, and if it weren't for their clothes, he would have entered her without a second thought. She wedged her hand between them into his sweats. His cock was hard, thick and barely kept in check by the sweats. She cupped his dick in her hand, stroking it from the crown of the head to the base. She could feel the wetness from his precum as he jerked, and pushed hard against her hand. Now she knew where he got the nickname Granite. He lowered her to the bench, continued to ravish her breasts. She released him, braced her back against the bench, wrapping her legs higher on his back, and could feel his thickness pressed against her. He pulled at the knotted string, tied to the waistband of her pants, in an attempt to pull them over the hips, when a banging at the door halted them.

Calisa banged again then yelled.

"Granite, Mama says we're leaving now. Did you hear me!"

He had to catch his breath. He looked at Vonda and tried to answer as calmly as possible. He released her and sat up managing to answer.

"Okay Lis, I heard you. Call me when you get home."

Secretly, Vonda was thankful for the interruption. They were at the point of no turning back. She knew she would have gone all the way to feel him inside her, and she didn't need this, or him to further screw up her life right now. She gently pushed him up off her, righting her clothes as she stood, and walked towards the car. She took a few deep breaths to steady her nerves. Her legs were weak as her body still pulsated with want. He looked down at the head of his cock peeping out over the top of his sweats and thought the erection may take days to go back to normal. He covered himself, then walked over to the utility sink, turned on the faucet then stuck his head under the cool running water.

She watched him, seeing his arousal, and knew it was time to go.

"Hart I better go," She said as she hurried towards the door, as he wiped the water from his face with his hands, but not before she saw his muscles tense.

"Oh, we're back to Hart now?" He asked turning to face her, and walking towards her then reached for her hands.

"Yes, that's the way it should be," She answered, as she gently pulled her hand from his.

"It doesn't have to be Vonda." His eyes couldn't hide the hurt he felt at that moment.

"Yes, it does. We're partners, and that's all. I got to go." She said and continued to the door. He didn't want to hear it, but it was true they were partners. He wanted more, much more, but knew she deserved more than a quickie on his weight bench in his garage.

"Wait; let me drive you home. It's kind of late to be taking a cab." He didn't want her to go, and waited for her answer, "I promise to behave." He added smiling; showing those dimples she knew had gotten him his way. Vonda stood, looking at him then reluctantly agreed, but was pleased that the patio was empty, as well as the house.

She used the guest bathroom to shower, and changed back into her clothes as he did the same in his room. When she came downstairs, he was waiting for her in the kitchen. He stood as she entered the room, handed her a bottle of water, and asked if she was ready.

His mother had put away all the food but left the dishes for him to wash. She offered to help wash the dishes piled in the sink, but he turned her down and said he would get them later. He set the alarm as they exited the back door. He activated the electric door opener, as they walked towards the garage. He held the car door opened for her to get in, and took one last look at the shapely legs in those skinny jeans, that was just wrapped around his waist, He was unaware that he licked his lips.

The drive to her house was silent; neither knew what to say. She sat with her arms crossed over her breast. The same breast Garrett feasted on just hours before. Thinking about it made her nipples harden again, and flushed her body with heat.

"Can you turn up the a/c?" she asked.

"Sure," he answered, and pushed the lever all the way in the blue zone.

"Thanks," She said as she adjusted the vent to blow cold air directly on her.

"You're welcome," He said, as he shifted in his seat, and continued to focus on the road. They pulled up in front of Vonda's apartment, and he turned off the engine then turned in her direction. God, he wished she would let him help her get through this. Her ex-husband hurt her badly, and it would take her awhile to recover if she didn't let someone in, to help her.

"Vonda, I want to apologize for the way things happened today. I don't want you to think I'm like that but... I don't know what came over me."

"Forget about it, Hart. It was just as much my fault as yours. You don't have to worry; it won't happen again." She answered, without looking at him, because she knew she was lying. She wanted it to happen as much as he did, and if she weren't careful, it would. "I let my guard down."

"But that's the thing. I wanted it to happen," Garrett ran his hand over his nearly bald head. "What I mean is there's something here between us, and I would like to see where it goes." He tried to explain.

"No! There is nothing between us. We're partners, and that's all." She reached to open her door, but his strong hand stopped her.

"Vonda look at me. Please." It took everything in her to look at him. "I've never been good at expressing myself unless I was angry," He gave a little chuckle, "But with you, I can talk to you about anything. Believe it or not, I realized it, your first day on the job when you checked me on the elevator. No one ever talked to me that way. I've been trying to deny the attraction, then and I know you felt it too, but there's something here." He touched his chest over his heart.

"No, I can't give my heart to another not now, maybe not ever. So, if we can't be just partners, then I guess you better ask for a replacement."

"I don't want another partner Vonda. I want you watching my back, on the job, and off."

"Hart no! I will talk to the Lieutenant in the morning and ask him to reassign me."

"Damn woman! Why do you have to be so stubborn?" He yelled as he hit the stirring wheel.

"Look, Hart, I'm not one of your street thugs. Your yelling doesn't intimidate me. So, you better lower that tone, mister." She opened her door, got out of the car, and walked towards her apartment door.

He hurried to get out of the car and ran after her. "Vonda wait! I'm sorry," he called after her. She turned to face him with her hands tight across her chest. He slowed his pace, liking how sassy she looked standing that way. He took her face in his hands and kissed her deeply before she knew what happened. He got his fill of her sweetness, then backed away and said, "I'll see you in the morning. Partner," Then he ran back to his car. She was furious with him. She screamed, stomped her feet, then turned and opened the door to her apartment, then slammed it hard. He watched from the safety of his car and watched her slam the door. He smiled, and he knew who put it there, Ms. Vonda Bradley.

Calisa was in bed for the night and had just picked up the TV remote, to watch her favorite late-night talk show, when her cell phone rang. She muted the sound, and picked up the phone off the nightstand, wondering who would be calling her this time of night. She smiled to see Glenda's picture and number on the screen.

"Hey, girl what's up?" She asked and put the remote down.

"Not much just wanted to thank you again for inviting the kids, and me to the cookout. We needed a break, and they had a good time." Glenda and Calisa had been best friends since forever, but when Glenda married, they kind of lost touch. It was by chance they ran into one another at the store a few weeks ago.

"You're my girl. No thanks are needed. I just wish Derek could have made it."

"I wish he could have too. But you know how he can be, and with him out of work, he hasn't been in much of a social mood," Glenda explained, but in truth, he was never in a sociable mood. Besides, she hadn't told him about the cookout. She didn't want him to embarrass her, or the kids and ruining their evening.

"Maybe Granite could help him get a job, or give him some leads."

"Calisa I see you still calling him Granite?"

"Yeah, because it ticks him off, and because he thinks he's so tough."

"Speaking of Garrett, who was that woman he was with today?" Glenda asked.

"That was his new partner, Vonda something or another."

"Partner, when did he start working with a partner?"

"Since Mr. Manning made him after he went all gung-ho and got himself stabbed a few months back."

"Wow, I didn't know that. Well, they look really close the way he was feeding her and all." Garrett always held a special place in her heart, and she was a little jealous to see him acting that way. Her main reason for coming to the cookout was to see him, and maybe get him to notice she wasn't that little girl that followed him around like a sick puppy.

"That surprised all of us. You know Mr. Hard as Granite never gets close to anyone, especially in public," She teased. "But from what I hear she won't be here for long. This was a temporary assignment."

"Girl you are crazy. He has always been nothing but nice to me." Glenda said with affection.

"You only say that because you had a big old crush on him." They laughed knowing it was true.

"Well, let me go I don't want to keep you up," Glenda stated.

"I'm glad you called, and we have to keep in touch. I want to hear more about this travel agency of yours."

"Sure thing, maybe I can book your family vacation or a family reunion?"

"Hey, that sounds great. I'll run that by my parents, and see what they say."

"Thanks again friend."

"You're welcome friend." Glenda laid the phone on the kitchen table and picked up the ice pack. She placed it against her face to calm the sting, and take down the swelling. Derek came home drunk, and mad that his dinner wasn't on the table. She told him she and the kids had gone to Calisa's for a cookout and had brought him back a plate. He became angry, and pushed the plate of food in her face, then started slapping her around. Saying how dare she serve him somebody else's leftovers, like a stray dog? She begged him to stop hitting her, and swore that she had made his plate before hers or the kids, and put it in the refrigerator. She was finally fed-up, and today after seeing everyone so happy, she knew she couldn't continue to live like this any longer. Glenda knew in her heart; Garrett was the man to help her and her kids out of this situation. Now all she had to do was to make sure Vonda was not in the picture.

Chapter

Thirteen

So far, today had been a great day for the two partners. Things were quiet, which allowed them time to complete more paperwork, that had piled up on their desk. The Lieutenant hadn't yelled once at anyone and stayed at his desk most of the day, which was so unlike him. Vonda had finally broken down and purchased a car. It was one of those new Hybrid vehicles, which wasn't anything fancy. But it met all her requirements, and beats that costly rental, or having Garrett pick her up in the morning, and took her home in the evenings. Despite what had almost happened between them, they were getting closer as friends, and comfortable being around one another, and she really didn't want that. She liked him as her partner because they had a lot of the same qualities and work ethics. Nevertheless, she just couldn't push away those feelings, sexual feelings away, and she didn't want to have them. Working so closely with him, she couldn't help but notice how handsome, and charming he was. Even the way he walked, had this sexiness in his glide that made her remember that day. Not to mention those deep, penetrating eyes, full luscious lips, and oh-my-gosh his pearly white teeth, hidden behind that sexy smile, that granted a rare appearance of his dimples. She got a knot in the pit of her stomach just thinking about him. When he smiled, it lit up his entire face, as it did when he was mad, a bitter hard coldness showed on it. However, when he graced you with that smile, he had a boyish way about him. He would look at you, turn away, then back at you, giving it all to you at once. The eyes, the smile, those even pearly-white teeth, she shuddered to think of it. On many nights, she awakened in a heated sweat from hot sexual dreams about them. Boy, if he was half as good in reality, as he was in her dreams, no wonder every woman in town came on to him. Vonda's lips tightened just thinking about him with other women, but why should she care who he had in his bed, as long as he had her back on the job. She watched as he returned to the car, with two cold drinks in hand from the corner store. He gave her a cup through the opened window, then opened the door and got in. She took a big sip, to cool down the heat racing through her body from thinking of her dreams. He looked at her and asked. "Wow, you were thirsty. Do you want me to get you a refill?" She wiped her chin and answered. "No thanks, I'm good." She watched him from the corner of her eye, as he placed the straw between his lips and drew in the cold brown liquid. She parted her lips and imagined her tongue replacing the straw as he drew it into his hot mouth. She quickly opened the door and almost fell out as she told him she changed her mind about the refill, after all, closing the door behind her before he could reply.

Garrett watched her hurry towards the store and wondered why she was acting strange lately. She spoke to the attendant behind the counter and shook her empty cup at her. The attendant gave her a strained smile, then looked up in the direction of the camera. She didn't think anything of it and continued to walk to the far wall of the store, where the drink fountains were located. She placed her cup underneath her drink selection, then glanced back at the attendant who was still standing in the same spot. A strange feeling came over her, and she felt in her gut that something wasn't right, but it was too late. As she turned around, a skinny punk attempting to rob the store, punched her in the jaw. She was stunned for a moment, but quickly gained her footing, then tackled the man running towards the exit door. They tussled on the floor until he got the upper hand, flipped her over, and attempted to punch her in the face again. She was too quick for him and moved her head out of the way, and his punch landed on the floor. He grabbed his hand and yelled out in pain, which gave her the opportunity to push him off her and get to her feet. She looked around for her gun, which was knocked from her holster in the struggle. This guy has to be on something, no one the skinny could be this strong. He attacked again, grabbing her by the neck with his forearm and held on. The attendant finally snapped out of her trance, running from behind the counter, and out the door screaming for her life. Vonda knew Garrett would be coming to her rescue at any moment, hopefully, before the man did any serious harm to her, or worst break her neck. She found the strength in her legs to push him against the coffee dispenser, knocking over several pots of hot coffee against his back. He released his hold from her neck long enough for her to get loose, and grab one of the remaining glass pots filled with hot coffee and crashed it over his head. He grabbed his face screaming and attempted to wipe the hot liquid from his face, as he fell to his knees. She loomed over him, as she touched her sore neck to catch her breath. She took a step back and with all her might, kicked him in the face knocking him over on his back. All the rage in her five-six frame was unleashed on this punk.

Garrett noticed the clerk running out of the store towards him calling for help. He jumped from his car, meeting her as she pointed back towards the building. Garrett wasted no time rushing in to help his partner, not giving any thought as to what he was running into. His heart beat wildly in fear at the thought that Vonda may be seriously hurt before he got there or worst dead. He rushed the door with his gun drawn, but what he witnessed utterly shocked him. Vonda was opening up a severe case of whip ass on the punk. She stood over the man lying on the floor; she was leaning down in his face yelling, and cursing at him, saying words he never heard any decent woman say. The man sat up against the drink machine, screaming at the top of his lungs for her to help him. "Help me, help me. My back is burning!" She stood over him and pushed the ice dispenser lever, and ice cubes poured out down over him.

"Vonda! Vonda! Detective Bradley, what are you doing?" Garrett asked, as he stared at her in disbelief, then looked around to see if anyone else was in the store.

"He said he was hot, so I was cooling him off." Garrett pushed her to the side, turned the man face down, and cuffed his suspect. A few moments later, some uniformed officers arrived along with the EMS team. He was lucky to only have sustained second-degree burns from the hot coffee and a broken nose. Vonda's neck, on the other hand, would be sore for a while, and there were a few cuts and bruises to remind her of the incident, but luckily, nothing was broken. She refused to go to the hospital to be examined. She rather take down the clerk's statement for the report. Garrett could still see the rage in her eyes, and it hurt him to think how close he came to possibly losing her, his partner.

By the time they got to the office, her face, and neck were showing signs of bruising. She sat in her chair and rested her head in her hands.

"You need me to get you something," Garrett asked.

"No, I don't need anything. Thanks." She replied with an edgy tone in her voice.

Vonda looked up to see Lieutenant Manning rushing from his office in her direction, "Shit," She cursed under her breath, rolling her eyes because she knew what was coming.

"Bradley what are you doing here! Get your butt over to the hospital and let them check you out!" He ordered.

"Lieutenant Sir I'm all right. I don't need to go to the hospital." She said.

"I don't think I asked you. Now Hart, drive her over to TGH, and report back to me as soon as you get there." Manning kept an eye on Bradley, as he gave his orders.

"Sir, I said I don't need to go..."

"And the last time I checked, I was in charge here! Now get your butt to the hospital! NOW!" Not allowing her to respond, Manning went back to his office and slammed his door, then abruptly opened it again and yelled, "And after you leave there, go home!" Garrett didn't say a word. He knew better, and so did Vonda.

The doctor gave Vonda the all clear and sent her home to rest for a few days, which in Vonda's eyes, was a life sentence. Garrett dropped her off at her apartment and told her he would pick her up tomorrow to get her car from the precinct lot.

She hadn't gotten much sleep that night, and by noon the next day, she was at her wit's end, after being alone in her apartment. She couldn't stand the quietness, and really missed being back in New York. It looked like her old habits, and temper had followed her to Florida. This would be her second incident in less than a year. Maybe it was time for her to seek counseling if she kept getting agitated at the littlest things. The other day, she nearly threw the vacuum out the door, because she couldn't get it to maneuver in the direction, she wanted it to go. And this morning, she kicked the trash can, because the wheels wouldn't roll on the grass. She realized her life was a mess, and so was she. She let her appearance go to hell. She hadn't had a pedicure or manicure in over a year, and her preferred hairstyle was a ponytail or braids. No makeup, not even lipstick. She had to get herself together and quick. Maybe she would go see her mom for the weekend. Being spoiled by her mother is just what she needed, but for now, a stiff drink would have to do.

Garrett stood on Vonda's doorstep with a large New York Style pizza, and a bottle of wine. After the week she had, she could use a friend right now if she wanted one or not. While the assault charges were being investigated, she was suspended with pay. Everyone in the department knew the charges wouldn't stick, but no cop needed any unwanted marks on their employee record, and Vonda was no exception. Garrett rang the bell a few more times and waited for her to answer. He knew she was home; her car was parked at the curb.

Vonda barely stepped out of the shower, when some crazy person began impatiently ringing the doorbell. She didn't know or care who it was because she didn't feel like any company. She hastily slid her short terry-cloth robe over her wet body as she headed to her bedroom, then grabbed her service revolver from the holster lying on her bed, and proceeded to answer the door. Not taking the time to look through the peephole, she snatched the door open and stood with her hand by her side holding the gun, and the other on her hip. To her surprise, of all the people that could be on the other side of her door, stood Garrett with those puppy dog eyes, staring at her with that killer smile. Her anger was quickly replaced with a heated sensation that surged through her entire body. She prayed for her wildly beating heart to slow down, and reminded herself that he was just another man, that she didn't want anything to do with.

"Hart, what are you doing here?" She huffed, as she took her finger off the trigger of the gun. "Did the lieutenant send you to spy on me, to make sure I'm not drowning kittens in my bathtub?" She asked, but didn't offer for him to come in.

"Is this how you greet all your guests? No wonder you don't have any visitors." She gave him a look and walked from the door back towards her bedroom.

"Funny, come in and close the door behind you," She said over her shoulder, "How do you know how I treat my guests? I should have shot you through the door. That would have saved me the trouble of having to do it later." He smiled to himself and watched as she padded barefoot back down the hall. He could see that her legs and feet were wet and assumed other delicious parts of her body were as well. Remembering her comment, he thought of asking her what she was doing in the bathroom but thought better. He admired her because even after a tough week she had she still walked like a woman with a purpose. From what he could see, by the sway of her hips, her sole purpose was to arouse him, and it was working.

Vonda couldn't wait to get out of his dangerous glare. She could feel those eyes looking right through her robe, causing her nipples to harden against the fabric. She wished he hadn't come over, the way her body was reacting. She asked herself why he was there, but in the same breath was happy he was. She had planned on breaking out that bottle of champagne, her parents had sent her when she moved to her apartment. And put on one of her 'I got the blues CD's,' she made of her favorite artists. She had just the one in mind, her somebody stole her dog, her man been cheating on her with an ugly bitch, and took all her money out the bank blues. That always put her in a depressing mood. Now she had to find a way to get rid of Garrett and get on with the evening she planned. She quickly dressed as she heard him yell.

"Hey, I brought a peace offering. Pizza, and a bottle of my best wine," He called out, as he walked to the kitchen adjusting his cock the best he could. He placed the pizza box in the middle of the table, took the corkscrew from his pocket, and opened the bottle of wine to let it breathe. He began searching the cabinets and found the plates, and wine glasses he was looking for. When Vonda returned, wearing a pair of jeggings, and a tee shirt that said, "I Love Myself – Curves & All," Garrett was standing with a kitchen towel thrown over his arm, holding out her chair. Noticing the plates and wine glasses, she sarcastically remarked, "Well, make yourself at home." She gave him the evil eye, but when she saw the large New York style pie, she closed her eyes and inhaled the heavenly aroma. She had been looking for a New York style pizza parlor for months and would have never thought to ask him if he knew of a location. She was still annoyed with him, as he pulled out a chair for her. She took a slice of pizza from the box, dropped it on a plate, then walked to the sofa and turned on the TV. He laughed, as he pushed the chair back in place, then put a slice of pizza on a plate for himself. He grabbed the bottle of wine, the glasses and joined her on the sofa. She sat with her legs tucked against her butt, as she tried to ignore him. He could tell she enjoyed that first bite of pizza. Her eyes closed, and her tongue darted out to lick at the sauce at the corner of her mouth. He enjoyed watching her seductive tongue trail across her lips and wanted to taste as well. He inhaled the body fragrance she wore, teasing his senses as he watched her wiggle her toes as she ate.

"Smelling good," He said before he realized it.

"It's just pizza," She replied, as she looked at her slice.

"I wasn't talking about the pizza. I was referring to you. I mean your lotion smells good. Obsession, right?" He questioned. For some reason, he was getting a little nervous, as he poured the wine. He took a sip, and then placed his glass on the coffee table next to hers.

"Oh, yes it is," She answered, as she tried focusing her attention back to the program on the TV. Then she asked, "You some kind of perfume connoisseur or something?"

He laughed saying, "No, I know what I like and I like Obsession. Did you know they also have one for men?" He rambled on nervously. "But not everyone can wear it." She gave him another strange look, then picked up her glass, took a small sip. To her surprise, she liked the taste of the bold deep red wine. She wasn't much of a drinker, but she had enjoyed a glass of white wine with Jerrod from time to time. Garrett continued his small talk, as she flipped through the channels until she got to the station airing WWE Raw. She paused for a brief look, then pressed the channel up button again.

"Hey put that back. That was Raw!" Garrett shouted with excitement and scooted to the edge of his seat.

"You're a wrestling fan?" She asked, not many people enjoyed wrestling as she did.

"Yes, I am the biggest. Besides my dad, that is," He said.

"Oh no, I don't think so! I've been a fan since I was nine!" Vonda announced proudly.

"No way! Me too!" He said with excitement and pointed to the screen shaking his finger, "I love this guy."

Vonda sat up announcing, "Triple H is the M.A.N!" They shared a laugh, continued watching the program, and commenting from time to time, as to whom they liked and disliked. By the time they finished most of the pizza, and the bottle of wine, it felt as if they were old friends. As they continued to watch the matches, they were starting to feel the effects of the wine. While the commercials were on, Garrett asked the direction of the bathroom. She pointed, then he headed off to locate it. Vonda was feeling hot and started fanning herself with a magazine to create a breeze. She looked up to check if the ceiling fans were on, and they were. She walked over to the thermostat panel to make sure it was working and saw it was set at seventy-eight degrees. She lowered the temperature to seventy-two and instantly heard the fans turn on.

She turned and came face to face with Garrett coming from the bathroom. He surprised her, and in a split second, she went into defense mode raising her arms to her face and balling her hand into a fist to defend herself. Garrett knew in his profession not to sneak up on any officer, but he wasn't thinking at the time, his thoughts were on Vonda. Being on guard always, was just part of the job if you wanted to keep on living. So, when she punched at him, he quickly averts the blow by grabbing her wrists, pinning her hands against the wall, as his hard body pressed against hers, allowing her to feel every inch of him.

He felt her breast pressed against his chest in response to their nearness, her nipples hardened, and ached for his touch. Every nerve in her body exploded at once, sending a flood of emotions racing through her. Her body had never reacted to anyone like this, not even Jerrod. Her sex life with Jerrod had been terrific before everything blew up in her face. However, this was something else, and at that moment, she didn't have the words to describe it. She gazed up into those penetrating brown eyes, that burned her to the depths of her soul, adding fuel to the already blazing fire.

He searched her beautiful eyes for any sign, nothing was revealed, but her body apparently screamed her needs. Her lips parted slightly, drawing air into her lungs as his presence tugged at her soul.

What was he doing, this was his partner, he thought as he held her to the wall with his body. His body told him to go for it, but his mind warned him to back off. He could still smell the faint alluring fragrance of her body wash, and it stirred the hardening of his shaft. His lips were just inches from hers, and it would be so easy to slide his tongue into its warmth, and feast on the lingering sweetness of the wine. He could still smell the wine on her breath, *"Yes it was the wine,"* he thought as he lowered his forehead to the wall behind her, to collect his composure. Memories flashed in his mind of her body spread out beneath him, so close to having what they both wanted. She was so vulnerable, and he needed her to want him as much as he wanted her. He couldn't take her fast, he needed to slow down, and prepare her for him. It had been a while since she had sex, and he wanted her time with him to be memorable. Because he didn't want any other man touching her.

Lowering his lips to hers, he took her mouth gently, slow at first, until her body melted into him.

Releasing his grip on her hips, he took a step back and looked down her body, then back to her lips. He turned her around, pressing her back flush against the front of his body. Leaving no doubt how she was affecting him. He angled her head so he could recapture her lips with his mouth as he palmed her breast through her shirt. She squirmed her ass against his cock, urging him to take her. His hands roamed freely over her body until he found the hem of the shirt, and ran his hands underneath it until he touched her hot flesh. *"Slow, Garrett slow,"* he repeated in his head as he raised her bra and cupped her breasts.

She arched her back, loving the feel of his hands on her. Vonda wanted him, all of him, and this time, there would be no interruptions. She inward swore she would kill anyone that came to the door. He played with her nipples with his thumbs and forefingers, pinching just enough to cause her to moan with pleasure. He held her body tight to him, as he eased his hand lower to the waistband of her pants to seek out her hot pussy. She slightly parted her legs, allowing him easy access to touch, and explore as he willed. He parted her vaginal lips and slid his finger down the slit until he found her clit. Her knees buckled, at the intensity of his touch, but he held her by her waist with his arm. He played with the bud, as her hips rocked back and forth to match the rhythm of his finger. She was wet, very wet and her hot juices covered his finger as he slowly entered her pussy. It was too much, she thought as her muscles tightened around his finger holding it in place. In and out, in and out he stroked cupping her clit with his palm. Vonda clamped his hand between her legs, as she neared her climax. He pulled out of her warmth, then inserted two fingers increasing his stroke. Garrett's dick strained to the point of climaxing himself, and when she moaned his name, he knew she was near.

"Garrett," She whispered, throwing her head back against his chest, gripping his pants at his hips in her fist. "Yes, tell me what you want. I'm here for you." He said against her ear, as he thrust his fingers into her faster. "Please, now." She pleaded for him to release her from the sweet pain of ecstasy. He strummed her clit with his fingers like a guitar, until the musical sound of her release, echoed in the air. Her body shook, riding out the intense climax. The sweet smell of her sex filled the air coaxing him to want more.

He turned her around to face him, saying before he fell to his knees. "I want to taste you." She was still in a fog when he pulled her leggings down her legs, and off her feet. He lifted her leg over his shoulder, exposing herself to him. He parted her sex lips with his thumbs, then licked his own lips in anticipation, of tasting her sweet juices. He dipped his head forward and nibbled at her clit with his lips before his tongue licked her. She tensed at the feel of his mouth sucking on her bud, applying just enough pressure, as he flicked his tongue back and forth, masturbating her to another orgasm. She screamed his name repeatedly, then slumped against his face, purring like a kitten. He greedily lapped up her sweet juices, as she came in his mouth.

He lowered her leg to the floor and stood bracing her against the wall. Vonda couldn't move her body; it felt like two tons of weights were holding her feet in place. She closed her eyes, to calm her breathing, and the throbbing between her legs. Finally, opening her eyes, to his intense gaze locked on her, as he fought to control his rapid breathing. The hunger in his eye showed he wanted more. He lifted her up and walked back to the living room. She needed another drink but thought better as he lowered her to the sofa. He kissed her kiss-swollen lips, then went to the bathroom. She could hear running water and assumed he was washing the scent of her from his lips and hands. She was worn-out but never felt better. She laid her head against the back of the sofa, trying to make sense of what had just happened. Besides the mind-blowing orgasm, she wondered how they went from sharing a pizza with him eating her out in her hallway, but it was fantastic. She snuggled the blanket tight around her shoulders and closed her eyes remembering the sensation.

Garrett looked at his reflection in the mirror, puzzled at how they got to this point. He wanted to take her entirely, but she had been through a lot the last few months, and having sex with her would have been too much to add to her troubles. Closing his eyes, he licked his lips remembering her sweet taste. He wanted to hold her in his arms and reassure her that everything would be okay. He would never mislead or deceive her in any way. He would protect her from harm, even if it were from him.

He pulled his self together, exited the bathroom, and found her curled up fast asleep. He noticed how peaceful she looked, and wondered if she was dreaming of him, as he had dreamed of her for the last few months. Somewhere in the last few months, things started changing in their relationship, from partner to something else, at least for him. He began thinking of her as a little more.

He talked about her to his parents, which was something he had never done before. He looked down at her, wanting to kiss her again, then make love to her all night. But instead, he straightened the blanket on her shoulders, then sat quietly next to her on the sofa. He reached for the remote to turn off the TV and stumbled a little from the effects of too much wine, so he sat back down, then leaned his head back on the sofa. He needed to close his eyes just for a second, to clear his head but drifted off to sleep.

Hours had passed, before he awakened with Vonda's half-naked body, stretched out on top of him. Her leg laid across his thigh, as her arm rested on his chest. At first, he thought he was dreaming, but in his dreams, they both would be naked as a newborn baby and engaged in the hottest sex his mind could imagine. He tried to shift his body to slip out from under her without waking her, but the way she laid it would be impossible. As not to startle her again, he softly called her name.

"Vonda," She didn't respond, only squirmed a little rubbing against his body. He gritted his teeth, calling her name again, "Vonda."

"Yeah baby," she answered, rubbing the palm of her hand across his chest. Her words surprised and pleased him at the same time, as a smile creased his lips.

"Wake up baby I got to go," He said. Vonda sleepily stretched her body, opened her eyes looking around, and then realized where she was laying. She jumped up and retreated to the other side of the couch. Her head throbbed from the wine, and her thoughts were cloudy, but she was sure she heard him call her baby. She rubbed her hand over her rumpled hair and realized she was naked from the waist down. She was a little sore between her legs, and the first thing came to mind was that they had had sex. She looked at him and met his heated gaze, fixed between her legs. She quickly grabbed a blanket to cover herself and blushed, asking.

"Hart, what the hell are you doing?" He thought, okay she's back to her old self, then he replied. "I must not have done a good job if you don't remember?"

"What do you mean by that?" She asked angrily. With a slight edge in his tone, he replied.

"Well baby, from my count, I had you crying my name three, maybe four times." He wanted to touch her smooth brown thighs and rub his hands up to her wet spot.

"Don't flatter yourself. It was the wine."

"Well, we're both sober now. Let's see what happens?" He placed the palm of his hand on the inside of her thigh, and slowly inched up between her legs. Her eyes widen in shock, as she clamped her legs together, and pushed him away from her. He just smiled and moved back from her. "I was trying to pry myself from under your body without waking you." She gave him a "Yeah right" look, and pulled the blanket over her breasts, hiding the view of her protruding nipples, as he continued. "I didn't want to wake you since some of us do have to go to work. Garrett caught a glimpse of pain in her eyes and regretted what he had said. He hoped she knew he didn't mean it. His words hurt her deeply, but she wasn't going to let on.

"That wasn't called for. I think it's time for you to go now." Vonda stood holding her chin high, and walked to the door, opening it as a sign for him to leave. He knew she was furious, and wouldn't listen to anything he had to say. He slipped on his shoes, then walked out the door, standing on the porch, he turned to apologize, but she slammed the door in his face, cutting him off before he could get a word out.

Chapter
Fourteen

Lamar left the city to lay low, soon after the incident with Garrett, at least just until things cooled off. His cousin, Jason, lived in St. Petersburg and agreed to let him stay at his crib for as long as he needed. If in turn, he was willing to work off his room and board by hustling dope on the street for him. Lamar wasn't a saint by any means, but selling crack wasn't his scene. Nevertheless, at this point, he didn't have a choice, he had no place else to go. He knew those St. Pete hustler dudes were no joke, and knew those jokers would kill you for the t-shirt off your back, let alone your dope stash. As a precaution, Jason always had his crews work in pairs. This way someone could be a lookout, watching your back, while the other made the sell. Jason made it clear that he was family, but if he came up short with his money, it was his ass.

Lamar had upheld his side of the agreement for months earning Jason's trust. However, on one night, in particular, Jason had him make a drop to one of his best customers' cribs. Bo needed some extra product on hand, he was celebrating his twenty-ninth birthday. His neighborhood wasn't the best area to be in after dark, but this was how Jason made most of his money. Jason said he only trusted him with this drop, because most of his boys had started using their own product, spending the money they made back on more dope. Which in Jason's case wasn't good for business, but every once in a while, one of them would try him, and come up short with his money, or claim they got jacked. One of those fools, even had his smokin' buddies beat him up to look convincing. Jason was no fool, and if he had to, he had no problem strong-arming them to keep them in line. With two-thousand dollars of crack hidden in the trunk, Lamar drove his car to the south side of St. Petersburg.

"Another dead end," Lamar thought. He wasn't familiar with the area and found himself lost, again. He was supposed to make the drop over an hour ago, and if he didn't find this address quick, he was going to be in deep shit with Jason. Bo wasn't a patient man and didn't like to be kept waiting. Lamar didn't have his cell phone with him. He was in such a rush that he left it on his bed. At this time of night, it was much too dangerous to stop and make a call from a pay phone. If you could find one. Either the cops would arrest you just for being black, or some gang would jack you for whatever they could get, and he wasn't taking that chance with Jason stash. He drove around for a few minutes more, then decided to pull over in a Shopping Plaza parking lot to rethink Jason's directions. As the car idled, he went over the information in his head, then realized he took a left at South 28th Street but should have made a right. Now with the directions clear in his head, he put the car in gear and drove off.

Once he located the street, he couldn't believe his eyes and leaned closer to the steering wheel to try to make out what the hell was going on in the distance. There was no mistaking the police cars' red and blue lights flashing in front of him. There had to be ten or more police cars, and the Swat Team van up ahead. He wasn't about to stop anywhere on this block, but he slowed his speed and drove right past the address he was to make the drop. *"Damn. A raid,"* he thought and cursed to himself. People were lying out on the ground in handcuffs, and some were already seated in the back of patrol cars. It's a good thing he had gotten lost because he would have been caught up in the middle of all this drama. He needed to get back and tell Lamar what went down as fast as he could. He cruised past the patrol cars and saw Bo cuffed, lying face down on the hood of the cruiser, cursing at the top of his lungs. Bo raised his head and looked over in Lamar's direction, giving him a mean mug look, and mouthed "I'll get your ass boy," as he nodded his head up and down. Lamar was just as surprised as everyone else. *"Did Bo think he or Jason had something to do with it?"* he thought. "Man, I should have stayed in Tampa, and let Garrett kick my ass, rather than be mixed up in this shit," he mumbled.

As the view of the patrol cars grew smaller in his rearview mirror, he hurried back to home and told Jason what went down. By the time he finished his story, the word on the grapevine was all over the street, that Jason had set Bo up for the bust. Jason knew Bo wasn't a man to be messed with and knew he had to make this mix-up right. He called down to central booking to see how much it was going to cost to bail Bo out but learned there was none. Bo with his past criminal history was considered a flight risk. Since he couldn't get to Bo, he had to get the word to his boys and clear up this misunderstanding before something bad happened to him, and Lamar. Jason told Lamar that he needed to go hide out until he could straighten this out and suggested he leave town and lay low. Because Bo was going to be looking for someone to blame this on, and since he saw him drive by, more than likely, it will be Lamar. Lamar was scared, really scared and didn't have a clue where to go, but as he packed his few belongings in a pillow case, then he thought of Calisa. He hadn't talked to her in months, but he knew she would help him without a doubt.

He and Jason said their goodbyes; then he got into his car and headed back across the bridge. He called Calisa's and hoped she hadn't changed her number. He was pleased to hear her voicemail greeting before the beep sounded. He hoped she would pick up when she saw his phone number, but it was late, and she probably had gone to bed. He left her a message, saying how sorry he was for not calling sooner, that he stilled loved and missed her very much. He omitted the part about being on the run again. He did say that he needed to talk to her, and he would call her tomorrow. He added if she didn't answer, he would know that she never loved him as much as he loved her. As he drove around St. Pete, he was always checking his rearview mirror to see if anyone was following him. Once he felt no one was, he headed in the direction of Tampa, and when he reached the Howard Franklin Bridge, he felt a little easier but kept his speed under the limit. For tonight, he decided to go hide out in his old stomping ground at the factory, and sleep in his car. The next day he would contact Calisa again, and see how things went from there.

Calisa held her hot pink cell phone. She couldn't believe Lamar's name, and phone number showed on the display screen. How could he have the nerve to call her, after all this time? She hadn't heard from him since that night he and Granite had a confrontation, and Granite practically ran him out of town. She looked at her bedside clock; it was two a.m., "Why was he calling her at two a.m.?" That had always been his problem. He never thought through anything. He just did as he pleased, and the hell with anyone else, even her. Well now, she didn't want to hear anything he had to say. Nor would she fall for any more of his lies. Was she kidding herself? She missed him so much that she cried herself to sleep most nights. She held the phone in her hand close to her heart, and turned over in bed, pulling the covers up over her shoulders to her neck.

Granite had no right to come between them like he did. She knew what she was getting into when she started up with Lamar. He was from the streets, and that's what attracted her to him in the first place. He was charming when he wanted to be, street smart, and even though he had his moments, he was a good person at heart, and she loved him. She buried her head in her pillow and started to cry. Just when she thought she was over him, here he was again. This time, their relationship would be on her terms, and no one would ever come between them, not even Granite.

Chapter

Fifteen

Lamar called as promised, asking Calisa to meet with him. Calisa agreed, but it had to be at a public location, just in case his old demanding ways flared up, and he wanted to hurt her. She sat at a picnic table at the park, located not far from a local college, where many of the students hung out after school, feeling that it was a safe place. She ran this meeting over in her head a hundred times, but couldn't talk herself out of seeing him. This was crazy, and she knew that in her heart, that the outcome wouldn't be good.

Lamar stood behind a tree watching Lis when she walked up. He didn't want to appear anxious, so he let her get there first. This morning he freshened up at the corner gas station and stayed out of sight. He didn't want to risk the chance running into some of his old homies that may rat him out. He took one last look around before walking in her direction. "Hi Calisa," Lamar said from behind her. She jumped, then turned to see the strained face of Lamar. He looked like he hadn't had a good night sleep the entire time he was away.

"Don't sneak up on me like that. You know I hate it." She scorned him.

"I'm sorry baby, I wasn't trying to scare you," He said, as he slid in next to her on the bench. He leaned in to place a kiss on her cheek, but she pulled away.

"Oh, it's like that now?" He questioned.

"Like what Lamar?" She answered in disgust.

"Your brother turned you against me? That's what." He was playing the part of a hurt lover. He knew she had a soft spot for him.

"My brother didn't turn me against you Lamar. You did that all by yourself. Now don't be wasting my time. What do you want?"

"First of all, I wanted to see you because I thought you missed me, as much as I have missed you. But I guess I was wrong." He lowered his gaze in a dramatic effect, then raised it to show his watery eyes. She knew Lamar could lay it on thick, but her heart out ruled her mind, and she gave in.

"Lamar I did, I mean I do miss you, but you left me without a word. Do you know how that made me feel? How much that hurt."

"Calisa, as I recall, you broke it off with me that day," He said and paused, waiting for her to answer.

"Yes I did, but it was to make you realize that you have some serious problems at times. And before our relationship could go any further, you needed to get help."

"I know baby, and since I've been gone, I haven't smoked one joint, and I'm working on my anger issues too. I'm trying to be a better man... for us." He knew that would do the trick. He leaned in again for a kiss and, this time, she didn't turn away. She responded as he hoped she would. Once the kiss ended, she looked around to see if anyone had noticed them, but she really didn't care.

"Where are you staying?" She asked.

"Well nowhere at the time." He said in a sorrowful tone.

"What does that mean Lamar?"

"Well my cousin Jason started tripping and, needless to say, we parted ways and not on a friendly note, so I have been staying in my car." Calisa looked at him to judge if he was lying, and after a moment of silence said.

"In your car? It's too dangerous. You can stay at my house until you find a place of your own."

"Don't you still stay with your parents? What would they say?"

"They can't say anything if they don't know you're there."

"Look, baby, I don't want to get you in any trouble, and I don't need Garrett on my ass again. If he finds out, he will kill me this time for sure." Things were going as planned, and tonight he would be sleeping in a soft bed next to his woman. Hoping if he were lucky, in the next few days, he would be hitting that sweet stuff like old times. They talked for the next few hours, and before they parted, she told him to be outside her house after midnight and wait for the signal. She would turn her bedroom light off and back on when it was all clear for him to come to the back door of the house.

Lamar parked his car a few blocks away, in the housing complex parking lot, then walked back to Calisa's house at midnight. There was so much traffic going and coming from the apartments, that his car wouldn't be noticed. He flipped the hood of his jacket over his head, slowed his pace, and stopped near her house. He looked up at the window to her bedroom and noticed the light was still on. Moments later her light went off, then back on as planned. He looked around once more before he made his way to the back of the house. After a few moments, she opened the door and motioned for him to enter. She placed a finger to her lips, signaling for him to be quiet, then led him up the stairs. They passed her parents' bedroom heading towards her room at the end of the hall. She hurried him in and took one last peek, to see if they had been heard, then closed and locked her door. Within the safety of her room, Lamar took the liberty of pulling her into his arms and placed an unexpected bone-shaking kiss on her. He held her body tight against his so she could feel the effect she was having on him. She broke the kiss, and took a step back, to calm the tingling sensation surging through her body. She needed to erase the scandalous thoughts from her mind and gain control of her body. Lamar was her first and only lover, his kisses, and lovemaking, always had an overpowering impact on her. She wasn't sure if it was because he was her first, and she didn't have anyone to compare him to, or if he was as skilled in bed as he boasted. Nevertheless, this time would be different. It was one thing to let him sleep here, but sex in her parent's house was totally disrespectful and out of the question. If it came to that, then he would have to get them a room in the next city, because her father and Garrett knew too many people for her to be caught with Lamar.

"Look, Lamar, I agreed to let you stay here for a few days until you find another place. But sex... in this room, it's out of the question," She motioned with her finger in a circle, putting her hands on her hips.

"I'm sorry baby, it's just that I missed you and all this," He said as he grabbed her hips, pulling her back into his arms.

"Well get, "it," out of your mind buddy. This is not yours any longer; you lost your claim when you left me. So keep that thing in your pants and under control." She whispered and pointed to the noticeable bulge showing under his jeans.

"You know he has a mind of his own when it comes to you. Besides, why are you letting me stay here if it's not mine any longer? Your new man must not be shit if I'm here." He said placing his arms across his chest.

"I never told you I had another man. I'm not like you. You just can't walk back into my life and think you can continue where you left off."

"I didn't think that at all Lis. I know I wasn't as good to you as I should have been. But I learned how much of a good woman I had lost, and I vowed if I ever got another chance, I would make it up to you." He placed his hands on her shoulders and looked into her eyes, and added, "And I mean it."

She was overjoyed with the thought that he wanted to change his life to make things right for them. But for now, he would be sleeping on the pad, she laid out for him on the floor.

Chapter

Sixteen

Another restless night, plagued with dreams of Vonda and him engaging in the most erotic sexual acts he could imagine, even in a dream. Garrett rolled out of bed soaked in sweat and went to the bathroom to take another cold shower. If this kept up, he could probably be the cleanest detective on the force. Still wet, he wrapped a navy-blue towel around his waist and walked to the kitchen. He took a cold bottle of juice from the refrigerator, and downed it in one gulp, then looked at the clock on the range and thought, *"Three hours until his work day began."* He decided to watch a little TV to pass the time, there was no way he was getting back to sleep in his state. He located the remote that was stuck between the sofa cushions. Once the TV came on, he began flipping through the stations. There wasn't much on at three in the morning. Mostly infomercials, on various types of exercise equipment, a few grills ads, and some 1-800 hook-up line phone number advertisements. Disgusted, he turned off the TV and switched on the stereo; then leaned back to let the music ease his mind. Before he realized it, he had fallen off to sleep. The ringing of his cell phone woke him with a jolt, and he fumbled to answer it.

"Hello," He answered without looking at the display.

"Hart, were you planning on coming in to work today?" Manning asked.

"Sure Lieutenant, I'll be there at six, but if you need me there sooner, I can come in now?" He replied in a haze.

"Now would be great, because I needed your butt here thirty minutes ago, Granite! It's six thirty!" Manning yelled. Garrett jumped to his feet and looked at the time on the cable box.

"Shit! Lieutenant, I'm sorry... I'll be there as soon as I get dressed." He said and ended the call, as he rushed to his bedroom. He pulled clothes out of his closet, throwing them on top of his rumpled bed covers. He cursed the entire time he dressed, he had never been late to work a day in his life. To think his first time was because of a woman, but it wasn't any woman, it was Vonda.

About an hour later, Garrett rushed to the Lieutenant's office and noticed he wore the usual scowl on his face, as he looked over the morning files. He knocked on the door and waited for the Lieutenant's two-finger wave, granting him permission to enter his office, then he pointed towards the chair in front of his desk. Garrett knew the drill. Manning closed the file in front of him, sat back in his chair, and removed his glasses.

"Hart, is there a problem?" He asked with concern.

"Problem? No problem Sir. I just had a hard time sleeping and didn't hear my alarm this morning." He explained without adding the cause of his restless night was over Vonda.

Manning placed his glasses on the desk and felt he wasn't telling him the entire truth, then asked, "How are things working with you and Detective Bradley?"

"What? Okay, I guess." He answered, unsure where this was going. "Why?"

"No reason, I wanted to make sure things were okay between the two of you. I know how hard it had to be on you taking on a partner, and a female partner at that."

Garrett thought carefully before he answered. He didn't want to say the wrong thing or imply that there was something between Vonda and him, which it wasn't. "She's a good partner even for a woman. I can count on her to have my back, and I have hers."

Manning looked him over, feeling he had vaguely answered his questions and asked, "Was Bradley the reason you were late this morning?" Garrett wasn't sure he understood the Lieutenant's question, then he made it clearer. "Are the two of you involved?" He asked.

Garrett sat straight up in his chair and didn't mix words. "Hell no! Sir," He stood to his feet and asked, "Would you be asking me that if Bradley was a man, and I was late to work?" He thought back on their "encounter" as he likes to refer to it. He still couldn't figure out what came over him.

Manning stood as well and replied, "Look, I have enough on my hands with the both of you out-of-control hot heads. I don't need to deal with anything else going on between the two of you." He looked out into the squad room to see if anyone was out there. "Now do I need to reassign you two to other partners? Because you know, no one else wants to work with either one of you hot heads." He replied with a touch of humor in his voice.

"No sir, we're cool," Garrett said and sat back down knowing Manning took him at his word.

"Ok, now get to work, and by-the-way, Detective Bradley is taking a personal day. You'll be working by yourself. Do you need someone to back you up?"

He was surprised to hear she was taking today off. She hadn't mentioned it to him, but why would she. He wondered if everything was okay with her, "No sir, most of our cases are closed. I just need to complete some paperwork on our latest case."

"Good, now get to work. The city's not paying you to sit in my office all day." Manning ordered and reopened the file on his desk, ending the conversation.

By lunch, Garrett couldn't take it anymore. He needed to find out what was up with Vonda. He stopped at their favorite deli, picked up a few turkey clubs and headed for her apartment. With bags in hand, he knocked on her door and waited for her to answer. He knew she was home, her car was parked at the curb. He knocked again, this time, a little more forceful that the door shook. After another no answer, he turned to face the street and thought if he should go around back, to see if he could see anything through the windows. As he stepped off the small porch, an unfamiliar car pulled up to the curb with Vonda inside. Garrett didn't recognize the man behind the wheel and felt a little jealous that she would take a day off to be with another man. His grip tightened on the bags in his hand as he viewed the exchange of conversation when she exited the vehicle.

Jerrod noticed Garrett standing on the steps, and asked if she needed him to come in. She looked beyond Jerrod out the driver's side window, and swore under her breath, *"Garrett,"* when she saw him standing on her doorstep. She had learned to read him pretty well, and from what she could see, he was mad as hell. She knew she should have told him she wasn't coming in today, but she didn't want to answer a bunch of questions. Besides, they were only partners, not lovers "per say" and she didn't have to answer to him. When Jerrod called last night, he had been very persistent about needing to talk to her. He was going to be in town on business and insisted they meet to talk about some unfinished business. If she was going to completely put him out of her system. Really get on with what was left of her life, then she needed to face him and finally end what had already ended over a year ago. She wasn't sure how she would handle seeing Jerrod, after all, this time. Would she still have feelings for him, or would she want to kill him on the spot? All these questions raced through her mind. Would she have the strength to say no, if he asked her to take him back? At lunch, she learned that his mother's home was part of the divorce settlement and had to be sold and half the money would go to her. Apparently, Jerrod had purchased the house using her money without her knowing it. It wasn't a secret how she felt about Jerrod when they divorced. However, his mother had always been kind to her. She wouldn't think of putting her out of her home, that just wouldn't be right. They agreed that he would buy her part of the house at a fair market price within the next five years. That was more than fair for everyone. After settling their business, she didn't want to hear anything else he had to say. Because not all the regrets in the world could fix the hurt, he and Tierra had caused her. She picked at her food, as they shared small talk, and when she couldn't take it any longer, she asked him to take her back home. He even had the nerve to try to kiss her, as he held her door open for her. She reminded him not to press his luck, and if she had her guns, she would shoot him for sure.

She got out of the car, closed the door, and waited for Jerrod to drive away, and back out of her life, but not before, he gave Garrett an unpleasant stare. He didn't dare say anything because Garrett's anger could be seen all over his face. She walked passed him on the steps and unlocked the door.

"Hart, what are you doing here?" She asked, and entered her apartment.

"Well, I was looking for you," He stated. "I had to find out from the Lieutenant that you were taking a personal day," He said as he followed her inside, and slammed the door behind them.

"Yeah, I had some business to take care of," She said, as she kicked off her wedge-heeled sandals shoes, and righted the shoulder of her blouse. She wore a one shoulder loose fitting top, and a form fitting skirt that hugged her hips. Garrett couldn't keep his eyes off them and grew madder thinking about another man's eyes on her.

"I can see that. You could have told me yesterday, or was this engagement last minute?" He asked as he placed the bags on the table and watched her walk around in her bare feet. His eyes glanced down towards her feet and thought how pretty her toes were with the coral color polish.

"I didn't believe I had to answer to you since I cleared it with the Lieutenant."

"I was just concerned since we are partners and all."

"And?" She said, turning to face him.

"Nothing," He replied and handed her one of the white paper bags. "Here I thought you may be hungry, so I stopped and got us some lunch."

"I'm not hungry. I've already eaten." She lied. "Jerrod took me to lunch..." She said before she could stop herself. She knew she had said the wrong thing and could tell by the stiffness in Garrett's shoulders, and the hard set of his jawline.

"Excuse me. Did you say, Jerrod, as in your ex-husband Jerrod?" He asked because he couldn't believe his ears. "After all he had put you through, you went on a lunch date with him? Garrett's eyes flashed a hardened shade of gray, as the anger cultivated inside him. For some reason, he felt betrayed, as if she had cheated on him.

"Yes, if you must know. He... we had some business to discuss, as I said before."

He could tell she was uneasy talking about the date, which made him think there had been something other than lunch going on between them. "Are you considering getting back together?" He asked and held his breath waiting for her response.

"Hell no! There's nothing in the world that would make me go there, and in my book, as they say, once a cheater, always a cheater." She wanted to change the subject, and took the bag from him, and asked, "What did you bring me?"

"A turkey club on rye with extra sweet pickles," he answered with emphases on extra pickles. A big smile grew on her face, and she removed the wrapped sandwich from the bag and placed it on the table.

"I think you're trying to fatten me up," she teased. "I'm going to have to put in some extra hours at the gym," She said as she rubbed her hands over her stomach and down her hips.

"I love a woman with curves in the right places better." He said, unaware he had stepped closer to her. She was well aware of his nearness, which caused her to shiver from being very uncomfortably close. The scent of his cologne surrounded her like a warm blanket on a chilly evening. His mind raced with all sorts of thoughts, as memories of their near-sex experience, and dreams struck him like a bolt of lightning. Vonda's breasts rose and fell as her breathing quickened, and as her desire grew. He held her gaze, as he slowly lowered his lips to hers. When their lips touched, all the suppressed passion and desire rushed through them with a fury. She closed her eyes and wrapped her arms around his neck, letting the fire consume her body. The desire was overpowering, as they fought for control over the other in a passionate kiss. Their tongues explored the depths of each other's mouth. His hands slid down her back, over her hips, cupping her soft behind, before lifting her, then lowered her onto the table. As he lifted her, she wrapped her legs around his hips, bringing the hard bulge in his pants closer to the warmth of her womanly center. He broke the kiss long enough to pull her blouse over her head and toss it across the room. She took advantage of the momentary interruption and loosened his tie; lifting it over his head and threw it across the room. She ripped open the front of his shirt and threw her head back laughing, as she watched the buttons pop from his shirt like popcorn. His hands hurried to release the front hook of her bra, and greedily took her ripe nipple into his hungry mouth. Her laughter quickly was replaced with moans of pleasure, as he skillfully sucked one nipple to the other. She reached for his belt buckle, unfastened it quickly, and then unzipped his pants. Reaching her hand into his boxers, she palmed his hard shaft causing him to tremble at her touch. He wanted her naked in front of him, right there on the table, before they came to their senses. He ripped the seam of her skirt.

"Garrett, that was my favorite skirt," She said, as she continued fisting his dick.

"Damn baby, I'll buy you another one," He replied as he pushed her back on the table. She laughed again just before he ripped off her panties with one quick pull. She was so beautiful lying there ready for him to take her. He slowly ran his fingers down the length of her body starting at her neck, between her breasts, over her flat belly to her womanly lips.

Thinking she must be crazy as hell to be doing this with Garrett. He was her partner for goodness sakes. Her mind cautioned her to stop this foolishness. But her body urged her to open her legs to welcome his touch. His thumb applied pressure to her passion spot, making little circles on it, it was too late to turn back. She grabbed the edge of the table, lifting her hips to meet his wicked hand. He watched as her pleasure expressed on her face, as he stroked her until she quickly released her climax. As she rode out the wave of pleasure, he couldn't wait any longer. He pressed the crown of his dick at the opening of her wet core, pushing in slowly then pulled back out, leaving in the head, then pushed forward again a little deeper. His hips moved in and out in long slow strokes, allowing her body to adjust to him. He threw his head back fighting to control his desire to be deep in her, as her muscles wrapped around him tight. It didn't take her long to adjust to him, as her hips moved in a steady rhythm, signaling she wanted more, and he quickly obliged.

He kept the tempo slow. He wanted to take his time and make it last because Vonda felt so good. He pulled her hips to the edge of the table and raised them to meet every stroke.

Vonda wanted him, all of him like you couldn't imagine. Her body had known no other man excepted Jerrod. However, from this moment on it wouldn't want any other besides Garrett. Her pussy muscles tightened around him, as her climax neared. It took over her body with an explosive charge. Her hips lifted from the table meeting his thrust. She gripped his arms and rode out waves that electrified her being. Garrett fought to delay his release but in the end, couldn't hold out as her pussy tightened around his shaft, and instantaneously they groaned their release. He smiled as he watched Vonda's body relaxing against the table, as she made a little whimpering sound as her orgasm subsided.

Garrett awakened in Vonda's bed, with her resting contently in his arms. He wasn't sure when they had fallen asleep, but after making love for the third time, their bodies were too exhausted to do otherwise. Gently he took his finger, and brushed a few wild strands of hair from across her face, as she continued to sleep. He looked at the bedside clock and was surprised that it was seven o'clock. He had to check in with the Lieutenant, or he would have his butt in a sling. He eased out of bed as quietly as he could, and searched through the remaining heap of clothing on the floor for his cell phone, then remembered he left it in the kitchen. Taking another glance in Vonda's direction, he pulled on his boxers, left the room in search of his phone, and found it on the floor next to the table's leg. He made a quick call to the Lieutenant, told him he had been following up on some leads, and lost track of time. Lieutenant Manning didn't question him. He was known for getting caught up in a case. Manning reminded him to be on time in the morning, then ended the call. Garrett placed his phone back on the table and turned to see Vonda wrapped in a sheet standing by the refrigerator. He presumed she was naked underneath but needed to do a little detective work to be sure. Smiling as he advanced towards her, he thought he had never felt like this about any woman in a long time. He could feel himself growing hard with every step. Vonda reached into the refrigerator and grabbed two bottles of water. She and then turned towards him, pushing one of the chilled bottles into his tented boxers saying.

"I think you need this." Smiling as she opened her bottle, and took a big sip, then put some distance between them. She could not explain what was happening to her. Had she lost her senses? She knew better than to get involved with a coworker, and especially not a gigolo like Garrett, He had every woman on this side of Florida drooling after him. "I think it's time for you to leave Detective." She added.

Garrett was perplexed as to what happened from the time he left the bedroom until now. "What... What do you mean it's time for me to go? I thought I could hang out, and maybe cook you a little breakfast in the morning, and see what we could get into."

"I mean you had your little fun, and now it's time for you to leave." She replied with her back to him. He was so confused by her reaction. He didn't want to leave her and wished to explore the new feelings he was experiencing.

"Just like that, you're putting me out? What did I do this time?" He asked throwing his hands in the air.

There was a moment of silence before she spoke, "It's not what you did, but what we did, and we did a lot, much more than we should have Detective."

"Stop calling me detective, it sounds so cold!" He shouted, then took a calming breath, looked at the ceiling, then back at her. "I see what this is all about. It's Jerrod, you're getting back with him, and I was just a last-minute fling." Vonda's eyes widened in surprise at his statement and then turned cold as ice. Here was a man that she was sure had stolen, and broken many hearts in his lifetime. And he was accusing her of having a last-minute fling with him. How dare he assume she was getting back with Jerrod of all people? "Look you, green eyed fool. How many times I must say I'm not getting back with Jerrod. He's my ex, and he is going to stay my ex for as long as I live. Anyway, I don't have to explain myself to you, or anyone else. Not even my parents. So, I suggest you put on the rest of your clothes and get the hell out of my house!" She yelled and threw her water bottle at him. He ducked and looked at the bottle as it flew past his head, hitting the kitchen cabinets.

"Okay woman, you need to calm down. Besides, I'm not leaving here with you mad at me again. So let's both calm down and talk about this." He said holding out his hands.

"Oh, I'm not mad! You haven't seen mad yet. Besides, I would never let a Gigolo like you get on my last nerve." Taken aback by her statement, he had heard it all. He had been called many things but never a gigolo.

"Look Vonda, I don't know what you've heard about me, but if you think I'm a gigolo, then you've heard lies. Just because you see a man that attracts a lot of women doesn't mean he's a gigolo. I have never ever played or used any woman. I have a sister and mother, and if someone did that to them... I would come very close to losing my badge." They stood looking at one another trying to assess the situation when Vonda said, "Just leave Hart," with a heavy heart.

"No, I can't leave us like this," He said, as he tried to take her in his arms. She pushed against his chest to keep some distance between them, but she could feel her desire growing.

"There is no us, and there will never be, so please leave." She fought to hold back the tears forming and hoped he didn't detect the crackle in her voice. Garrett held her hand against his aching heart. The heart he knew would only belong to her. He leaned down to taste the sweetness of her mouth one last time.

The kiss they shared was full of passion, tenderness, and longing to be loved. He fought the need to take her back to her bed and make love to her repeatedly. Until their bodies and minds were satisfied to the fullest, and could no longer function, then gave up once again to exhaustion. Instead, he feasted on her lips, filled his lungs with her scent, and then went to dress. When he returned to the kitchen to gather his phone and keys, she was sitting on the sofa with the sheets pulled tight around her body. Neither could find the words to say goodbye, so he left and closed the door behind him.

Behind the security of a locked door, Vonda broke down and cried her heart out for giving herself to a man like Garrett. She was only fooling herself to believe he could want, let alone love someone, whose life was as messed up as hers. How could she face him in the morning, and the days to come? She hadn't felt this foolish since the day she walked in on Jerrod and Tierra. *"Why was her life such a mess?"* She thought as she lay with her head resting on her arm, inhaling the faint scent of him that still lingered on her. Leaping to her feet, she rushed to the bathroom to wash away any traces of him from her body, and hopefully her heart.

Garrett sat in his car for a moment, trying to wrap his mind around what had just happened between them, before he headed home. For the first time in his life, he wanted to wake up in the morning with a woman lying beside him, and do all the things couples did together. Couples... when did they go from partners to couples? He realized that things were going too fast for the both of them, but now that he tasted her honey, he couldn't get enough of it. He started his car, as he glanced at the door to her apartment. He had to restrain himself from going back, and banging on it until she let him in. For now, he decided to go to his parents' house, a place where he always felt at peace, and check on them before going home to another restless night.

♥ ♥ ♥

"Hey, Mom, anybody home?" He yelled as he entered the house that he still called home.

"Yeah baby, I'm in the kitchen," His mother, Carol, called out. He found her standing at the kitchen table and gave his mother a kiss on the cheek. He walked to the refrigerator and looked in as he had done his entire life, looking for his special bottle of juice she kept for him. Locating the last bottle of pineapple juice hidden in the back, he opened it and then sat at the table. Carol scraped the mixture of macaroni and cheese into the glass cooking dish. She watched Garrett play with the top from the bottle. After placing the filled dish in the oven, she smiled to herself knowing something was on his mind. He never realized it, but as long as she could remember when he was troubled about something, he would sit at this table with his juice and play with the bottle top. She wiped her hands on the dishtowel hanging on the door and pulled out a chair at the table across from him. She watched him for a moment before he realized she was watching him. He smiled and asked, "What?"

"I should be asking you the same thing, mister." She gave him a motherly touch of her hand and stopped him from spinning the top again. "Tell your mother what's on your mind." She asked.

"What makes you think something is on my mind?" He asked her.

"Boy, I'm your mother. I know my children, and something is troubling you." He looked at her puzzled, then dropped his gaze towards the table.

"Man, how did you know? Are you a mind reader or something?" He laughed, looking into her caring eyes.

"Let me let you in on a little secret. For as long as I can remember when something is troubling you. You would sit at this table and spin the top from that juice bottle, as if the faster it spun, the faster the answer would come to you."

"I have?" he asked.

"Yes, you have. Now tell me what's up?" she asked. Garrett didn't want to tell his mother that he spent the day with his partner having mind-blowing sex with her. So instead, he told her there was a woman he liked, that didn't feel the same way. Carol laughed, reminding him of all the little girls, and women, that came to her crying, that they were in love with her son. But he didn't feel the same way. They were all heartbroken too, and in his heart, he knew she was right. He would have never thought the time would come when circumstances would be reversed.

Nevertheless, if he was going to fall for someone, why did it have to be his partner that had stolen his heart? The person he would have to work with every day. He continued to talk with his mother as she finished preparing dinner, and when everything was ready, he made a plate to take home. Calisa arrived home as he was leaving and walked past him without speaking. She was still mad at him for butting into her personal life, but he was her brother. It was his job to protect her, and he took that responsibility very seriously. Yes, she was a grown woman and could handle herself, but sometimes love can blind you from the truth.

She greeted her mother, then headed towards the kitchen to make a plate to carry to her room, where Lamar was waiting. After Carol and Garrett had said their goodnights, she entered the kitchen as Calisa was leaving. She looked at the plate in her hand and wondered where she was putting all the food she seemed to be eating lately. One thing she could be grateful for was that Calisa was cleaning up her own room and doing her own laundry. Thank God for small favors, she thought, shaking her head in disbelief.

Garrett endured another restless night of sleep, filled with thoughts of Vonda and their lovemaking. He swore he could still taste her sweetness on his lips and smell her scent. Just thinking of her, caused his breathing to increase, and the blood to rush through his veins down to his shaft. For once, he hated himself for being so reckless and jumping into a situation without thinking first. He didn't have time for a steady relationship with any woman. Let alone someone as fragile as his Vonda. He was at a point in his life where he should be thinking about settling down and having a family. Maybe a few kids by the time he reached forty were what he needed. He smiled at the thought of a little Garrett running around here, or maybe a sassy girl like Vonda. He sat up in bed at the thought of kids, then remembered he hadn't used any protection in their haste when they made love. He slowly lowered his body back to the bed and thought, *"Made Love... not just sex."* That was a first in the book of Granite, referring to sex with any woman he had slept with as making love. Until he talked to her in the morning, that was another thing, he had to worry about. If she were pregnant, what would she do? Would she tell him or would she abort it, and act as if nothing ever happened? Immediately, he was on his feet pacing the room. He balled his hands into a fist and thought, *"How dare she get rid of my baby. Who did she think she was, not wanting to have my baby?"* He stopped pacing, laughed at himself, and got a grip. He didn't even know if she was pregnant, it might be too soon to tell. Sitting back down on the bed, he wanted to call her just to hear her voice and put his mind to rest about this issue. He knew she wouldn't pick up the phone so he settled in and tried to get some sleep.

Garrett arrived at the station early and waited for her car to pull into the employees' parking lot. He opened his door, got out and headed in her direction. He noticed she didn't appear to be in any better mood, than the last time he saw her. He put on a strained smile and waited for her to exit her car.

Vonda turned off her engine and sat for a moment before she opened her door. She hadn't gotten much sleep last night and wasn't in the mood for any of his mess. She wondered what he was up to when she noticed the silly smile on his face. Opening the car door, she sucked her teeth in discussed and exited her car.

"Good morning Vonda," He said as pleasantly as he could under the circumstance.

"Detective," she replied and clicked the automatic lock on her doors.

He looked out over the parking lot to see if anyone was looking at them, he then thought what would they see other than two partners talking.

"We need to talk... about last night." He said.

"What about last night? From where I stand nothing happened that we can't put behind us, and I want to leave it that way." She replied and walked away.

"Look, I need to ask you something, and if you don't want everyone in our business, then I suggest you get in my car." His temper was starting to rise, and he fought to keep it under control, but she was making it very difficult. She could see the set determination in his eyes. He wasn't taking no for an answer. She walked over to his car, opened the door and got in; slamming the door closed. Garrett clenched his teeth at the sound of his door slamming. He took a few deep breaths and then got in behind the wheel. He glanced over at her and wanted to start the car, drive back to his place, and make love to her until he wiped that smug expression away.

Vonda asked staring at him. "Now, what was so damn important that you would show your ass, and threaten to put my personal business on the street?"

"First, last night was our personal business and as much my fault as yours. But you don't see me acting like a spoiled child." He waited for her to respond, but when she continued to look out the window, with her arm folded across her chest, he went on. "Neither one of us was prepared for what happened, nor did we take the proper precaution to prevent... you know." He struggled to express the right words.

"No Hart I don't know. Will you please spell it out so I can get to work?" She almost shouted at him. He didn't know any other way to put it, so he asked. "Could you be pregnant?"

Offended by his question, she asked. "What the hell are you talking about?" She exploded at the idea that she may be having his baby. Garrett gripped the steering wheel then slammed his elbow against the window.

"Vonda don't act like you don't know what I'm talking about. We sort of was caught up at the moment. I didn't use a condom, and unless you are on the pill or something, there is a chance that you're pregnant."

She gave a small chuckle then said, "You don't have to worry about that. I have that covered with a Hormonal Implant. Do you know what that is?" She asked, then explained. "It's a device that prevents me from getting pregnant. My doctor recommended it years ago due to the type of work I do. I didn't want to unexpectedly get pregnant, and lose it by being gut-punched." He loosened his grip on the steering wheel as he calmed at the news, but deep down he felt a little disappointed. "You happy, now can I get to work?" She exited the car without allowing him time to answer. He wanted to tell her more as he watched her enter the building. He wanted to tell her how he felt but knew it would just make her furious. He gathered his things and placed his thoughts of Vonda Bradley in the back of his mind, but knew they would never be far away.

Chapter
Seventeen

It had been a little over a week since the raid on Bo's house. He still didn't have a clue as to who dropped a dime on him, but he would bet his last dime it was Jason and his punk ass cousin, Lamar. Nevertheless, if it weren't, they would have to pay the price and set an example. Bo knew they were monitoring his calls, so the only person he had spoken to was his lawyer. These Fed's thought they were smart but not as smart as he was because anyone could be bought, and these guys were no exception. Bo paid one of the guards a grand, to sneak him a pre-paid cell phone to make a few calls, and no one would ever know. He made two calls; the first was to his man Dee. Dee was his go-to guy if he needed someone to come up missing. Dee would make sure it was done, and no one could trace it back to him. If the price was right, he didn't ask any questions, and Bo made sure he would be paid well for the job. He gave Dee the names of the two snitches he wanted to disappear, asked him his price, and told him his money would be there within twenty-four hours. Next, he called his lawyer and told him where and when to drop off ten g's to Dee and to pay a grand to the guard. He gave the phone back to the guard, told him his money would be dropped off at the location by tonight. He also told him that if he double-crossed him, that he knew where he and his family lived and left it like that.

Dee had one of his boys pick up his money from the lawyer, and bring it back to him. He didn't need to count it because he knew no one was crazy enough to short him on a deal. He placed the backpack in his safe, sat back in his chair, and finished his expensive cigar. What he didn't tell Bo was that he was going to be out of town for a few days on business. He planned to expand his business to other states and had made contact with this group of interested investors on the east coast. He would be entrusting this job to some of his new boys, as sort of an initiation ceremony. How hard could it be to whack a couple of dudes like Jason and Lamar? The young twins had already earned a name for themselves on the streets. They wanted to move up to bigger and more profitable things, and they had to prove themselves if they wanted to be one of Dee's boys. He had heard that some twins did everything alike, but what were the chances they both were bad to the bone and had an appetite for the street life. He gave them the information and told them where their two subjects were the last time he saw them and sent them on their way.

Jason tried unsuccessfully to get the word to Bo that he wasn't the one that dropped the dime on him. Why would he do that to one of his best customers? Now the word was out that Dee was looking for him and Lamar. Which only meant one thing; Bo had put a hit out on them, and once the money exchanged hands there was no calling it off. Dee didn't work that way or gave refunds. As a precaution, Jason had posted a few of his boys, Toot and Turk, out front of his house as lookouts. He knew that Bo and

Dee were tight. There was a possibility that Dee would be handling the hit himself, but the word was Dee was out of town on business, and wouldn't be back for a few days.

Jason took that as a blessing and sold as much product as he could, and planned to leave town like Lamar, but he would be going further than across the bridge. As Jason picked up his duffle bag and headed for the door, he heard a popping sound, *"Gunfire,"* he thought. He dropped his bag and pulled his gun from his waistband.

"Who's there?" He asked as he turned around to see if he could see anyone. "Toot, Turk where the hell are you!" He yelled, but neither answered. He fired off two shots in that direction then asked, "Who the hell is out there?" His hands slightly shook as he aimed the gun; picking up the duffel bag and backed back down the hallway, firing off another round into the darkness. The house was dark, and he could barely see. The back door seemed to be his only way out, and the only thing standing between him, and it was fear. Jason was a badass in the hood and had no problem kicking ass if his money came up short. If he had to kill someone to prove his point, he would, but this shit was on another level. It was him on the receiving end, and he had to make a run for it.

He straightened the duffel bag on his shoulder, took a few deep breaths, and made a run for it. The back door couldn't be more than 30 feet from where he stood, but it sure felt a lot further for him to reach the door. He quickly turned to glance behind him, when something caught his legs, and he hit the floor like a ton of bricks. His head hit the floor, knocking him dizzy for a second, but before he could regain his senses, two dudes were on him. One kicked the gun out of his reach, while the other jerked him up by his collar, throwing him against the back door. To make sure they had his attention, one of them pulled his gun and shot him. The pain ripped through his leg as the bullet entered and exited in a matter of seconds. He screamed for help but knew they would go unanswered in this neighborhood. They dumped him in one of the kitchen chairs; duct taped his hands behind his back, and his legs to the chair legs as well. They only asked one question, "Where is your cousin Lamar?" Jason knew they were going to kill him, but hoped he could talk his way out of this by offering them money, plus the info they wanted. He told them that Lamar was hiding at his old lady's parents' house in Tampa. He didn't know the exact address but gave them enough information that they wouldn't have any trouble finding him. He also told them about the money and offered it to them in exchange for his life. They picked up the bag, opened it, and found it full of cash.

Nevertheless, they told him they couldn't double-cross Dee, and that this was just business. One took a device from his pocket, a leather strap attached to two wooden sticks. He placed it around Jason's throat, then twisted it until his body jerked trying to free himself, and from lack of oxygen. The other took a joint from his pocket, lit it and took a deep drag from it, then closed the money bag. Once Jason's body stopped jerking, he removed the strap, reached for the joint and took a puff, then passed it back. They picked up the rope they used to trip Jason then looked around to make sure they didn't leave any evidence that could be traced back to them. At the door, one stopped and looked back, pulled his gun and shot Jason's body twice in the chest, then looked at one another.

"Just wanted to make sure," he said and closed the door behind him. It would take days before Toot, and Turk's bodies were found behind the house, as well as finding Jason.

They returned the money to Dee and got the okay to go after the cousin in the morning. He praised them for a job well done, gave them a handful of cash from the bag, and told them to go to the club and have some fun on him. Before they left, Dee suggested they steal a car for the job, so when it was done to dump it and Lamar's body in the river.

The twins left Dee's, went to the club to have a little fun before they finished the job. They called their crew and told them to meet them for a night of drinking, women, and sex, their treat. Some of their boys were already at the spot when they arrived. When they entered, a few of the regular customers finished their drinks and left. The twins had a rep of being big trouble, and if you were smart, you didn't want any parts of it. They bogarted a table at the back of the club and ordered several bottles of rum and a setup, which consisted of cups, a bucket of ice and the chaser of your choice. The waitress placed the tray on the table and took the money and a hefty tip for the order. She smiled, told them thanks and said she would be back to check on them in a while. They watched as her big booty crammed in a short tight skirt walked away, then gave each other some dap and laughed. They added more chairs as other crew members arrived to join the celebration. The twins were a product of parents of the street. Their father was a drug addict, as well as their mother who sold herself to afford their habit. Since they didn't look like either one of their parents, they assumed that the man they knew as their father wasn't, but you wouldn't dare tell him that if you wanted to live. They lived a very dysfunctional life, but the bond was strong. They took care of each other, and no one came between them. Their mother died of an overdose when they were about ten, and when the County Coroner's office took her body away, everything went on as usual. At least, she was out of her misery. Their father tried to make sure they went to school. But like their mother, the drugs and them, soon got out of control, and soon afterward, they were kicked out of school. They continued to hustle the streets and became good at it. Soon, they grew tired of standing on the corner hustling for someone else. They wanted to move up in the business and knew that Dee ran things in the city. If they wanted to take their operation to the next level, he was the man to start with. They thought it was ironic that they were hired to kill two dudes that were blamed for setting up Bo. When in fact, it was them; that had turned a dime on him to save their father. You do what you need to do for family, so when The Feds approached them a few months ago after their father was caught transporting drugs across state lines to support his habit. Usually, if he were picked up, he would have been booked and released. But this time, because he had twenty grams of drugs on him, there was no bail.

They closed down the bar, bidding their friends' good night, and went home to sleep off their high, before they started out in the morning to find their target. They entered their rundown apartment and found their father lying on the floor with his crack pipe lying beside him. They lifted him and laid him on the sofa; then covered him with an old blanket and headed to the room they shared. As always, they bumped fists, which was their way of saying goodnight and turned out the light.

Chapter

Eighteen

Calisa gathered up the dishes from her room to return them to the kitchen, while Lamar took his shower. Her hands were too full to close the door completely so she closed it the best she could with her foot. She checked the hall then hurried past her parents' room then down the steps. She didn't know how long she could keep this up before her parents found out about Lamar. Besides him being cooped up in that room all day, was making him irritable, and he was getting on her last nerve trying to make a move on her every chance he got. She had to come up with another living solution for him and get him out of the house. She scraped the leftover crumbs in the garbage disposal then loaded the dishwasher. She took a moment and sat at the kitchen table to rest before leaving for school. She was carrying a full schedule of college courses and working at the mall part-time, was getting to her. She once loved Lamar, so she thought, but now that they were spending so much time together, she could see another side of him, that everyone else saw, and she didn't like it very much. He was running up her cell phone bill calling some of his old friends, and playing those online games. She even thought of telling Garrett about him but didn't want to give him the satisfaction of being right about Lamar. She rested her head on the table and closed her eyes just for a second.

Carol just couldn't seem to get going this morning and needed another cup of coffee to give her that boost.

"Honey, do you want another cup of coffee while I'm getting me one?" She asked Charles from the doorway. He shook his head no. As she closed the door, she heard noise coming from Calisa's room, then thought they hadn't seen much of each other lately. Maybe she would come and have a cup of coffee with her so they could get caught up on things. She lightly tapped on the door as she entered Calisa's room. She was baffled to see a pad of blankets on the floor next to the window. As she walked further into the room, she could hear humming coming from the bathroom, but it wasn't Calisa, she was sure of that. She pushed the bathroom door open, and to her surprise, there stood Lamar of all people with a towel wrapped around his waist.

"What the hell are you doing here?" She screamed at him. He was so shocked to see Mrs. Hart that he backed up and fell over in the tub pulling the shower curtains down over him. Mr. Hart came rushing in to see what all the commotion was about, and couldn't believe his eyes. He rushed past his wife and tried to grab Lamar from the tub, but the curtains got in the way.

Calisa heard the screaming, jumped to her feet, rushed up the stairs to her room and into the small bathroom where everyone was.

"Mom, Dad, what are you doing in my room?" She asked, as she rushed to Lamar's side and helped him to his feet.

"Lis, what the hell is this boy doing in your room?" Charles asked as Carol held him back from getting to Lamar. She didn't need Charles having a setback now that he was recovering so well.

"Charles calm down. You don't need to be getting yourself all worked up. Let's give her a chance to explain." Carol said trying to defuse the situation.

"There's nothing to explain Carol. I can put two and two together, and it comes out to he's been staying here for a while. Now it all makes sense. All the extra food she piles on her plate and brings up here to this fool. She's locking her door every time she leaves and goes to bed at night. I'm no fool, woman!" Charles states angrily. Lamar didn't know what to say, so he just stayed quiet and out of Mr. Hart's reach. He decided things were getting out of control. He rushed out of the small room to the bedroom and dressed as fast as he could, while Calisa and Mrs. Hart continued to hold on to Mr. Hart.

"I'm going to call Garrett," Carol said and hurried to her room to the nearest phone.

"I don't need Garrett; I can take care of this punk myself. Come here you fool. I'll teach you to take advantage of my daughter!" Charles shouted as he reached for Lamar again. But the slippery boy managed to avoid Charles grip, running pass him and out of the room, with Calisa now close on the heels. They took the steps two at a time until they reached the bottom, then continued out the front door onto the streets.

♥ ♥ ♥

The twins combed the neighborhood looking for the street where Lamar was last seen. From the description they were given, there he was up ahead, waiting for them to snatch his sorry ass up. The driver smiled at the thought of what was to come He stepped on the gas until they were next to Lamar, and some hot chick then slammed on the brakes. The twin in the passenger seat opened his door, jumped out, pointed his gun in Lamar's face, and demanded they get in the backseat. Calisa was terrified and tried to run, but she was grabbed by her hair and pushed against the car.

"Get in, or I'll leave you dead on these streets!" He demanded as he pushed the barrel of the gun to her head.

"What's this all about man? We don't have any money, look," Lamar said as he turned the pockets of his jeans inside out. Realizing what was going on, he pleaded, stepping between the gunman and Calisa. "Come on man, leave her out of this. I know who sent you and what you want."

"Well, if you know so much, then you know I can't let her go. She saw my face. Now get in!"

Carol and Charles opened the door and was horrified to see their daughter and Lamar, being pushed in the backseat of a car at gunpoint. Charles' law enforcement and fatherly instinct took over as he rushed down the steps to help them without thinking of the consequences. He was able to get the part of the license plate number, that wasn't covered by mud as it sped away. Realizing she had a phone, Carol entered Garrett's phone number and prayed he would answer.

Garrett and Vonda left the station on their way to follow up on a domestic case they were working on. The tension in the car was thick in the small confines of the vehicle. Garrett struggled to concentrate on his driving and keep his eyes on the road and off Vonda. He thought she looked especially beautiful today, which he hoped he contributed to her having that radiant glow about her. He wasn't one to boast, but he had put it on her last night, and he had the bite marks on him to prove it. The corners of his lips curled in a slight smiled, as thoughts of her screaming his name one minute, then whimpering like a puppy, after she calmed down from her climax. Just thinking about it, had him wanting her again.

Vonda glimpsed out of the corner of her eye and noticed Garrett with a smug smile on his face. She wondered why in the hell did he keep looking at her. The blaze in those eyes was playing havoc with her nerves, among other parts of her body.

After he had left her apartment, she could still feel his powerful pleasure that lingered for hours. It had been a long time since she had sex like that, and last night he made her aware of just how long it had been. Moreover, what she had been missing.

"Hart, what are you looking at?" She finally asked.

"What, what are you talking about woman? He replied with a humorous tone in his voice. Giving him a hardened look, before she was about to give him the tongue-lashing of his life when his phone rang. He laughed and said as he removed his phone from the case on his belt, "Hold that thought," and looked at the display on the phone. "Hello Mama," He greeted warmly, but the smile soon dropped from his face. Abruptly, he slammed on the breaks not caring if any cars were behind him upon hearing the alarm in her voice. He managed to pull the car off the road.

"Calm down Mama, I can't understand what you're saying." Vonda could hear the panicked tone in his voice, as he struggled to make sense of what was said. "What's wrong?" she asked but got a wave of his hand. "Kidnaped who was kidnaped?" He asked trying to piece together what was happening. "Calisa, Lamar? I'll be there in a minute." He dropped the phone on the seat, pulled the car back on the road. Trying to explain to Vonda what he could gather from his Mother about what was going on and within minutes, they were pulling up in front his parents' house.

Chapter

Nineteen

"Come on man, let her go! I told you she didn't have anything to do with this, and she won't talk. Ain't that right Calisa?" Lamar begged again for them to spare Calisa's life. He hadn't wanted this to happen, especially not to her. She was good people and didn't deserve to leave this world like this. He now saw that he was all wrong for her, and they shouldn't have ever gotten involved. His entire life he had been a user, but this was the only time that he could remember that he regretted. His way of life was one of the streets, a do to others, before they did it to you, motto.

"He's right, I don't know anything. So please let me go, and I will keep my mouth closed. I promise, please." She cried, as she pulled at the cloth tied around her hands. She should have listened to her parents. Lamar hadn't changed. He just learned how to hide it better, or was she that blind by her love for him.

"Man I'm sorry, but your lady must suffer the consequence along with your snitchin' ass. Snitches get found in ditches, and that's just where they're gonna find you two in a few weeks or so." He laughed as he waved the gun in their face.

Garrett and Vonda arrived at his parents' house as fast as they could. Charles and Carol were waiting for them outside on the steps. The car came to a screeching halt at the curb, and they stood as Garrett rushed up to them and asked, "Now what's going on? What do you mean Lis was snatched and pushed in a car?" Charles spoke first, "She had just run outside with that Lamar…"

"Lamar! What was she doing with him?" Garrett asked, but felt in his gut that this wasn't going to be good that Lamar was back in the picture.

"We discovered that she had been hiding him in her room. Your mother found out when she went to her room this morning." Charles said.

"Damn both of them. I told Calisa to stay away from Lamar," Garrett slammed his fist in his hand and looked over at Vonda, who was standing quietly by his side. Carol stood with her arms wrapped around her waist. She was worried that her daughter would be seriously hurt, or maybe killed. And from the look of the man with the gun, killed was more like it.

"That doesn't matter right now Garrett. You got to find my baby and bring her back home safe." Carol cried, as she took Charles hand and leaned on him for support.

"Don't worry, we will find her," he said to comfort his mother. They gave Garrett a description of the car and the man, and then he said. "We'll start combing the streets looking for them, and call the Lieutenant and give him the same information you gave me. He'll take it from there." Garrett and Vonda got back in his car and took off down the street. Garrett had a gut feeling that they should start at the old factory on the other side of town. It was still a hotspot for all sorts of criminal activities. If you wanted an isolated location to kill a person, that was the place. Garrett loved his sister more than he loved anyone, and if anything happens to her, God helps the person that harmed her. His intense gaze in his eyes was set on the road. The tight set of his jaw, let her know that he was on the verge of exploding if he didn't find her soon. She just hoped they would find them alive. Vonda assured him as she entwined her fingers with his and offered a weak smile. "Don't worry; she's going to be okay baby."

Two blocks from the factory, Garrett slowed to a stopped and turned off the engine of his car. He knew this area well, and the best advantage point for looking down into the factory, and not be detected, was from the north side. They quietly advanced towards the building, and he was right; they could see four people, but it didn't mean there wasn't more. His sister and Lamar were tied up and leaning on an old car. They couldn't hear what was said, but by the expression on their faces, it wasn't good. The guy holding the gun hit Lamar across the face, then pushed him to the floor. Garrett clenched his fist as the man turned his attention towards Calisa. Calisa had a lot of heart like Garrett. She could be mean as a snake and would fight to the end if she had to. Before he had a chance to hit her, she kicked him in the groin, dropping him to his knees. *"Way to go Calisa!"* He thought.

However, he feared that little stunt would cost her, and it did. Once he recovered and got to his feet, he slapped her across the face, hard enough that it flipped her over on her back. Garrett

218

jumped to his feet to run to his sister's defense. But Vonda grabbed him by the arm, holding him back to keep him from charging in and killing the man that dared hit his sister. She reminded him that they had to use their heads if Calisa was to come out of this alive. Garrett knew it wouldn't take long before Manning would figure it out, as he did and he the others would arrive. He couldn't afford any mistakes. This was his sister's life on the line, and he had to make his move, but he needed to get Vonda out of the way first. He asked Vonda to go back to the car, wait for the others, and he would stay and keep an eye on them. Vonda didn't think twice about his request and did as her partner asked. No sooner than she walked off; one of the men grabbed Lamar by his collar, dragging him as he pleaded to the back of the car. He was made to get into the trunk as the other thug watched, keeping his gun pointed at Calisa.

She knew her parents had called Garrett by now, and he was out looking for them. She stared at the barrel of the weapon and prayed that for once Garrett would stick his nose in where it didn't belong and would come rescue them.

Vonda waited by the car for Manning and his men a few blocks from the factory. The lights from the parade of patrol cars were flashing as they sped towards her with their sirens off. At least, half-dozen men in squad cars stopped behind Garrett's car. Manning asked as he jumped out of his car, storming toward

Vonda, asking. "Detective Bradley, where the hell is Detective Hart?"

"He told me to meet you here while he kept an eye on the suspects, and bring you back to the factory." Just as the words touched her lips, she knew what he had done. Garrett wanted her out of the way so he could do something stupid. "Damn!" She shouted and ran back towards the factory with what appeared like an army of men hot on her heels.

Garrett had made his way close enough to the door to see that there were only two of them. Both held a 45 in their hand, and by their unstable behavior looked to be high on something. Thinking this was the perfect time to make his move on the man standing at the trunk of the car. Lamar's begging and was making so much noise that it made it easy for him to sneak up close enough, to tap the man on the shoulder. When he turned around, Garrett punched him in the face with his fist, knocking him unconscious. Garrett placed a finger against his lips to signal for Lamar to be quiet. Lamar didn't know whether to be happy, or terrified to see him, but decided Garrett was the best option of the two. Lamar got out of the trunk, then Garret pushed the unconscious thug inside, and lowered the lid. They leaned down behind the car and Garrett pointed to the exit, instructing him to leave, as quietly as possible and run to the highway where his partner was waiting. Once he had Lis, they would join him. Lamar took off running towards the door and was almost to safety when his pants slid down his skinny butt tripping him to the ground.

"Hey man, what's going on back there?" The other guy asked as he raised his gun in their direction. Garrett cursed silently, stood to his feet, and closed the trunk.

"Okay man, it's over. Put the gun down and put your hands on the top of your head." Garrett said as he walked towards him not bothering to show his badge. The young thug called out to the other man but got no response. "He's not going to answer you," Garrett replied. So do as I say and you can keep on living."

"Fuck you, man!" He nervously shouted and pointed his gun towards Calisa's head, then back at Garrett. Calisa knew that expression on Garrett's face and knew it wasn't going to be good. As she broke free of his grip, she fell to the ground, rolled underneath the front of the car as far as she could, and tucked her body in tight. Garrett had no other choice, but to fire off two rounds at the young man, one hitting him in the shoulder causing him to drop the gun, and the other in his leg.

Vonda and the others heard the gunfire coming from the direction of the building. The men ducked, not sure if someone was shooting at them. Vonda, on the other hand, drew her weapon and charged forward. Her heart beat wildly, scared to think Garrett might have been shot. She entered the building as Garrett handcuffed a wounded suspect. She hoisted her gun, as she walked towards Garrett and tried to calm the anger steadily rising in her.

Calisa crawled out from under the car, rushed towards Garrett and jumped into his arms, hugging him tight as he did her.

"Granite I knew you would come. Thanks, big brother." She said as she held on tightly to him.

"If you don't stop calling me Granite maybe next time I may leave you to fend for yourself," He laughed. "But you know I always got your back sis," He replied as he continued to hug her. Vonda stood next to them, waiting for their moment to pass when Manning and the others entered and attended to the injured man. "Sir, there's another one in the trunk. He's out cold. Be careful, he's not cuffed." Garrett advised.

"Hart that was another fool stunt you pulled to add to a list of many, but since Calisa wasn't hurt, I guess you did well." He said and turned his attention to Calisa. He pulled out his cell phone to call her parents, who were waiting for news of her safety. Vonda touched Garrett on the shoulder and motioned for him to step outside. He looked at his sister again, turned, and then followed her outside a few feet away from the commotion. Garrett turned to face Vonda and for the first time noticed the anger in her eyes. He knew she would be upset for that stunt, and nothing he could say would probably calm her, but he had to try.

"You lied to me! How could you do that!" she huffed, with her fist balled at her side.

"I know I know you're upset, but I had to do..." Before he could finish his explanation, she slapped him, across the face. It rocked him for a moment. However, what she did next shocked him even more. She grabbed him by the shirt, pulled him to her body, and kissed him passionately, right there in front of everyone. He melted against her body, encircling his arms around her waist, pulling her closer to him. He returned her kiss with as much passion as she gave him. The kiss was broken by Manning shouting. "Hey, you two! Cut that out!" She looked around at all the eyes staring at them and quickly walked away from the building, leaving Garrett standing there shocked.

"Garrett, I think you better go handle your business," Calisa remarked.

Dazed he looked as if he didn't understand her meaning at first, then smiled and ran after Vonda. She was so embarrassed that she didn't want to talk to anyone, especially Garrett Hart. He called out to her several times, but she kept on walking. He knew she heard him, so when he caught up with her halfway to the car, he stepped in front of her.

"Hart get out of my way," She said through clenched teeth.

"Wait. We need to talk." He pleaded.

"We have nothing to talk about," She said as she stepped around him and continued walking.

"I think we do after that kiss." He reminded her as he gently grabbed her arm, and turned her to face him.

"It was a moment of insanity. Don't worry about it. It won't happen again."

"I rather enjoyed it, quite a bit," He added, as he placed an open palm on the side of her face, staring down into her tear-filled eyes. "We don't have to hide how we feel anymore."

She studied him for a moment, then as if a weight had been lifted from her shoulders. The fear that she had at the thought of losing him showed as she looked up into his face and said. "You could have been killed." He regretted deceiving her the way he did, but he didn't want her implicated if his plan didn't go well. He could see the fear, the love in her eyes for him. "But it didn't. I'm here. I'm okay." He reassured her as he reached for her.

"Don't," She demanded as she pushed his hand away. She stood on shaky legs in front of her partner, the man she realized she cared for, even loved.

"Why? You didn't mean it when you kissed me?" She couldn't answer. She just stood looking into those eyes that had captured her heart. "What was that all about Vonda? Answer me, please." He almost begged.

"I... I don't know Hart. It just happened."

"Oh, so it's Hart again? You need to stop fooling yourself because I'm not anymore." He said. He knew there had been this thing between them for some time now. "I've felt it, and now I'm sure you have too." She averted her gaze from him to the ground. She didn't want him to read her thoughts or see the truth in her eyes. He placed a finger under her chin, lifting her face to his and continued, "For me, it started that day you and Jerrod went to lunch. It felt as if you had cheated on me. I was so angry with you, I could have exploded, but instead, I made love to you. I wanted to remove any feelings you had for him by loving you so hard, so long, I would be the only man you ever wanted again. So, let's stop playing games and let's see where this goes."

"I can't take that chance again. I just can't." The tears welling in her eyes rolled down her cheeks, as she thought of Jerrod's betrayal.

"Look Vonda, baby, I'm not your ex-husband. I would never hurt you like that. Now I can't promise you if we give this a try, where it would lead, but I'm willing to give it my all. What about you?" Garrett knew he wanted to try and make things work with them, and he indeed would give it his all. But she couldn't keep judging him, or every other man by what Jerrod had done. Vonda's heart and mind raced with so many emotions and thoughts. She wanted more from Garrett than just being his partner but did she dared risk her heart being hurt again to find out. She searched his face and saw truth and sincerity there.

"Okay, Garrett. I'm willing to try." She replied and was delighted to see him smile, and he asked.

"Say it again," He asked.

"Say what?"

"My name, I love the way it sounds rolling off your lips," He said close to her ear. She smiled at his silly request but put on her sexiest voice, and she repeated

"Garrett... Garrett... Garrett," and each time she said his name she followed with a kiss, which he gladly returned.

Chapter

Twenty

Garrett's hips slammed into Vonda's ass as he thrust in and out of her. She gripped her headboard with one hand for balance, as she grasped his ass cheek with the other, to push him further into her. Pleasure surged through them as he moved faster and harder as he neared his climax. Her vagina muscles clenched around his thick shaft, and she screamed his name as her climax hit. He thrust one last time deep into her and moaned his release as he filled her with his hot seed. Her body collapsed under his weight fighting to catch her breath, as she spiraled down from the incredible feeling. He couldn't move from her body, she felt good to have her muscles milk his cock empty. He laughed with joy, lovingly kissing her shoulders and neck.

"Baby, you got to stop doing this to me."

"Hey, you're the one that started this." She reminded him and wiggling her ass against him. She squeezed her muscles against his penis still inside her. He sucked in air through his teeth, as sheer pleasure shot through him again. Reluctantly, he withdrew himself from her warm body and rolled over on his back with a satisfied smile on his face. Vonda continued to lay on her stomach unable to move from their third round of lovemaking. They were acting like a sex craved young couple unable to get enough of each other. They kept it professional at work, but as soon as they were behind closed doors, they were all over each other like wild animals in heat.

"Yeah I know, but I just can't get enough of this sweet stuff." He said, rubbing his hand over her butt, giving it a good smack.

"Hey cut that out, Granite!" She protected and turned on her side to face him.

"Baby why do you insist on calling me that. You know I don't like it, especially coming from you." He asked, pulling her closer to his sweaty body.

"I know, and I don't like that slapping on the ass thing either." She smiled and pushed the palm of her hand against his chest.

"I'm sorry," He said with a sad expression on his face, "Let daddy make it better." Reaching around her hips and rubbed the spot he slapped. "Is that better?" He whispered while placing soft kisses on her earlobe. Then played with it with his tongue. A submission moan rose from her throat that told him she was ready for round four.

"Stop baby. You know what that does to me."

"I know. Why do you think I'm doing it?" He asked.

"Your nasty self." She playfully said, pushing away from him, flipping on her side with her back to him. He slid to her back, cuddling close. "Stop, this bed of mine can't take another round. We almost broke it this time.

"Then let's take it to my house. My bed is more than sturdy and can handle anything we do on it. I'll even let you use your handcuffs on me." He teased. They had been sleeping together for months, and they had never made love in his bed. He offered on many occasions, and not once would she agree to spend the night at his place.

"No, it's all good. I'm comfortable right here."

"Baby, I'm starting to get a complex. What's wrong with my place?" He asked as he leaned up on one elbow. "Every time I mention you coming to my place you always have an excuse."

"Don't be silly. I just prefer my place. Besides, I don't want to sleep behind all those other women you had in there." Her statement shocked him. He pulled back from her and sat up on the edge of the bed.

"Vonda what do you mean by that?"

"Nothing Garrett, I'm worn out. Let's just go to sleep. Okay?" She knew she had said too much. She didn't mean to hurt his feelings, but it bothered her that he had other women in his bed, even though it was before they started up.

"Damn woman you make me sound like a man whore." He stood looking for his clothes. She turned, saw him putting on his pants, and knew she had said too much.

"Garrett I told you I didn't mean it like that." She sat up in bed, pulling the sheets up to cover her breast, and tucked her knees up to her chest.

"Well, that's the way I took it," He replied with an edge to his tone. "I take pride in my home, and no matter what you think, I didn't have a bunch of women parading through my place," He kneeled looking under the bed for his shoes and found one. He grabbed his T-shirt off the floor, jerked it over his head and shoulder then stormed to the living room to look for his other shoe. Vonda got out of bed wrapping the sheet around her body to go after him. She knew she shouldn't say things like that to him, but ever since Jarrod tainted their bed having sex with her friend, she had this hang up about sleeping behind other people. Her leg was caught up in the sheet, and she stumbled to keep from falling. Shaking her foot clear, she took off behind him.

"Baby wait up, I said I was sorry. Garrett!" He was fully dressed and had his hand on the doorknob to leave. He wasn't in the mood to be insulted and decided he would spend the night in his own bed. "Garrett!" She yelled.

He stopped, exhaled the breath he hadn't realized he was holding but didn't turn to face her.

"Vonda I'm going home."

"Baby I didn't mean it the way it came out. I just feel more comfortable in my own bed. Can you understand that?" She asked. "Now come back to bed, and I'll give you more of this," she let the sheet slide from her body to her feet. He turned his head to look over his shoulder. Any other time seeing her naked would have caused an instant hard on, but he was hurt.

"No thanks, I'm not in the mood." Then he closed the door behind him.

Vonda stood stunned; she had never seen him like this. She had indeed hurt his feelings, and she didn't know how to fix it. She picked up the sheet and walked back to the bedroom throwing herself on the rumpled bed. She had to find a way to work through her issues, or she was going to lose him. She had never been happier than she was with Garrett. She'll wait until he calmed down and talk to him. She pulled the sheet over her head and cursed under her breath.

****

Garrett arrived home, and his mood hadn't improved, by the way, he slammed the door. He loved that woman, but sometimes he wanted to call it quits. He didn't know what he could do to convince her that he had never been some womanizer, as she was led to believe. He could count on one hand, the number of women he had sex with in the last year before they met. He climbed the steps to his bedroom and removed his shoes and shirt. He needed a shower. He could still smell the sweet scent of her sex on him and regretted leaving her. Just thinking of her made his cock twitch in excitement. His cell phone in his pocket vibrated. He rushed to answer, hoping it was her. He wanted to forgive her, rush back to her place and make love to again. To his disappointment, it was his father.

"Hello dad," He answered in a dry tone.

"Hello to you too son. Did I catch you at the wrong time?" Charles asked.

"No, dad. I'm sorry. I just left Vonda, and we had sort of a disagreement."

"Is that all? Son if you live long enough you two will have lots of disagreements. You'll work it out." He laughed. Garrett was silent for a moment then asked his father.

"Dad, can I ask you a question?"

"Sure you can, but didn't we have that talk when you were about fourteen. I don't have anything new to add." Garrett finally laughed, relieving some of the tension.

"No, I don't need that kind of advice, but it is about women.'

"Ok shoot."

"Vonda had this hang up about coming to my home and spending the night."

"Okay, why?"

"She thinks I use to have a bunch of women jumping in and out of my bed before we got together."

"Where did she get that idea from? Have you given her a reason to think that? Charles asked.

"What do you mean? No, I haven't."

"Look, son, you have to see it from her point of view. You have been a single man for some time now and being a Hart man, with all that charm and good looks, women are bound to throw themselves at you. Now most men wouldn't pass up the opportunity to jump in the bed with as many women as he could." He paused to let what he said sink in.

"But I'm not like that."

"I know that and you know that, but taking Vonda's previous history with her ex and all, don't you think it would be on her mind."

"I didn't think of it like that. So how can I convince Vonda?"

"Well, first of all, women are funny when it comes to laying behind other people. Where we wouldn't give it a second thought. Clean sheets are all we need, sometimes, but women think beyond the sheets. They think about the entire bed."

"So what do I do?"

"Man, do I have to spell it out for you? Get another bed. Get rid of everything."

"Everything?" Garrett asked.

"Only if you want to get that woman into that bed," Charles stated.

"Everything huh,"

"Ev-ery-thing..." Charles emphasized.

"Thanks, dad for the advice. Was there a reason you called?"

"Oh yeah, I called to see if you wanted to pick out some new camping equipment with me tomorrow?"

"I would, but I have a new bed to buy."

"Smart choice," They talked a while longer before they ended the call. Garrett knew what he had to do if he wanted the woman he loved to trust him and know where his heart lied.

Chapter

Twenty-One

They worked side by side for the next few days, and Garrett hadn't brought up the last time he was in her apartment. He just acted as if it never happened. She wanted to talk about it but didn't know how to start. She invited him over for lunch, but he declined and told her he had other plans. It pained her to think she may be the cause of them breaking up. If that happened, she would surely not recover from it.

"Hey Vonda baby, I need you to do me a favor," He asked with a big grin on his face.

"Sure honey what is it?" she happily asked with a glimpse of hope they could get past the little bump in the road.

"I need you to go to my house tomorrow and sign for a delivery," He asked still grinning. She just stared at him as the smile faded from her lips.

"Your house?"

"Yes, you're still off tomorrow right?"

"Yes I am, but..." She watched the expression on his face change. "I have plans."

"I know babe, but it shouldn't take more than a few minutes. I should be there around five, but the window to deliver the package is four to five o'clock. I don't want to take a chance of missing them." She took a deep breath, looked into his loving eyes and thought she could do it. She didn't have to go up to his bedroom. She would just stay downstairs and sign for the package, then leave as soon as he got there, or the package was dropped off.

"Okay."

"Thanks, babe. Here is the spare set of keys to the door. Just let yourself in. There are plenty of cold drinks and food in the frig, make yourself at home." He dropped the keys in the palm of her hands and gave her a quick peck on the lips.

"Sure."

Vonda lounged around her apartment most of the day dreading going to Garrett's place. She had run her errands and was back home by noon. Her imagination was running wild, thinking of the things he had done to the other women in there. She had seen the den of sin. All the candles, pillows and plush rug in front of the fireplace. And that bed, that four post bed, was large enough for two people to achieve every conceivable position on it. *"Snap out of it woman!"* She shouted in her head. She looked at her watch; it was three-thirty. If she were going to be on time, she should leave now.

****

She stood on his front porch and jingled the keys in her hand. She stared at the door and reached for the handle, inserting the key in the lock, unlocking it and stepped inside. She just about knew where everything was, from the one and only time she was there. She removed her jacket, then went directly to the kitchen, and sat on a barstool at the counter.

"Okay, this is good," She said to herself, crossing her arm over her breast and waited.

****

Garrett parked his car in the garage out of sight. He heard Vonda unlock the door and come in. He couldn't be sure, but he thought she went straight to the kitchen. He loved that woman and would do anything to ease her mind and any fears that she was the only person for him. The delivery truck driver called to let him know they were on schedule and would be there in fifteen minutes. Garrett had taken his father's advice and purchased a new mattress, box springs, and bed. The bed was the same as the one he has now, but it was brand new still in the box. If that is what it took to get Vonda to spend the night with him, then he would do it again. He heard the doorbell ring and prayed his plan would work.

****

Vonda nearly jumped out of her seat when the doorbell rang. She was glad they were on time so she could sign for the package and get out of here. She rushed to the door and opened it without asking who was there or looking through the peephole.

"Is this the Hart residents?" The pleasant young man asked.

"Yes, it is," She replied and looked at the large truck parked at the curb.

"It shouldn't take us long to set this up, and we'll be out of your hair in no time." He turned to walk away.

"Hey wait! I thought I just need to sign for the package."

"You do after we set it up."

"Set what up?"

"The bed."

She was confused. Why would Garrett order a bed when he had a perfectly good bed already? Four men headed towards the door carrying two big boxes. One was labeled headboard and the other footboard.

"Wait. I'm not sure where they are supposed to go?" She stated as the men pushed passed her.

"I have instructions to set it up in the master bedroom upstairs, last room on the left. Just step aside ma'am and let us do our job," Which she did without any further questions. She watched the four men disappear up the stairs, and moments later back down again to the truck, to get another two boxes marked bedpost, then finally the mattress and box spring. One carried a toolbox with him up the stairs, and the next thing she heard was furniture being moved. She closed the door and paced the floor until she couldn't take the suspense and braved the stairs to go see what was going on. These guys were fast. They had taken down the old bed and replaced it with a new one of the same style. She didn't know what to think. The men gathered their tools, cleaned up the mess, and started taking the old bed downstairs to the truck. She watched in awe as they hurried to complete the job. But then again it was nothing compared to seeing Garrett out the corner of her eye, standing near the wall next to the bathroom.

"Garrett... what, what are you doing here? I didn't hear you come in." She stammered. He signed for the bed and thanked the men. He picked up the large plastic bags at his feet, carried them towards her, and dropped them on top of an unmade bed. There was a comforter set in the same colors scheme as the one laying crumpled on the floor, with the coordinating sheets.

"Hey, baby can you help me make up the bed?" He asked as he unzipped the bag.

"What is this all about?" She asked dumbfounded.

"A new start," He replied stopping to look at her. "Look Vonda, I want this relationship between us to work. So I'll do whatever it takes to make you feel comfortable in my home."

"I didn't want you to go out and buy a new bed. I only meant... hell, I don't know how to put it without you getting mad again." Water welled up in her eyes, and she dropped her gaze to the floor," I don't like us to be upset with one another, and I'm sorry. I've missed you."

"I'm the one that should be saying I'm sorry. I should have understood your reasoning. Now, I get it, with the help of someone wiser. Now help me make up this bed so we can get to some serious making up sex. I missed you too." She closed the distance between them, coming to stand toe to toe with him. She removed the sheet from his hand and dropped it to the floor giving him a devilish smile.

"Who need sheets with all this plastic? Get the baby oil, and I'll meet you in the middle of our new bed." She reached her arms up around his neck, pulling his face down to hers. He didn't resist. The hunger was too strong; he takes her mouth in a deep kiss. It had been four days since they made love and he instantly responded. He lifted her up, and she wraps her legs around his waist, pressing her center to the bulge in his jeans. Four days felt like a lifetime of longing to have her.

"Damn the baby oil. We'll get to that later." Sitting Vonda on the edge of the bed, he pulled his shirt from the waistband of his jean and lifted it over his head in one smooth motion. He proceeded to slowly unbutton her shirt, taking his time, letting his hand warm the flesh he touched. His gaze never left her as his hand unfasten the last button just below her navel. He spread his fingers and pushed her shirt aside revealing her purple lace bra. A slow whistle sounded from his lips, followed by a broad smile showing his pleasure at what he saw. Pushing the shirt off, he placed kisses on her shoulders, as he pushed away her bra straps, and then kissed her neck to the other shoulder. She leaned her head back enjoying the sensation his mouth created against her skin. He urged her body back on the bed allowing him full asset to her. Leaning forward, he inhaled the sweet scent of her body as he gently kissed and licked just below her breast. Continuing down to her midsection, to her belly button, then stopped to unfasten her jeans.

She purred, as she wrapped her legs around his waist, grinding her sex against the strained shaft under his pants. He was driving her wild, she wanted him, and she wanted him in the worst way. Garrett slipped his hands around her back, grabbing the waistband of her jeans and slid them over her hips and down her legs, tossing them to the floor. Taking a moment to drink in her beauty, he reached and unhooked the fastener on the front of her bra, exposing her lovely round breasts. His body could hardly contain his need to be embedded deep inside her warmth, but he wanted this to last. Dropping to his knees, he spreads her legs and kissed her inner thighs to the slit of her pussy. He brushed his thumb over her sexual ripe bud. She grabbed a fistful of the plastic needing something to hold on to besides his head. Lowering his mouth to the spot that made her groan, and grinds her hip against his face. Her body tensed as he worked his tongue up, down and over her swollen bud. He loved her taste on his lips, in his mouth and he would taste ever drop of her juices.

"Garrett please," she moaned, "Please, I need it now,"

He freed his shaft from the confines of the material as he pushed his pants down over his hips. He curved his arms around her thighs, lifting them over his shoulders. He ached so bad, he fought the need to take her fast, and hard. Instead, he pressed the crown of his penis against her opening, slowly moving in a few inches, and back out again. He shivered at the feel of her tightening around him. The sexy sounds she made mimicked his own, urging him to drive deeper and faster. She was almost there; she could feel it. Every nerve ending in her screamed its release when he hit her G-spot.

"Oh... oh... oh... Oooh!" she tensed, screaming as her climax struck. Garrett wasn't far from his own. Her muscles clamping down on him, was too much for him to bear any longer. His rhythm increased faster and faster until he couldn't stop his release. He collapsed on top of her but kept his weight balanced on his arms. Breathing heavy against each other, she wraps her arms around his damp shoulders, hugging his close, kissing the top of his head. He laughed, raising his head to look up at her, then pecked her on the lips. She smiled feeling his shaft twinge inside her body ready to get started again.

"I love you, Vonda Bradley."

"I love you too Granite." She declared. He pushed up further into her and said. "I got your Granite right here." He laughed and began moving inside her again.

Vonda laid straddled across his body after their third round of lovemaking.

"I love this bed," She stated, lifting her head to meet his gaze. He laughed and replied,

"I thought you would."

Chapter

Twenty-Two

Garrett was excited about taking Vonda on their first official date. He wanted this evening to be special. They tried their best to keep their relationship as discreet as possible. But, they were sure a few people knew, and they preferred to keep it that way. He didn't want to take any chances of them running into anyone they knew in Tampa. He planned a thrilling train ride to Orlando, then they would catch a cab to the hotel, and spend a romantic weekend together touring the City Walk. That morning he booked two coach seats, on the Amtrak train leaving Tampa to Orlando. The trip should take about two hours, and from there, they would catch a cab then check in at the hotel for a night of fun and romance.

Garrett had his father drop him off at Vonda's apartment so he wouldn't have to leave his car parked at the station over the weekend. At her apartment, she had a million and one questions, when he told her to pack a bag for the weekend, that he had a surprise for her. He wouldn't tell her where they were going, only to bring casual clothes, and that sexy little number he loved to see her wear. Reluctantly, she finished packing her bags and was further surprised to learn they were waiting for a cab to arrive. She grew more suspicious when the taxi dropped them off at the train station on the outskirts of Ybor City. Garrett paid the elderly driver and retrieved their luggage from the trunk, then they went inside to check-in. Vonda had ridden the subways in New York numerous of times, but this train station was something out of an old movie production.

The high vaulted ceilings and wooden benches gave the place a vintage feel. She was surprised to see so many people, including families, waiting to board the train. She would have never thought this many people rode the train as an alternative. She guessed it made sense, no traffic, and no stress or road rage, just sit back, relax, and let them do the rest. They boarded the train and Garrett located their seats and let her sit by the window. Once they settled in, the train slowly pulled away from the station. He had picked up a pamphlet providing historical information on the station and read it to Vonda to pass the time.

The Tampa Union Station is a historic train station that was built in 1912. It was served by three railroads (Atlantic Coast Line RR, Seaboard Air Line RR, and Tampa & Gulf Coast RR), thereby creating a "union" of the three lines. The pamphlet also stated that the "Union Station" was named from its function as a location where two or more common carriers (railroads) arrive and depart, allowing the transfer of passengers and express alike. However, due to structural deterioration closed in 1982. The Tampa Union Station was donated to the City by the rail freight company, CSX. CSX took title to the landmark station back from the preservation group after forgiving the mortgage on the property. Tampa Union Station Preservation and Redevelopment Inc. is a non-profit company, owned the property, and had overseen renovations to the two-story brick building since 1991. Altogether, more than two and a half million dollars in grants and loans had been spent for the purchase and improvement of this site. At the completion of the restoration in 1998, the station reopened to Amtrak passengers and the public. CSX donated the station to the City of Tampa that same year.

During the restoration, numerous abandoned documents from the Pullman Company, Tampa Union Station Company, and the Seaboard Air Line Railroad were discovered. TUSP&R volunteers sorted the documents and preserved them by archiving them at the University of South Florida Library (USF) Special Collections Department and in the case of the Pullman Company materials, the Newberry Library in Chicago.

James E. Tokley, Sr., The City of Tampa's official Poet Laureate, in 2009 authored a poem, "The Epic of Union Station" which commemorates Tampa Union Station's history. Mr. Tokley performed a dramatic reading of the poem at Union Station on May 9, 2009, as part of National Train Day festivities held at the station on that day.

Currently, Tampa Union Station operates as an Amtrak station for the Silver Star line. It also provides Amtrak Thruway

Motorcoach services to Orlando, Lakeland, Pinellas Park-St. Petersburg and other neighboring cities.

The station was originally built with eight tracks. However, only one is in regular use today and designated as "Track 2, with adjacent Track 3 used for private railroad cars and special display trains on occasion (as was the case on National Train Day 2008 and 2009, when Amtrak equipment was presented on Track 3). Although the other tracks remain in place, they are out of service, and some have been severed from the main track. Original track bumpers, constructed of poured concrete, are also still located at the end of several of the remaining tracks. Adjacent to each of these bumpers are flower pots that have "TUS" imprinted on them.

Vonda was so engrossed in the information he read to her, that when the train slowed to a stop, she was amazed at how quickly the trip ended.

They caught a cab from the Orlando train station for a short drive to the magnificent Orlando Waldorf Astoria. Vonda anxiously waited for the taxi to stop before she hopped out, and marveled at the grand hotel.

The Epitome of Orlando luxury, The Waldorf-Astoria, is the crown jewel unlike any other, which nested in the heart of over 482 acres in Bonnet Creek. She had temporarily forgotten Garrett was with her, as she wandered into the grand lobby, as he paid for the cab, while the bellman unloaded their luggage.

Hearing the magnificent clock chime, as she stepped into the elegant lobby, welcoming them to The Waldorf Astoria. As Garrett checked in, she waited and watched the sunset on the resort pool from a comfortable chair in the lobby. Garrett, with their key in hand, walked up to her interrupting her tranquil moment, but as she looked up into his handsome face, she thought there was no sunset that out-shined the smile on his face. She stood and placed a tender kiss on his lips.

"What was that for?" he asked.

"No reason, I just wanted those envious women eyeing you, to know who this sexy hunk of a man belongs to." He turned and noticed a small group of women dressed in their party gear staring their way. He laughed and led her away hand-in-hand.

Once in their deluxe suite, she rushed from room to room like a little kid at the playground, not knowing which ride to get on first. He watched her in amazement. It delighted him to know she was pleased, and he already knew what he had in mind for her to ride tonight. He tipped the bellman, and went in search of Vonda and found her lying stretched out, spread eagle style, on top of the California king size bed. He couldn't wait to join her as he ran, and jumped on top of the bed beside her, causing her to laugh as she tried to move from his grip. He held her close, and playfully nibbled at her neck, which quickly turned into a hot romp in the hay as the old saying goes. There would be no site-seeing tonight only room service, and a long night of heated sex.

In the morning, Vonda laid on the bed with the Egyptian cotton sheets pulled up around her body. Waiting for Garrett to finish his shower, she noticed how peaceful the room appeared. The soothing colors and classic fabrics selected for the warm décor was very appealing to the eye. She looked for the television remote on the nightstand but found it lying on the floor next to the bed, with their clothes and a few pillows. She had just turned on the local weather channel to get the temperature for the day, when Garrett entered the room, wrapped in one of the hotels plush cotton towels around his waist. Her first thought was to pull him back in bed and make slow passionate love to him again. And, from the look in his eyes, he was thinking the same thing, but that would have to wait until tonight. She rose from the bed with the sheets wrapped around her body, then walked up to him, and on tippy toes placed a quick kiss on his lips, then continued to the bathroom for her shower. He dared not move because he would act on the thoughts racing through his mind at that moment. He couldn't resist turning his head to watch her enter the bathroom. She turned to face him, with a wicked smile on her face. She slowly released the sheet, letting it fall to the floor at her feet, giving him an eye full of what was to come later. She slowly closed the door as he greedily watched.

She eyed the marble soaking tub and longed to lower her body to her neck, in a warm bath. Knowing if they wanted to get started on their tour, she better take a quick shower instead. She turned on the water, then unwrapped one of the complimentary, Salvatore Ferragamo scented soaps and stepped into the shower under the warm running water. The "Signorina" fragrance filled the room with its irresistible scent. She made a mental note to purchase some, while they were out shopping. She closed her eyes, rubbing the bubbly lather over her skin, letting it roll down her body. She thought she was in heaven when a knock interrupted her thoughts.

"Woman, how much longer are you going to be? I'm starving." Garrett questioned.

She let out an exasperating breath and answered, "Just a few more minutes. Please!" She begged.

He laughed at her whining tone and replied, "Five more minutes and that's all. I'm wasting away out here."

After enjoying a delicious breakfast of crepes, omelets and Oscar's re-interpretation of the American classic Eggs Benedict. They took a cab to City Walk, but not before, they did a little shopping at The Mall at Millenia. She thought Garrett was crazy to want to go shopping at the mall in Orlando when there were so many Outlet Malls closer to Tampa. But when the cab dropped them off, she just about ran Garrett over getting through the doors, when she saw the sign advertising Tiffany's. She felt a rush of excitement, at the thought of reliving her many days of shopping at Tiffany's in New York. He bought her a bracelet, and she got the matching necklace. Then off they went to the Gucci store, where he purchased a pair of Gucci shades for himself. By the time they left the Coach store, Vonda had added two bags and a wallet to her credit card. They took a break for lunch and put out the fire that had burned a hole in Vonda's credit card. Garrett knew his limits and refused to buy one more thing. He would have to be satisfied with window-shoppin' the rest of the day. They were on their way to the exit, to wait for the cab to return when they passed the Rolex store. He couldn't resist going in and taking a quick look around. Rolex watches are one of the finest, cutting-edge technology pieces of its time, and the craftsmanship was exceptional. He always wanted one, but he could never bring himself to buy it. He walked around, looking dog eyed, through the glass cases, then thanked the clerk, before leaving the store. She watched as he admired several styles of watches. With the encouragement of the sales clerk, he went as far as to try one on, but overall, they left empty handed. As they sat on the bench waiting for a taxi, Vonda needed to go back in, and use the restroom, telling him she would hurry back. Once inside, she rushed back to the Rolex store and asked the clerk how much was the watch Garrett was looking at. The clerk removed the watch and showed her the five-figure price tag. She reached into the tote bag, placed her Platinum Credit card on the counter, and said, "I'll take it."

Chapter Twenty-Three

That evening back in their suite, they took a quick shower, changed clothes and left for City Walk. They purchased tickets to the Blue Man Group show for that night and had a few hours to kill before it started. Neither was up for walking after combing the mall today, so they decided to go to the Bob Marley Restaurant and enjoy some Jamaican Cuisine, and a few Jamaican inspired drinks. They shared an appetizer of Buffalo Soldier Jerk Wings and Jammin' Chips, and of course, Garrett had to have extra salsa.

The wildly popular, Blue Man Group show was excellent, and she didn't want it to end. From the time the lights dimmed, they were enthralled with original music by a live band, instrument selections, and inventive comedy with audience interaction. The entire experience was incredible, and when the curtains came down, she couldn't wait to return and experience the whole performance again. Still feeling a little buzzed from too many Jamaican Rum Punch drinks, Vonda held on to Garrett's arm as they left the theater. With ticket stubs in hand, they used their free admission to City Walk and enjoyed a few venues before returning to the hotel.

Garrett lovingly watched Vonda sit on the edge of the pool, with her feet dangling in the cold water. He was glad he planned this trip for them to be together, without running down a suspect or dodging bullets. It was well worth the money. They had one more day together, and he wanted to spend it in bed making slow sensual love to her all night. He loved knowing he put that smile on her face. After all, she had been through enough with Jerrod breaking her heart the way he did. Sometimes men don't think of the consequence of what happens to a woman, that gave her heart and soul to loving them. Hopefully, the woman can overcome the pain and move on with her life. But in Vonda's case, it was too much for her to bear, and he knew he had to reassure her every day that he would never hurt her.

Vonda let the cold water of the pool soothe her aching feet. She had never danced as much as she had done tonight with Garrett. She would have never thought, of all people, that he would be such a great dancer. She thought as she glanced over at him in the lounge chair and smiled, that the old saying, *"Lite on your feet, bad under the sheets,"* didn't apply to him. Just thinking about making love with him made her blush, causing the fire to tingle in her body. She never thought she could ever love another man after Jerrod had hurt her so, but here sat the man that changed all of that, and she thanked God for him. In many ways, they were a lot alike; they loved their careers, their family, wrestling, and they loved hard. They held nothing back to satisfy their partner in and out of bed, and they were both good at it. With him, she could be herself, telling him what was in her heart as they made intense love. They shared their dreams as she laid in his arms afterward.

She stood, picked up her shoes, and walked towards him as she held his gaze. She straddled him, lowering down onto his lap and he cupped her hips. A sultry moan escaped her when her eager tongue invaded the warmth of his mouth. She broke the kiss and gazed into his intense eyes, that matched her own. Smiles spread across their lips at the silent acknowledgment of what they both wanted. She stood, and helped him to his feet. They kissed once again before heading to their suite for another night of passion.

They shared a hot steamy shower to wash away the night of sweat from dancing. Their first round of love making started under the spray of warm water in the tub, then in the master bed, continued in the lounge chair in front of the high definition television. Then on top of the elegant dining table and finally, again in the king size bed before exhaustion took over and they fell fast asleep, wrapped in each other's arms. They didn't want to leave the comfort of the bed to feed the hunger aching in their empty bellies. So ordering room service was the best option for breakfast, and lunch before packing to catch the train back to Tampa.

Garrett placed her bags in the bedroom, as Vonda looked through the shopping bags and located the watch she purchased for him. When he returned, she was sitting on the sofa with her legs tucked under her, and a big smile on her face. She beckoned him to join her, and when he sat down next to her, she pulled the bag from behind her back and handed it to him. He looked from her smiling face to the bag in her outstretched hands.

"Here, take it, it's for you." She said excitedly.

"What is this? I see someone was doing a little side shopping." He joked.

"Something like that," She beamed with happiness. He took the bag and saw the Rolex name printed on the outside then looked up at her grinning expression. Reaching in, he pulled out the classic box and held it for a moment in disbelief.

"Go on, open it," she urged.

"Baby I know you didn't buy what I think is in this box." He asked then slowly opened the lid. His eyes grew as big as saucers at seeing the watch he admired a day ago.

"Do you like it? Is that the one?" She asked one question after the other.

"Vonda baby, I love it!" he said, as he removed the watch from the box, "But this is too expensive. I can't accept it. You'll be paying for this for the next few years."

"Don't you worry about that? I wanted you to have it because you deserve it and so much more." She said then leaned over, cupped his face, and placed a tender kiss on his lips.

He returned the kiss but added with a smile, "As much as I want to, I just can't take it." Then he placed the jeweled watch back in the box. She gently cupped her hands around his and knew it was time to let him in on her secret about her inheritance. She hoped he would take it well, then proceeded to tell him. He took in everything she said and was speechless when he heard her ask.

"So will you accept my gift?"

"Vonda?" he said with a questioning expression.

"Garrett just consider this a thank you for showing me, that I could still trust someone with my heart. No strings attached." She said as she pushed him back on the sofa, and laid her body on top of him. She began placing kisses on one side of his face to the other ending with a passionate kiss on his mouth, his neck, and further down his body.

"Baby I can't think while you're doing this." He said.

"Good, now stop thinking, and give me what I'm craving, and we'll call it even." She said as she continued her assault on his body. As she kissed her way down his chest, she unfastened his pants, sought out her prize, and took it into her mouth greedily. He was on the verge of surrender when the doorbell rang, and he cursed himself for forgetting he had called his father to pick him up.

"Baby wait, I got to get that. It's my father." He requested through labored breath. She sat up, gave him a sinister smile, as she slid back to the other end of the sofa. He hurried to right his clothes and rushed to the door as he heard her say.

"Hurry back," removing her blouse. Garrett partly opened the door and startling Charles.

"You ready son," he asked as he started to step inside, but Garrett blocked him.

"Hey Dad," he said as he stood in front of Charles. "Um, there's been a change of plans. Vonda's going to take me home later, and I'll pick up my car then. I have my spare set of keys, so you don't have to stay up waiting for me."

"Hey Mr. Hart," She called the singsong voice. "Would you like to come in for a minute?" She asked teasingly.

"No!" Garrett almost yelled, "He needs to get back home and get his rest." He answered looking over his shoulder in her direction.

"Hey, Vonda, Garrett's right I should be getting back home to my loving wife. I'm sure we could find something to do. Like the two of you." He shouted past Garrett then winked at him and whispered, "Have fun, son and use protection," then walked away. Garrett kept watching until his father got safely into the car. He closed the door and turned, to see his beautiful woman sitting on the arm of the sofa naked, as the day she was born. Her legs were slightly parted, giving him just a glimpse of her womanly treasure. There was a hint of mischievousness combined with lust showing in her eyes, and he knew he could never deny her anything. He would take the watch, and everything else she wanted to give, especially her love and give his all in return.

Chapter

Twenty-Four

Garrett and Vonda's relationship was going hot and heavy, and no one was the wiser in the department. However, they did have their suspicions that Lieutenant Manning knew about them, and was quite sure where he received his information. Of course, their parents knew and were thrilled with the idea of them being together. Garrett was exceedingly happy when Vonda declined an offer to transfer to the Los Angeles Crime Unit. He didn't know what he would have done without her watching his back on the street. Even more, he didn't know what he would do without her in his life and his bed each night.

Things were a little rocky once the word got out about them. A few jealous ex-girlfriends learned he had moved in with a woman, which meant things were serious. He hardly ever spent the night with any woman, or if you were lucky to know where he lived, spend the night at his place. However, she insisted that he keep his townhouse. Just in case, things didn't work out, or they needed some time apart. He wanted her with him all the time, and for now, that was fine with her. Vonda tried to keep her cool in the beginning when women he knew would come up to him on the streets acting as if she wasn't standing there, and totally disrespecting her. Garrett being the man that he is, would introduce her as his woman, and advise them of his intentions towards her.

Nevertheless, when the phone calls started coming in the middle of the night, she had to put a stop to it. She asked him to change his phone number to show her he was serious about their relationship. He didn't exchange words.

They were aware of the hazards of the job. How it could consume you with long grueling hours, emotional stress, and the uncertainty dangers, days on end. Nevertheless, they were partners and lovers, which allowed them to spend their day and nights together. Tonight, Vonda was home nursing a cold, while Garrett was called in to assist on a murder case when the phone rang at one o'clock. She didn't look at the number, she was expecting Garrett to call and check on her, as he had been doing every hour on the hour.

"Hello baby," She answered through a stuffy nose.

"Isn't that sweet, but I'm not your baby." A woman voice said.

"Who the hell is this?" Vonda weakly asked, sitting up in bed.

"Don't worry who this is, but if you need to know. I'm the other woman." The woman stated.

"Look, I don't know you, and don't care to, so don't call here with these lies," Vonda demanded as she wiped her nose with a tissue.

"Think I'm lying if you want to, but do you actually think you are woman enough to handle Granite by yourself? A man like him needs more than you can give. But I know what he likes." She said with a snicker to the tone.

"GO TO HELL!" Vonda screamed into the receiver and slammed the phone down on the cradle with such force that it bounced off the base and landed on the floor. This was getting to be too much. The late-night calls from this woman accusing Garrett of all sorts of things. The dead air calls, when she answered the phone. She mentioned the calls she had been receiving to him for the last few months. It would just upset him even more, than the last time she told him about them. She thought she could handle the pressure, but now she wasn't so sure. She knew she wouldn't be able to go back to sleep, with such thoughts racing around in her head. She tossed back the covers and climbed out of bed with as much strength as she could gather.

She went to the living room wrapped in a blanket to warm her from the chills. The last time she checked, her temperature was 102 degrees, which had only gone down two degrees from this morning. She couldn't remember the last time she had been sick enough to miss work. The doctor said it might take a day or so for the antibiotics to start working; until then she was to get plenty of rest and drink plenty of fluids. With a large bottle of juice in hand, she plopped down on the couch, turned on the TV, and started flipping through the stations. Her mind went back to the caller and wondered who she was, and why was she, so hell bent on breaking them up. It didn't make any sense to her. Garrett assured her repeatedly that nothing was going on, and he would get to the bottom of it.

She soon drifted off to sleep, and at one point in the night, was awakened by the light nudge of Garrett's hand on her shoulder. Through sleepy eyes, she glanced up at him as he felt her forehead and said, "Hey baby why are you out of bed? Come; let's get you back to bed." He helped her to her feet, led her back to their bedroom then tucked her in and took her temperature. He was pleased to see it had gone down several degrees from the last time he talked to her. He noticed the phone receiver on the floor. He picked it up, but before returning it to the cradle, he checked for messages. There was none, so he checked the phone log, and noticed several private caller entries. He turned to ask her who were the calls from, but she had fallen off fast asleep. Lying there without makeup, her hair wildly hanging loosely over her head and face, he still yearned to crawl into bed and make love to her in the worse way. Instead, he gently kissed her on the forehead, pulled the covers over her shoulders, and then went to shower before getting into bed.

Garrett now washed clean from another long day crawled under the covers, pulled Vonda close to him. He brushed the hair from her face then kissed her goodnight. Lying with her in his arms like this made life worth living, and wishing he could live the rest of it with her. He had been thinking about it long and hard, and he knew he wanted to make her his wife. A big grin raised to his lips, as the realization of what he wanted in life. He would ask her to marry him, but the moment had to be right. Somewhere special to pop the question. He would come up with a plan, but tonight he would sleep and hold her near.

Full of excitement, Garrett awoke early, cooked Vonda a hearty breakfast before starting his day of ring hunting, and he knew just the place to start. A new jeweler recently opened in the Brandon area, which imported some of the finest pieces and rarest stones to Florida. He hated going behind her back, lying to her when she asked him where he was going so early, but he couldn't tell her the truth. So telling her, he had some paperwork to finish wasn't quite a lie, because he needed to go to the office and do just that.

She couldn't understand why he was so happy going to the office to do paperwork. Normally, he tried to get her to complete theirs after each case was closed. Nevertheless, she couldn't let those phone calls put such doubt in her mind. She needed to get well so she could get back to work on Monday. She would have to be content, sitting enjoying the delicious breakfast he made. When they first moved in together, she was surprised to learn that he was such an excellent cook. He kept his house clean as well as any woman she knew. She scraped and placed her dishes in the dishwasher before she went back to bed. She smiled, thinking how lucky she was to have a good man like him to love and take care of her.

The store was much more than he expected, and after some deliberation, he finally decided on a three-carat oval-shaped diamond. He wasn't a Rockefeller by any means, but he wanted her to have a ring she could be proud to wear and show off. Now he had to find a place to hide it until he was ready to give it to her. It had to be someplace that she couldn't find it. He thought and thought then came up with the person he could trust the most, his sister Calisa. He knew he could trust her to keep his secret from his parents because she had done it for what seemed like forever. He called Calisa to make sure she was home before he drove to his parents' house.

He knew it was going to be tough for him not to shout his joy out to the world that he was asking this woman, his woman, to be his wife. Calisa was happy hearing the news and was proud that he would entrust her with his secret, and her to keep the ring safe. She promised not to say a word, and could not wait to be a bridesmaid or maybe the maid of honor at the wedding. They talked for a while longer, discussing this and that, until their parents returned home.

He left his secret in safe hands then went to spend time with his parents in the kitchen. They told him the news of his father's appointment, which was good. Charles had made a full recovery, but the doctor warned him not to overextend himself for another few weeks. Garrett looked at his watch and knew it was his time to make a hasty exit once his father suggested, he and his wife steal away for a second honeymoon, then steered the conversation towards grandchildren.

Vonda was starting to feel better. She called the office to ask Garrett to bring home more soup and another box of club crackers. When he didn't answer the desk phone, she called his cell thinking he may have left the office, and was on his way home. His voice message came on, and at the beep, she said, "Hey I couldn't get you at work. I guess you left already, so can you stop at the store, and pick up some soup and club crackers. Thanks, love you." She paused before she hung up the phone, wondering where could he be, and why hadn't he answered his phone. Well, for now, she would put it out of her mind and take a long hot bath, to ease her tension.

With the excitement of selecting a ring, Garrett hadn't checked on Vonda all day. He reached for his cell phone at his side, and it wasn't there. He looked on the floor of the car, and couldn't find it, then he realized he must have left it on the desk at work. He drove back to the office to get it, before heading home.

Vonda was lying on the couch when Garrett arrived home past six pm with the items she requested. She wasn't too happy and didn't have a problem letting him know it as soon as he stepped in the door. "Where have you been all day Hart?" He knew he was in trouble when she addressed him as Hart. He couldn't tell her the truth, so he stuck to his original story.

"Remember baby, I told you I was going to work, and afterward stopped by and visit my parents and Lis." He explained trying to keep the unsteadiness out of his voice. She had a way of reading him very well, and he didn't want to draw any suspicion to him.

"Well, I called you at the office and on your cell phone. I guess you were too busy to answer either of them." She stated without looking at him. She didn't want to see the look on his face when he realized he was busted.

"I forgot my phone at the office when I left to go visit my parents. I did tell you I was going there?" He waited for her to acknowledge him and when she didn't, he asked, "Baby you want me to heat you up some soup or something?"

"No... I couldn't wait for you to come home. I didn't wish to starve to death, so I warmed up the last can in the cabinet and ate that... thanks."

"I'm sorry baby; can I get you anything else?" He asked as he put the cans in the cabinet.

"I said no. I'm good." She wanted to confront him about his whereabouts but knew the way she was feeling, it would turn into a full-fledged argument.

"Well, I'm going to take a quick shower and come join you," He said then left the room. She heard that was a sure sign that a man had been with another woman when as soon as he got home, he had to take a shower to wash off any trace of her sex. She had to steady her breathing to ease the pain, ripping through her heart as it broke in two. Just the thought of him cheating, hurt more than anything she could remember, even her divorce. She wiped at the tears with the end of the blanket, as Garrett came and sat down next to her, then pulled her into his arms.

Whoever this woman was, she must have fucked him senseless, because she had his sorry ass humming some cheerful tune. She stiffened as his arms tighten around her shoulders. The expression on his face was of satisfaction and pure happiness as he smiled down at her. He placed a gentle kiss on her lips then pulled her closer to his body. She couldn't remember what they were watching as they sat in silence. The cameras panned a beautiful view of a Hawaiian beach appeared on the screen. She leaned forward, admiring the clear blue water of the ocean, glistening white sandy beach, and tall green palm trees and exotic flowers. She could imagine herself lounging in one of those beach chairs, with a fruity drink in one hand, a book on her lap while listening to the ocean waves rolling up on the shore. She leaned back on Garrett's shoulder and said just above a whisper, "God, that's so beautiful," then closed her eyes.

He smiled, as an idea came to him to take her on a cruise to Hawaii and propose to her on the beach, but how was he going to keep it a surprise? He would have to think of some way to make it happen, he had too.

"It is beautiful, but I can't see myself going all that way to Hawaii to sit on the beach when we have so many great beaches here in Clearwater. Water is water and sand is sand, no matter where you go. Don't you think so baby?" He added. Vonda couldn't believe he just compared Hawaii to Clearwater Beach. *What an ass,* she thought.

"I'm going to bed. Goodnight." She said as she stood without even a goodnight kiss.

"Goodnight baby, I'll be there in a minute." He gently grabbed her hand and asked, "You feeling all right? You've been mighty quiet tonight?" She could see the concern in his eyes. She gave a weak smile and leaned down and kissed him on the cheek then said, "Yeah, I just got a lot on my mind lately."

"Ok, if there's anything I can do for you let me know." He had noticed a change in her the last few weeks but contributed it to the long hours of work, and her coming down with this cold. He watched as she walked down the hall to their bedroom, and couldn't wait to call the travel agent in the morning and book this trip.

Chapter

Twenty-Five

Vonda woke early, feeling better than she had in weeks, and decided to cook Garrett his favorite brunch since it was almost noon before he rolled out of bed. Today was another day, a fresh start to put all her insecurities behind her, and she planned to spend it with her man. She wore a tank top, no bra and a pair of short shorts that left no doubt that she didn't have on any panties. She was ready for her man, and couldn't wait to show him how much she missed him. By the time, she finished with his ass today, he couldn't think about another pussy but hers. Garrett hurried from the bedroom, kissed Vonda on the lips, grabbed a few strips of bacon, two homemade biscuits from the table, and placed them on a paper towel.

"Hey, where are you going? I made you breakfast." She asked as she placed a plate of eggs on the table.

"I'm sorry baby. I'm late, I don't have time to sit down and eat. I won't be out long." He said as he rushed from the apartment. He phoned Lis and asked her to call Glenda that was a travel agent and asked her to do him a favor and come to her office. He wanted to look at some packages for cruises to Hawaii. He knew Glenda, she and Calisa were best friends in junior high. They were almost like sisters and seemed to be inseparable. To let his sister tell it, Glenda had a serious crush on him, and she still did. She was at their house all the time. He remembered teasing her about it on several occasions. He even told her she was going to have to start paying rent if she didn't go home. Although she was married with two kids, he still felt she still had a little crush on him. He noticed how she looked at him when they bumped into one another on the street. Well, that was in the past. She was eager to open the office on the weekend, saying she really could use the commission.

She couldn't believe her ears, as she looked at all the food on the table. They had never put any real demands on one another in their relationship. They could come and go as they please without any stipulation, but hell, this was ridiculous. She sat down at the table disgusted by the amount of food that would go to waste. In her anger, she picked up the plate of pancakes dripping in syrup and threw it across the room against the wall. She had to laugh at the sight of one pancake sticking to the wall, then slowly slid to the floor. Now she had more of a mess to clean up. She then thought since she cooked, she would leave the clean up to Garrett when he returned. This entire relationship was getting on her nerves these last few days. She needed to talk to someone before it ended badly for them both. She changed clothes, then picked up her purse, located her keys and headed out the door. She didn't want to confide in her family but thought of Calisa. They had become good friends since she and Garrett started dating. She called Calisa to make sure she was home and asked if she could come over for a little girl talk. Calisa assured her she would love the company since her parents were out of town.

Garrett hadn't realized how much time he had spent with Glenda going over travel packages, but in the end, it was worth it. They finally reserved the cruise he thought would be Vonda's dream vacation and the perfect place to ask her to be his wife. The only problem was they would have to fly to California and depart from there. It was worth a little inconvenience and every penny to see the smile on her face when he showed her the tickets. Glenda assured him she would have everything finalized in the next week, and then they would be on their way on a voyage filled with love and happiness.

He thanked her for all her hard work, and for giving up half her Saturday for him. She said she was happy to do it, and that her commission on the sale would help her out a lot since Derek, her husband wasn't working. She gave him the half-truth, her husband was laid off his last job, and was having a hard time finding work in his field. But they were making it on her salary, and his unemployment for now. Her heart swelled with joy at the thought that Garrett was concerned about her and her children. He would make a great father and husband one day.

After he had left the office, she packed up her laptop and cleaned off the desk she shared with another agent, that only worked part-time. She set the alarm, turned off the lights, locked the door, and dreaded going home after she picked up the kids from her mother. She never knew what kind of mood Derek would be in from day to day. It was to the point the only time he showed her any affection was when he demanded to have sex with her. She suspected he was getting it from somewhere else, because he bothered her less and less lately, which was fine with her. She prayed he would just leave her and the kids, and go make someone else's life miserable.

♥ ♥ ♥

Garrett arrived home to an empty house and a kitchen that looked to have been ransacked by thieves but had left the remainder of the house untouched. There were dishes piled high in the sink, as well as on the table, but he couldn't figure out how pancake syrup ended up on the wall? He called out to Vonda, but got no answer, nor could he find a note from her anywhere. He then remembered how abruptly he left her this morning, and it all started to come together. She had to be at the least disappointed, that he hadn't taken the time to eat the breakfast she prepared for him, just out of her sick bed. Realizing his mistake, he knew he had to make it up to her big time, so he started by cleaning up this mess.

It took him hours to wipe down the wall, wash all the dishes and then get everything put back in place. He tried to call Vonda again, but she didn't answer nor return his calls to let him know where she was because she was mad at him. He was beginning to worry about her, so he called his sister to see if she had heard from her. Vonda and Calisa had become good friends since the incident with Lamar. They often talked and sometimes referred to one another as sisters. If anyone knew her whereabouts, it would be her.

Calisa and Vonda sat drinking raspberry tea on the patio as Vonda talked about how insensitive and distance Garrett had become lately. Calisa assured her that Garrett loved her, and he was dedicated to making things work with them. He had called Vonda several times, but she refused to answer. She wanted to show him how it felt to be ignored. Calisa's phone rang, and she wasn't surprised who it was. He would call her after not receiving an answer from Vonda. Knowing he was worried, she answered her phone on the first ring.

"Hi, mama!" Calisa replied cheerfully, not wanting Vonda to know she was talking to Garrett. He was puzzled for a moment as to why she was referring to him as their mother. He knew she had his number programmed into her phone as Granite, then thought that Vonda must be there.

"Lis is Vonda there?" He asked.

"Yes, mama. I'm okay, just sitting on the patio with Vonda having some girl talk." She said.

"Is she mad at me?" he asked, but knew the answer.

"Big time," She replied and added, "Well you and daddy have a great time in Atlanta, and tell everyone I said hello." She ended the call. Garrett was pleased to know Vonda was safe but knew he had to do something special to make up for ditching out on her this morning. What they needed was a little romance, and he was just the man to give it to her. He knew it would be nightfall before Vonda returned home, and that would give him enough time to set the mood in the apartment. He grabbed his key, rushed from the house to gather the things he needed to make this night special.

Vonda should be arriving any moment now. Calisa called him to let him know Vonda had left her house and should be on her way home. Garrett looked around the apartment, pleased with his efforts in transforming their apartment into a cozy, romantic haven, at least for tonight.

The white and red candles in various shapes and sizes illuminated the rooms in a warm glow. No TV tonight, only soft provocative music to heighten the experience, and if everything goes as he hoped, he will be making love to his baby, until the early morning sunrise. The thought of making love to her stirred a reaction deep in the pit of his stomach. He smiled, averting his thoughts, to the delicious aroma of the homemade lasagna baking in the oven. He set the wine out to breathe, ran her bath water, and add the vanilla scented bath crystals, then sprinkled the water with rose petals. He had showered and slipped on a pair of black silk pajamas pants when he heard her key turn in the lock. Smiling, he rushed to greet her at the door; ready to give his all to make things right with them.

Vonda opened the door and was greeted by soft candlelight, and the smell of her favorite dish lasagna, baking in the oven. If this was his attempt to smooth things over after how he dipped out on her this morning, then it wasn't working, she thought. She looked down the hallway, and her knees buckled when she spotted the most magnificent sight of her man, half-naked and walking in her direction. Garrett's body was perfect in every way. His solid, broad chest flexed as his arms swung back, and forth to match his steady stride. His six-pack stomach was so toned and solid you could bounce a grape off it into your mouth. Her gaze lowered to his hips, and it was evident what was on his mind, by the tent of his pants.

Her mouth watered at the thought of what she could do with it. She loved his muscular arms, strong arms, that held her tight while she slept. *"No, no, no you don't,"* she thought. But there it was, that smile inching up at the corner of his mouth that could melt away any resistant she had.

"Hey baby, welcome home," He said, as he picked up a glass of wine from the table, handing it to her, then kissed her on the cheek.

"What's with all the candles, did I forget to pay the utility bill? She said, placing her purse and keys on the kitchen counter.

He smiled, made a chuckling sound, and knew she wasn't going to make it easy, so he ignored the comment and replied.

"That's funny. I just wanted to show you how sorry I was for leaving you the way I did this morning. I came home, cleaned up the mess, and decided to make tonight all about you. Now, I drew you a nice hot bath to soak in, and afterward, I prepared your favorite meal, for us to enjoy by candlelight." He positioned himself behind her, and pushed her hair to one side, allowing him access to place tender kisses along the base of her neck. She wanted so much not to give into his advances, but her body had a mind of its own. She melted against his bare chest and felt his erection pressing against the small of her back. Sliding his arms around her body, he reached the front of her shirt, then worked at unbuttoning her it. He gently cupped her breast until he felt the buds of her nipples harden in his palms.

"Let's get the rest of those clothes off, and you in that hot tub," He whispered as he guided her towards the bathroom.

Upon entering, a light fragrance of vanilla teased her nose. She was more stunned to see the bathtub surrounded by the flickering glow of candles, as red rose petals floated on top of the water. She turned to face him, and he had a big grin on his face and said.

"This is all for you baby. I wanted to apologize again for this morning, and any other day I may have hurt your feelings, and made you doubt my love for you." He paused to gauge her reaction, then continued. "You know I love you, right?" He stated more than asking a question. She looked up into his eyes and saw love in them.

"I know," she replied, turning to kiss him lightly on the lips. With their love confirmed, he slowly removed her clothes kissing her body as each piece discarded on the floor. He took a moment to admire her body in her red silk undergarments. He knelt in front of her, sliding her silky panties down her gorgeous thighs. She barely remembered stepping out of them when he kissed her navel.

She stood naked in front of him as he looked up at her. The warmth of his breath was her only warning before his fingers parted her, and his tongue tasted her sexual bud. She held his shoulder, as her legs buckled from the sensation of his mouth eagerly devouring her sweet juices already starting to flow. She widened her stand, enjoying the pleasure he masterfully delivered. She moaned her pleasure as the sensation built and her release neared. Her fingers tighten on him, her head tilted back in anticipation when suddenly, he stopped his feasting and stood to his feet. He lifted her over the tub into the bath water. He kissed her again on the lips and left her to bathe. Her skin tingled as she slowly lowered herself into the tub of warm water. The water surrounding her helped take some of the edge off her aroused body. She thought before she closed her eyes. *"God, she loved that man."*

Garrett was as aroused as she was, and had to leave her alone before they both ended up in the tub making love. In the kitchen, he took a big swallow of wine from his glass then refilled it again. Inhaling a deep breath to calm himself, he grabbed the mittens from the counter, removed the hot lasagna dish, and placed it in the center of the table. He thought back to the first time they made love at this very table and smiled at the memory. With everything in place, he picked up Vonda's glass and headed back to the bathroom to continue his night of seduction.

Her pulsating body started to calm down and was almost back to normal when Garrett entered the bathroom holding a glass of wine. Just looking at him stirred every part of her body to heat. He knelt, holding her gaze as he placed her wine glass on the side of the tub, then picked up her favorite Sheep Wool Sponge. He seductively wiped it across her neck, to the mounds of her breasts. He lifted her arm out in front of her, and kissed from her shoulder to her fingers, then squeezed drops of the scented water from the sponge over her skin. He made sure he didn't leave one sweet spot unexplored on her body. He then moved on to her feet, legs and to the sensitive valley between her legs. She slightly raised her hips to meet his wandering hands and released a deep sigh of pleasure when his fingers entered her. This day would be etched in her memory every time she used her sponge.

At his insistence, he dressed her for dinner in the new black silk lingerie, with matching robe, that he had laid out on their bed. She picked up the lingerie and examined the silky garment. It was a little too short and left little to the imagination, and that wasn't saying a lot. While she examined the items, he removed from the dresser her vanilla scented lotion, and walked back to her and unwrapped her towel. He squeezed some of the cream in the palm of his hand and tossed to bottle on the bed. He rubbed his hands together to warm the lotion, then proceeded to rub it seductively into her body. Paying particular attention between her thighs. Whatever anger she felt, faded away with each stroke of his hand. Turning her around to face him, he continued to do the same to the front of her. He licked at her nipples before sucking one, then the other into his mouth. Once they couldn't take any more of his teasing, he stood, then kissed her mouth. Slipping the negligee over her head and down her body, she whispered.

"Garrett, I can dress myself."

"I know, but I like doing it. Any objection?" He asked, running his finger between her legs, lingering on her sex bud.

"Hmm, not at all," She purred. He ached, to feel his shaft bedded deep inside her, but held back until the moment was right. He had to remind himself it was all about her tonight. He helped her guide her feet into the opening of her panties, then slid them up her thighs to her hips. Admiring her in the sexy negligée he selected, he took her by the hand giving her a little twirl, pleased with his creation.

As the evening progressed, she noticed he went out of his way to make physical contact with her body. Such as holding her hand for a second longer than needed, when he handed her a glass. Using his finger to brush a strand of hair from her face, and passionately kissing her until she was dizzy. Even when he sat next to her at the table, he made sure their legs touched. She was indeed turned on by everything about him. Because she had been sick with the flu, they hadn't had sex for a few days, but right now, it felt like months as her body ached to have him inside of her. After dinner, he removed the dishes from the table, as she remained seated. He had teased her body into a frenzy, and she didn't know if she could stand any more of this pampering.

"Did you enjoy dinner?" he asked as he stood behind her rubbing her shoulders and arms.

"Yes Garrett, everything was excellent." She replied, in truth and tried to stand, but his gentle hand stopped her and said,

"Not so fast. There's dessert." Going to the refrigerator, he took out a three-layer red velvet cheesecake and held it out to her. But the cake wasn't what caught her attention. It was the strained bulge pushing against his pants. Her gaze moved from his erection, to focus on the delicious cake he held. Her mouth watered at the thought of the sweet creamy-rich combination spread over the head of his shaft, tantalizing her taste buds.

He didn't think it was possible for his erection to get any harder, but the way she was eyeing him, he couldn't wait to feel her warmth wrapped around him. With each pain-stricken step towards her, he placed the cake on the table, then retrieved the cake knife and the plates he had put on the counter.

Vonda didn't know how much she could take before she threw him on the floor, and took what she wanted. She craved to feel him deep inside her, putting out this fire he started, with this seductive evening of romantic torture. Her body had betrayed her every attempt to ignore him, as he had done to her this morning. She wanted to make him suffer a little before she gave in, and she knew she would, but the question was how soon.

"Garrett I'm too full for dessert. I think I'll pass." She said while he sliced a piece of cake. He turned her chair to face him and lifted her legs across his.

"Come on baby… just a little bit." He asked as he held the fork up close to her lips. She knew what he was doing, and it was working all too well. Sitting in this position exposed the black silk fabric between her legs to his hungry eyes. "Come on. Open wide, I know you will love it." He said with an undertone of his meaning. She hesitantly parted her lips, allowing him to slide the tip of the fork in, then out. Her eyes closed as the sweet sensation exploded in her mouth, and she licked her lips with her tongue to capture the tiny traces of frosting.

This time, he took another piece of cake between his fingers and held it up to her. She didn't hesitate to let him insert his fingers into her mouth. She closed her lips around them, then sucked the red sweetness. His free hand traveled up her inner thigh until he reached the moist fabric that covered the dessert he craved.

Garrett couldn't hold back any longer, he needed to have her now. Rubbing his knuckle up and down the fabric against her clit. She gripped the side of her chair, raising her hips to meet his touch. Her body ignited into flames that only he could put out. He pushed his chair out of the way, kneeling between her open legs. Jerking at the fabric, giving him full access to what he wanted, and he wanted her. He toyed with her passion bud until the rhythm of her hips matched the pace of his thumb. He captured the nipple of her breast through the silk fabric with his teeth then sucked it into his mouth bringing the nipple to full bloom.

Through labored breath she couldn't speak, only gasp his name as the rush of an orgasm seized her from her feet to her head. He watched as she climaxed under the guidance of his hand. He wanted her to remember this night forever and how much he loved her and branding her his for a lifetime. He dipped his finger in the icing from the cake, then spreads it in her female folds between her legs. He positioned her legs across his shoulders, lowered his face and kissed what he branded his.

Still reeling from the first orgasm, Vonda felt another building as he pushed his tongue deep into the channel of her walls. He stroked in and out with such vigor, she grabbed his head and held it in place as she was overtaken by another earth-shaking orgasm, "Garrett..." She cried, as the thrill subsided. She looked down into the face of a man on a mission. He righted his chair, and he sat down, smiling allowing her time to catch her breath. He stood and kissed the lips which moments ago, moaned his name.

Desire showed in his eyes, as he untied the string at the top of his pants, letting them fall to the floor, exposing his hard-on. He excited every part of her, even in her weakened state. She wanted to be the only woman to fulfill his needs. She reached for him, wrapping her warm fingers around his shaft. A sharp intake of air rushed into his lungs, as she kneaded him with her hands. He watched her massage him while raking her perfectly manicured nails across the sensitive base, before licking the head with her tongue, then taking it in her mouth.

He threw his head back, moaning her name, as she used her mouth to bring him pleasure. Garrett didn't want it to end, but he felt himself about to explode and tried to pull back, but she refused to let him get away so easily. She increased her hold on him and deepened the thrust into her mouth. He locked his hips and came with a force, that rocked his very soul as she took every drop.

With a satisfied grin on her face, she leaned back and watched him drop down into his chair. He gave her a devilish grin of his own before he picked her up to straddle his lap. He slid his shaft into her warmth, which she eagerly embraced. Tonight, was no different than any other. They would spend hours pleasing one another, not seeming to get enough, only stopping when their bodies couldn't take any more pleasure, and they succumb to sleep.

Chapter

Twenty-Six

Glenda was hurt, no outraged, when she heard that he had settled down, and was serious about this woman. She loved him from the first time she laid eyes on him, back in junior high school. She knew she was too young then, but once she was older, she hoped things would be different, but nothing changed. He still treated her like a little sister, which she hated more than anything in the world because she wanted to be so much more. As she looked over Garrett's travel itinerary, she grew more envious that it wasn't her accompanying him to Hawaii. It was very hard for her to pretend to be happy for him, as he boasted telling her about Vonda. She had to admit, he appeared happier now, than she had ever known him to be in the past.

"Glenda! Glenda get your ass off that computer, and come fix my plate!" Her husband yelled. She cringed hearing his voice and immediately jumped up. She rushed to the kitchen finding him sitting at the table with his hand's palms down. She didn't make eye contact, as she hurried to the range and made him a plate of food. "How many times do I have to tell you to have my plate waiting for me, when I get home?" He warned her.

"I'm sorry babe; you said you were going to be late. I... I didn't want your food to get cold sitting on the table." She explained and placed the plate in front of him, taking a step back out of arms reach, just in case he had a mind to grab her. Derek was in a foul mood, which was the norm for him the last six months. She tried to understand how he felt, but he shouldn't blame her for being out of a job. It had been a year since he last worked, and his unemployment was cut off when he refused to look for another job. Or waste his time going to the unemployment office. She did love him, but she didn't know how much longer she could take the physical or mental abuse. She was trying to keep her family together, but he was making it very difficult.

They met in high school; he was funny, charming, but had a tendency to be very demanding and jealous even then. If another man even looked at her, he would fly off into a rage, which ended in a fight with someone, usually her. He swore it was only because he loved her so much, and wanted her all to himself. However, that never stopped her from secretly loving Garrett. Even though Garrett teased her, he always showed her love and cared for her with the utmost respect. As she waited for Garrett to realize she was the woman for him, she got pregnant by Derek her senior year. He wasn't Garrett, the man of her dreams, but she married him at the insistence of her parents. That was the beginning of a life of hell.

She was jolted from her thoughts, when he slammed his hands down on the table, then cut his eyes over in her direction, questioning. "What the hell is this shit?" She wasn't sure how to answer his question. It was obvious what it was, but she knew if she said nothing it would infuriate him more.

"It's Hamburger Helper; it's all I could afford to buy." She stammered bracing herself for a blow she thought was to come.

"You would think that fancy job of yours would bring in enough money to pay for a decent meal."

"It's been slow, but it would help if you went down to the day labor office..." She said without thinking and knew she had said too much. He balled his hands into fists and turned to face her. She wanted to avert his anger and said. "I just finished booking a cruise for Garrett," She stopped what she was about to say after mentioning of another man's name, "You know Garrett Hart, Calisa's brother. He's getting engaged, and wanted to propose on the cruise ship." She said and waited.

"Yeah, I remember him, he's a detective, right?" He asked, but she didn't say anything. "Yeah, and I also remember you had a major crush on him back in high school." He added leaning back in his chair. Crossing his arms over his chest, he stared at her. "Well, I better not hear or even think that you are trying to get something started with him, or I'll make you regret it!" He stated, as he hurled his plate in her direction and stood." Now clean up that mess before our kids get home. I'm going out and get me a decent meal."

Glenda watched him as he exited the house, and was thankful that he hadn't hit her this time. She knew she had made the right decision in making those calls; accusing Garrett of having an affair to break them up. It was a bonus that Calisa had recommended her for making his travel arrangement. "By this time next year, I will be Mrs. Garrett Hart," she boasted to herself, "After I figure out a way to get rid of Derek." She smiled as she took a roll of paper towels from the holder, got down on her knees, and began cleaning up the mess and thought, *"Patience Glenda, patience."*

♥ ♥ ♥

"Garrett, I don't want to spend my vacation cleaning, and repairing our place," Vonda complained as she tidied up her desk and turned off her computer.

"Oh Vonda, I think redecorating will be fun. You're the one who is always complaining about how the white walls are so depressing. Well, this is our chance to remedy that. Tomorrow we will go to the paint store, choose a new color for each room, and start painting. And if it makes you happy we can buy some fancy accessories." He added. He was so excited that he wanted to burst into a song and dance and shout to the world how much he loved her.

"Well, the next time I open my big mouth and put my foot in it, remind me of this day, okay." She said as she stood and pushed her chair under the desk.

"The next time you open that sweet mouth of yours, I'll put something in it beside your foot." He seductively said for only her to hear, but she looked around to see if anyone was looking and answered,

"I can't wait," then licked her lips with the tip of her tongue. A big smiled lit up Garrett's face just thinking about what those lips had done to him just last night.

"HART! I need to see you before you go," yelled Lieutenant Manning from his office. Vonda rolled her eyes to the ceiling and told Garrett she would see him at home.

"Yeah, you will definitely see me at the house," He thought as he watched her walk towards the exit.

♥ ♥ ♥

Excited Garrett left the Lieutenant's office, then checked out at the duty officer's desk to start his two-week vacation with the woman he loved. He couldn't wait to surprise her with the cruise tickets to the Hawaiian Islands. He had to make a few stops before heading home, one to Glenda's office to pick up the tickets, and the other to the liquor store to pick up a few bottles of their finest champagne.

With Vonda convinced that they were going to do some painting around the house and work in some much needed alone time, *"Boy was she going to be surprised when I show her the tickets,"* he thought. Glenda was a blessing and had worked with him to choose the perfect package, and not break his bank account. Vonda may have been loaded, but he still had his limits, but this wasn't one of them. He also made a mental note to send Glenda some flowers to thank her, and maybe he would throw in a dinner gift card for her and her husband to spend some time together.

He and Vonda had only known each other for about eighteen months. There had been a few rough times in the beginning, but he knew in his heart she was the one. He spared no expense for this little trip; it was first class all the way. Also, to complete the perfect voyage, he rented a cottage on the beach for one night. He wanted to wine and dine her at one of the finest restaurants on the lagoon. Then take a stroll on the beach under the big Hawaiian moon, and end the evening with him getting down on one knee with a proposal of marriage. And to think this trip was inspired by a commercial advertising a cruise to Hawaii. When she commented on wanting to go there one day, that gave him the idea.

He realized his purpose in life was to make Vonda happy or die trying.

He stopped by his parents' home to pick up the ring from Lis that morning on his way to work. He made Calisa promise again not to tell anyone, especially his mother. Because she couldn't hold water if her life depended on it. He told Calisa how proud he was of her, and he wanted her in his wedding, as much as he knew Vonda would.

Glenda pulled out the prepaid phone to call Garrett's house. Even though he had changed his phone number, he had to list an alternate number just in case she needed to reach him. He had just left her office picking up the tickets, and she smiled at the thought of the commission she made. It would keep her and the kids going for several months after she left Derek. This would be her last chance to put the nail in the coffin, that would break up the happy couple. After Vonda's last outburst, this would inevitably push her over the edge. Glenda being the good family friend that she was, would be there to comfort him through this entire ordeal, and he would be there to comfort her through her own problems. A match made in heaven. She placed the phone to her ear as it began to ring, but no one answered, so she dialed again. She knew Vonda was there because he mentioned that he had just spoken to her, so she hung up, and pressed redial and waited.

Vonda rushed to the phone hoping it was her mother calling her back, but when she picked the receiver off the cradle, the number displayed, as unknown caller. A knot formed in the pit of her stomach and in her gut, she knew it was that woman again. Before she made a hasty decision, she had to be sure. She pressed the talk button, then lifted the phone to her ear and said, "Hello?"

Glenda knew she had to make it right, so she laid it on thick, "Hello yourself, bitch, it's me! Is Garrett home?" She asked in a sexy voice.

"No, he's not home, and I got your bitch. What do you want with him?"

"I want more of what I just got. I must say, he sure knows how to lay down the pipe," She paused and waited for a response and when none came, she continued. "Hello, cat got your tongue? If you don't believe me, when my man gets there, check his dick, and see that it still smells like me. Better yet, see if his lips still taste like my pussy!" Glenda said laughing into the phone. Vonda couldn't - didn't want to listen to this crazy woman anymore. All she could say was, "You can have him, you stupid bitch!" She yelled.

"Don't be like that honey. I'm willing to do anything to please my man. Maybe that's why he keeps coming back to me." Glenda paused for effect, "Listen... let's be fair about this, maybe we can have a threesome, and I can show you just what he likes. How does that sound to you?" Glenda taunted.

"You both can go to HELL!" Vonda screamed, throwing the phone across the room against the wall. She fell to her knees and cried her heart out. A little voice in her head screamed for her to get up off that floor and get it together. It was evident Garrett had found someone else, and she wasn't going to stick around and be made a fool of again.

Glenda sat back with a satisfying grin on her face. Suddenly she heard from behind her, "I knew you were fuckin somebody else bitch!" Derek shouted as he rushed towards her with his fist clinched. "You want a threesome! I got your threesome right here!"

He said, as his punch landed to her face, knocking her out of the chair to the floor.

"No, Derek! It's not what you think, NO!" She screamed as she threw up her hand in front of her to defend herself.

♥ ♥ ♥

Vonda finally pulled herself together. This was the last straw. Although he said he wasn't cheating on her, and she really wanted to believe him. She just couldn't take any more of these calls from this woman. She had so many questions racing through her head. Who was this woman? How did she get their new home number, when it had recently been changed? Even though she had been cheated on by Jerrod only once, she promised to never let anyone do this to her ever again. If it was possible, she loved Garrett more than she had loved any man, but the lies, the deceptions, she wasn't going to take this from him or any other man. She rushed to the closet, found her luggage, and threw them on the bed. She called Garrett on her cell phone to tell him she was moving out, leaving his lying ass for good. *"God why couldn't I find me a good honest man?"* she thought as her heart broke into a million pieces. He answered on the first ring and was shocked to be greeted with the hysterical screams from Vonda.

"Garrett, I'm leaving! I can't take this shit anymore!" She screamed into the receiver.

"What are you talking about Vonda?" He asked confused. "Calm down and talk to me, baby." He pleaded, something terrible has happened, that he was sure of by the tone of her voice.

"That woman! Your woman, that's what I'm talking about. I received another call just a few minutes ago. She is the most vulgar woman I have ever spoken to. You know what she asked me to do. I'll tell you, she asked me if I could taste her - her pussy on your lips!" Vonda rage was uncontrollable as she paced the floor. She wanted to get her hand around the woman's neck, and squeeze the life out of her, and Garrett.

"What the hell! Vonda, did she tell you her name? Did you get her phone number?" He asked more confused than he was in the beginning.

"No, she didn't leave her number, and this wasn't the first time she has called you," Vonda shouts, as tears streamed down her face. She continued to throw her clothes on the bed on top of her suitcases.

"Vonda, what are you implying? Baby, you know me better than that. I would never cheat on you... I love you!" He shouted back at her. He received a curious look as coworkers walked passed him.

"Well keep your love for that other woman! I'm out of here Garrett!" She said as she paced in circles, trying to think of what to do next.

"Baby don't do anything. I'm headed home now. We need to sit down and talk this out. Please don't leave before I get there! I love you." He was on the verge of crying at the thought of her walking out on him. After all, they had been through, didn't she know how much he loved her? The parking lot was starting to get busy as people left the building at the end of the day. He didn't care who heard him confess his love to her.

"No, don't come. I don't want you here! I'll be gone by the time you get here!" She demanded, hanging up the phone.

He can't let her leave him. She was his world, his everything. He loved her with every fiber of his being. He had to convince her to stay until he finds out about this foolishness. "VONDA! VONDA! SHIT!" He screamed in disbelief as he jumped in his car. He turned the key, and the engine of his Mustang GT roared, as he stepped on the gas. The wheels spun trying to get traction before gripping the pavement then sped out of the parking lot into traffic. He continued to press redial on the speakerphone, and it repeatedly rang a few times then went to voicemail. He prayed she would answer her phone. They could get through this. They just needed to sit down, and calmly talk about it. If it took the rest of his life, he swore to get to the bottom of this. His jaw tensed as his lips tighten in anger. How could things change so quickly? One minute he had built his hopes and dreams around a woman he truly loved and the next his world had come tumbling down around him.

She snatched clothes still on the hangers from the closet and tossed them to the bed. She then went to the dresser drawers, pulled out items, and hurriedly threw her things in the open suitcases with her other clothes. She grabbed her overnight bag and carried it back towards the dresser. With her arm, she raked bottles of cologne, lotions, and a small jewelry box into the with her other personal item, not caring if anything broke or not. She raced from one side of the room to the other as fast as possible. She gathered what she could find, she was running out of time. Garrett would be there soon. She paused at the sound of her cell phone ringing and knew it was him. She froze, should she answer it or not. Should she give him a chance to explain? *"No,"* she thought, *"No more lies."* Once it stopped ringing, she put the phone in her pocket and zipped the bags close.

Garrett cursed again, hitting the steering wheel with his fist, then pressed redial again. *"Please. Please. Please, baby, pick up."* He cried inward. Garrett's heart raced as fast as his car. He pushed the car well past the speed limit, as he dodged in and out of traffic. *"Why wouldn't they move the hell out of the way?"* He thought. He had to make them move, and there was only one way to do that. He placed the siren on the dashboard and turned it on. The blue light instantly began flashing as the siren blaring, warning the other drivers to allow him through. He felt his was making some headway but hadn't noticed dark clouds forming above, which matched his mood. Large drops of rain slowly fell from the darkening skies onto the windshield. Within a few moments quickly turned into a downpour. He looked towards the sky and thought, *"When it rains it pours,"* In his case was true.

Vonda placed her bags at the door and took another quick look around the apartment. Making sure she hadn't left anything. But if she had, the hell with it, he could keep it and give it to his other woman. Pulling the carry-on bag strap over her shoulder, she then picked up the other bags and struggled to open the door. She could hear a siren in the distance and had a gut feeling that it was Garrett. "What the hell is he thinking?" she spoke aloud. He could lose his job for misuse of department equipment, but what did she care? He was no longer her concern. A heavy downpour of rain was starting, as she stepped out on the porch, and eyed the distance to her car.

She could now see the blue flashing lights of the squad car fast approaching. She closed the door behind her, and rushed down the few steps, fumbling with her luggage from the weight, and dropping one in a puddle of water on the grass. She was getting soaking wet from head to toe, as she quickly picked up the bag, and rushed towards her car. She had to get to the car before he reached her first. Her heels of her shoes sunk into the grass from the bags weighing her down, as she rushed forward.

Through the downpour of rain, he spotted her car still parked at the curb on the street, *"Thank God,"* he thought. He looked towards the house and saw her running towards her car with her suitcases in hand. He couldn't let her get to her car. He wouldn't let her out of his life without a fight. He floored the gas pedal, speeding towards her. Suddenly, he jerked the steering wheel sharply, causing his car to tailspin in the middle of the street. He crashed into the driver's side of her vehicle. The passenger side of his car grinded and smashed into hers, removing half of the bumper with it.

She heard the squeal of the tires, as the brakes locked before it collided with her new Hybrid car. Dropping her bags into the mud-covered ground, she screamed in fear he had seriously hurt himself. She covered her mouth with her hands, to stifle her screams and she watched in disbelief. The piercing sound of the siren echoed in her ears, as the blue lights blinded her rain-drenched face. She couldn't move, as she feared the worse when no movement came from the car. She could see his motionless body lying against the airbag. *"Move... Garrett move damnit,"* she willed. As if reading her mind, he lifted his head, moving ever so slightly.

Garrett was stunned from the impact of the airbag deploying in his face, thrusting his body back into the car seat. In a daze, he managed to remove his seatbelt, forced open his door, and stumble out into the flooded street. His only injuries that he could tell were a deep cut on his forehead, above his left eye. His chest felt like it was on fire, and his lungs and ribs hurt like hell. He was lucky to be alive considering the condition their cars were in.

"Vonda, Vonda baby wait... you got to listen to me!" He shouted with labored breath, stumbling around the front of the car towards her. He held onto the car's hood for support, as he removed the travel ticket from his pants pocket. He attempted to step up on the curb but fell to the ground. He gripped the bumper of the car and pulled himself to his feet. He stood for a moment to get his balance and try to keep from passing out.

She stood in place, still shocked at the sight of her damaged car and at the stunt Garrett just pulled. *"Is he out of his mind or what?"* She thought.

"Garrett, what the hell did you do? You fool, you could have killed yourself!" She yelled.

"I don't care!" He shouted over the siren and thunder that rolled through the air. Rain and blood rolled down his face into his left eye, impairing his vision. He used the hem of his shirt to wipe his face as he continued to walked towards her on wobbly legs. "Baby, there must be some kind of mistake. I would never do anything to make you unhappy. I love you Vonda!" He pleaded.

She backed away from him towards the house, "No, no Garrett I've heard this all before. Now get away from me before I call the police!" She demanded.

"We are the police!" He laughed delusionally. "But if you want, go ahead call them. I'll do anything to keep you from leaving until we've had a chance to talk."

"Garrett, I don't want to hear anything you have to say. I don't want to talk to you! Now please let me leave!" She couldn't take any more. She grabbed her hair in her fist then looked to the heavens and asked. "Why is this happening to me again?" She was overcome with a million emotions all at once. She wanted to scream, cry, fight and most of all give up on life. Anything to take away the pain she felt in her heart. Her clothes were soaked and clinging to her body. Her hair was plastered to her head and face from the rain, but she didn't care. She pushed the thick strands from her face allowing her to see Garrett clearly for the first time. "GARRETT!" She screamed at the sight of his blood-soaked shirt. His breathing was shallow as he desperately tried to pull air into his lungs. He painfully took a few steps towards her then collapsed to the ground.

Forgetting all else, she rushed to his side, falling to her knees, placing his head on her lap. She pulled out her cell phone and dialed 911. She frantically advised the operator of the situation and gave her the information she asked. She also advised the operator that she was an off-duty police officer, and so was the injured person. She looked down at the gash over his eye and looked for something to press against the wound. His blood soaked her pants leg and silently prayed he would be all right. She tore at the sleeve of her shirt until the material gave way. She balled it in her hand and pressed it against the cut. He moaned at the pain shooting through his head and tried to push her hand away. Even if their relationship was over, she didn't want to see him like this, helpless. He gazed up at Vonda and by the expression on her face; he knew he looked pretty bad. This may be his only chance to tell her how he felt about her. He gathered as much strength as he could and said.

"Vonda, I'm sorry," he inhaled.

"Don't talk baby. Help is on the way," With shaky hands, she wiped his face the best she could, and looked up for signs of the ambulance.

"No baby, I - have – something – I - need to - say." He paused to get his breath, "I love you. With all my heart and would never ruin what we have." His chest expanded trying to force air into his lungs. The pain was so severe he struggled to speak. "I had plans for us."

"I know baby. Don't talk, help will be here soon," She tried to be brave for his sake, but her own tears poured like the rain down her face. He gently rubbed her hand to the side of his face, while she held his head in her lap.

"I couldn't tell you. I wanted it to be a surprise." He said as he pushed the crumpled papers in her hand. She opened the blood stained envelope, pulled out the tickets, and read the writing.

"Cruise tickets, to Hawaii?" She asked.

"Yes, I had booked it for us to finally take some time to be alone. When I gave you this," He reached into his pants pocket, pulled out the black velvet box that held the engagement ring. He opened it for her to see the three-carat diamond inside. Her hands flew to her mouth in astonishment. She knew how she felt about him, but never had she suspected anything like this from him. At that moment, neither had noticed the ambulance pulling up to the curb, until the attendant rushed to her side as he slid the ring on her finger.

"Step aside Miss," the attendant almost pushed her out of the way. The rain was subsiding, but the storm wasn't nearly over. Vonda stood nearby never letting Garrett out of her sight as they evaluated his injuries. After a quick examination, he was lifted up on a stretcher then moved to the confines of the ambulance, for further assessment. Following the EMT's, she spotted the lieutenant headed her way, and he didn't look too happy. She had to think quickly to keep Garrett and herself out of trouble.

"Detective Bradley, what the hell happened here?" Lieutenant Manning asked, with his stern look on his face. He stood in front of her with his hands jabbed into his pockets. He really didn't want to hear her excuse, but he had to ask.

"Hi Lieutenant, how is Garrett?" she asked stalling.

"That's not what I asked. So don't start dicking me over and answer my question. What the hell happened here?" Vonda gave him a nervous grin and tried to answer with a straight face.

"Well you know Garrett, sir. You see he was in a hurry to get here so we could leave to go on our cruise and it started raining. And the streets were wet, and when he.... tried to stop, he slid and hit my car." She pointed to her car and the bags on the ground.

He held up his hand, "Stop, stop, just stop!" He demanded, "As much as I hated to ask in the first place. I really don't want to hear any more of this lie. So stop trying to make it up as you go."

She knew she was pressing her luck, but she asked, "Can I go check on Garrett sir. Before they take him to the hospital?"

He could see how much she was hurting to get to Garrett. Everyone in the precinct knew they were having a relationship, but he continued to let them work together as partners. Which may turn out to be the biggest mistake of his career?

"Go on, but I expect to have a full report on my desk first thing in the morning. Vacation or not!" Before he got the last word from his mouth, she was running towards the ambulance.

She quietly stood and watched them work on him and tape a large bandage around his forehead. They had started an IV drip and had cut away his shirt. "How is he?" She asked the attendant as she climbed into the back of the ambulance next to the attendant.

"From what I can tell it's not as bad as it looks. He has a broken rib and, of course, the cut above his eye. But the docs at the hospital will have to give the official call. Just to make sure he doesn't have any internal injuries."

She looked at him and fought back the tears as she watched him struggle to breathe. "Why is he having trouble breathing?" She asked the EMT worker.

"Probably the broken ribs, but like I said, the doc's will look him over so don't worry. We'll take good care of him." He gave her a reassuring smile. "We gave him something for the pain, but you can have a minute with him before we have to leave." The attendant moved out of the way to let her sit closer to him. Vonda scooted over next to Garrett and gently held his hand in hers. She had to fight back the tears welling up and realized it was time for her to stop running. She had to face her fears head on. Running almost cost her to lose the man she loved. She wanted to live the rest of her life with him.

"Hey." She said and forced a nervous smile.

"Hey you," He answered weakly. The painkillers were starting to take effect. "Baby..." he paused then swallowed the lump in his throat, then continued. "You didn't answer my question?" He asked as he gently squeezed her hand.

"Garrett..." She went silent.

"Baby do you love me? He asked as he tried to focus on her face.

"Yes, more than you know," She answered truthfully.

"Then what's my answer?" He attempted to sit up, but she placed a gentle hand on his shoulder to stop him. She looked at her beautiful ring then smiled at him with love in her eyes.

"Yes, Garrett. Yes, I'll marry you." She answered proudly and with so much love in her heart.

"Detective we got to go." The driver said. Garrett gave a weak grin, then pulled her to him kissing her to seal the deal.

Chapter

Twenty-Seven

Vonda waited in Garrett's room in the ER while he was taken to radiology for x-rays of his chest. As a precaution, they wanted to confirm that his lungs weren't punctured and see the extent of the fracture to his ribs. She never did like hospitals much, and tonight everyone in town was in here for one thing or another. Also, these little curtained-rooms didn't provide any privacy, and she saw more behinds than she cared to remember. As she shifted in a very uncomfortable chair, wishing this night was over. An extremely outraged man could be heard screaming at the top of his lungs as they wheeled him in on a stretcher, and placed in a room not far from where she sat.

"I'll kill that bitch when I get out of here!" Derek yelled as he fought against the restraints.

"Sir you have to calm down and let us examine the wound on your arm. You're making the bleeding worse by all this moving around." Calmly said the ER doctor. An assistant attempted to hold Derek's injured arm, flinging about while his other arm was securely handcuffed, to the railing of the stretcher. Vonda stood, peeped out into the hall, towards the room a few curtains down, as uniformed officers entered the room.

Derick eyed the two uniformed officers with disgust, as they entered the room. "Okay Mr. Stevens, do you think you can calm down enough to tell us your side of the story?" The officer asked as he stood with a pad and pencil in his hand.

"My side! My side! Now you want to hear my side of the story! Okay then, my side is, I caught her cheating on me, and I beat the shit out of her!" He answered, as blood oozed from the gash, where the letter opener was embedded.

"You caught her in the office with another man? Is that what you're saying, because there was no one, but the two of you in the office when we got there?" He replied.

"No man is you deaf! He wasn't there at the office. She was on the damn phone with him making plans for a threesome! A threesome! Can you believe how many times I tried to get her to do it for me?" He shouted as he attempted to explain his side of the story.

"Well, she is pressing charges against you..." The officer was interrupted by Derek's outburst.

"What! Why the hell is she pressing charges against me? She's the one that stabbed me." He pointed to his arm as to prove his point.

"Sir, you attacked her first, and she had to defend herself."

"Bullshit!" Derek said as he lay back against the pillow, out of breath from all the shouting.

"Doc, once you stitch him up, will he be able to be booked, or will he be spending the night?"

"I won't know until we get the letter opener out of him, but it looks like it missed anything major. So, I'm confident he can be discharged into your custody." Vonda shook her head at the man lying on a stretcher and thought how lucky she was not to have to deal with that on a daily basis. No sooner had she taken her seat, the lab tech rolled Garrett back into the room. She smiled and stood to get out of the way. Once the bed was secured, she wanted to stand by his side, placing a gentle hand on his forehead. Garrett moved the oxygen mask from his nose to speak.

"Hey baby," He said with a weak smile of his own, as he struggled to get his words out. She replaced the mask over his nose and told him, "You don't need to talk right now. Just rest until the doctor comes in." Garrett, the stubborn man that he was, removed the mask to speak.

"Vonda I saw a friend of Calisa's in one of the exam rooms," He paused to take a breath, "around the corner will you go check on her?" He asked with labored breaths.

"Only if you promise to keep that mask on and stop talking." She told him and asked her name.

"Glenda Stevens," He answered without removing the mask this time.

Vonda nodded her head and placed a kiss on his forehead, then walked out of the room. She knew how Garrett felt about his sister, and if this woman was a friend of hers, then she was a friend of his too. She wandered around the exam room looking for a woman named Glenda but had no earthly idea what she looked like. As discreetly as she could, she peeped into each room and was glad to see that most of the patients were men, which made the search easier. She ruled out anyone over thirty years of age, due to the fact he said it was Calisa's friend, which would make her in her late twenties. She rounded another corner and swore she heard a familiar voice, but wasn't sure where she heard it from before. She searched her mind, repeatedly when it hit her like a brick wall. She pulled the curtain back to see a young woman in her mid-twenties talking with a female officer. They both turned their heads looking in Vonda's direction, and the officer asked,

"May I help you?" Vonda pulled out her shield, showed it to them, and said.

"Yes, I'm Detective Bradley, are you Glenda Stevens?" she asked looking at Glenda.

"Yes," Glenda answered while holding an ice pack to her face.

"I'm Detective Hart's partner. He saw that you were here and asked me to check on you." Vonda paused, giving her a knowing look then asked, "Do I know you?"

"No," Glenda nervously replied, shaking her head then shifted on the bed. The officer turned her attention back to Glenda and replied.

"I'll be finished here in a minute Detective. Now, Mrs. Stevens, I have a few more questions." Vonda waited until the officer finished her questioning, and once they were alone, Vonda had a few questions of her own. The most important one running through her mind was.

"Why?" She asked. Vonda had already put two and two together and linked the irate man in the room down the hall to Glenda. Glenda knew there was no sense in denying what they both knew. She was the caller on the other end of the phone. She shrugged her shoulders, as tears rolled down her cheeks and she answered.

"I love him; always have. I always had hopes that he would love me too." Then her gaze became hard when she continued, "But then you came along and changed him. You made him want to settle down. You took what I have been waiting on for ten years. I want him to take my children and me from the horrible life with Derek." Vonda grew furious, and if she weren't on the right side of the law, she would have punched her lights out right there in the hospital.

"You know that little stunt nearly cost Garrett his life." Vonda hesitated to gain control of her rage, "He was in such of a hurry to get to me to stop me from leaving, he crashed his car." Glenda dropped the ice bag as her hand flew to her mouth. Vonda could clearly see the black and blue bruises on her face and a split lip. Her heart went out to Glenda because no woman or any person deserved to be treated like that. "By the grace of God, he came out of it with hopefully just a broken rib. We're waiting for the results now." Realizing she had been gone far too long from him, she made her final remark. "Glenda, I don't know you, and you don't know me, but if you come near my man again or call our house, you will get to know me in the worse way. You understand me!" Vonda stated and left the room.

Vonda arrived back to Garrett's room just as the doctor walked in with his chart in hand. She went and stood by his side as the physician read the x-ray report. She held his hand praying for the best news possible.

The doctor looked to Vonda then to Garrett and asked, "Is it okay to speak in front of her?" Garrett nodded, and the doctor continued. "Well, he has a few fractured ribs, but none are broken. He will have to take it easy for the next few weeks, and I want him to follow-up with his primary care physician. However, just as a precaution, we will be keeping him for a few days. Any questions?" He asked, and when there was none, he excused himself.

"Baby that's great news!" Vonda said, excited as she squeezed his hand.

"Yeah it is, but not as great as having you as my wife," He tried to raise and kiss her. The pain in his side hurt like hell, and he moaned, laying back on the bed.

"Hold up there, lover boy, there will be plenty of time for that. Now you rest." She assured him and planted a kiss on his lips. When the kiss ended, he gave her a half-dazzling smile and asked.

"How was Glenda?" Vonda didn't want to get into any details. She wanted to wait until he was better to explain that whole situation.

"She was fine, something about a domestic situation. Now enough talking you need to rest." He was about to ask another question when his parents and sister rushed in, followed by a nurse.

"Mrs., Sir you can't come in here without a pass." The nurse explained. His family ignored her completely and entered the room.

"I suggest you get out of our way. I got to see my baby." Carol demanded and rushed to Garrett's bedside.

"There are too many people in here. Two of you have to leave."

"I'm not going." Stated Calisa with her arms folded across her chest.

"Nurse, please give them a minute. They're his family." Vonda asked.

"And who are you?" She asked. A big grin grew across Vonda's face, and she proudly held up her hand.

"I'm his fiancée," Showing off her engagement ring.

"Praise God!" Carol shouted. "When can I expect some grandbabies?" She asked.

"Well let's get him out of the hospital first." Vonda laughed, receiving her congratulations before she left the room, to allow them to visit with him. She could hear Charles questioning his son as to how he was feeling, and Carol telling him to leave Garrett alone. She smiled to herself as she walked to the waiting room.

Chapter

Twenty-Eight

Vonda cared for Garrett for the next week of his recovery, then reluctantly returned to work. Since they were officially engaged, and she was wearing the ring to prove it. They decided to take a week of their vacation and visit her parents. Her parents were ecstatic to learn of the engagement, and moreover surprised to know that things were that serious between them. Garrett was put on a week of administrative leave without pay for the stunt he pulled, with the misuse of the sirens, which could have resulted in someone other than himself being hurt. Nevertheless, the next month after he was cleared to travel, they booked a flight to New York. She wanted to introduce him to her parents properly. Garrett knew it was going to be hard to convince her father, that he meant the best for his daughter. He loved her and would never break her heart. He was still a little sore and would at times have a difficult time getting around, but today it seemed like he could hardly get out of bed.

"Baby, are you feeling okay?" She asked after witnessing his slow movement while holding his side.

"Yea, I'm just a little sore this morning," He replied and gave her a smiled that didn't reflect in his eyes.

"Garrett Hart don't you try to bullshit me. I can tell that something is wrong. Now come sit your butt down, and talk to me." She said and patted the empty spot next to her on the bed.

He did as he was asked, and took a deep breath and blurted out. "What if your parents don't like me? What if they judge me by what happened between you and Jerrod?" For the first time, he was scared of the "what if's."

"Don't worry about that. They're going to love you because I do. However, I just want to warn you my dad can be a little hard at times. I'm marrying you no matter what and I love you." She meant what she said. She knew he was the right man for her, and she would give it her all to make it work.

Garrett looked into her eyes and saw nothing but love glowing in them. He knew she was right, that's all he needed to reassure himself. He leaned in and placed a tender kiss on her lips, that quickly became much more. He pulled her in close, laid her back on the bed, and let his hand roam up and down her body.

"Oh no, baby we only have a few hours to get to the airport to make our flight, and you know how you are," She stated.

"Me, me hey I'm good for a quickie anytime. All I need is thirty minutes. It's you that's greedy, and can't keep your hands off me." He reminded her with a playful slap on the butt.

"I never heard any complaints before and as I recall you were the one begging for more at two o'clock in the morning." She said and pushed him off her.

"Well I had a late-night craving for something sweet, and you were the first thing that came to mind," He replied as he tried to pull her back into his arms.

"Well, I hope the late-night snack was enough to hold you until we get back because there will be no snacking, while we are staying with my parents." She reminded him as she stood to her feet.

"What? What do you mean no snacking until we get back? Do you realize how long we will be gone?"

"Yes, I know, I'll be with you."

"A week! An entire week! Somebody shoot me. I don't think I can last a week." He shouted and rolled on his back with his hands above his head as if signaling that he gives up.

"I may be grown, but I still respect my parents, and you will too." She looked at Garrett and had to laugh at his antics, rolling around on the bed like he was having a temper-tantrum. "Oh stop it, and help take these bags to the living room.

♥ ♥ ♥

Vonda and Garrett rented a car at the airport and drove the forty-five-minute drive to her parents' home in Long Beach, New York. She didn't want them to have to sit at the Airport and wait for their flight just in case there was a delay. Garrett had been to New York many years ago, for a business conference for the force. He didn't get to see many of the sites, so he was excited to have his own personal guide. They were glad they booked an early flight, so it would still be light when they arrived at her parents' place in Long Beach. Vonda drove and decided to take the Long Island

Expressway. It may not have been the fastest route, but she thought it provided the authentic experience of being in New York.

She turned the car onto her parents' building's parking lot on West Broadway. She located a parking space not far from the entrance to the building. Garrett thanked God because Vonda brought enough luggage for a month's stay. From the car, she called her parents' High Rise to let them know they had arrived. However, before they reached the entrance, Aaron and Gina were there greeting them with open arms. At least, Gina was. Garrett could tell he had his work cut out for him to gain the respect of her father. He knew without a doubt that it was mainly because of Jerrod. At that moment, Garrett had a reason to hate Jarrod a little more. Vonda rushed to her mother's outstretched arms, and they shared a warm embrace. Her father, on the other hand, gave her a warm embrace but didn't take his eyes off Garrett. Introductions were made, and Gina gave Garrett a warm welcome to the family hug, while Aaron nodded his head and grunted a response.

"Aaron, help him carry all those bags," Gina stated, as she and Vonda headed back towards the building.

"He looks like he has it under control," He replied as he continued to size Garrett up. Gina and Vonda turned towards him and said unison.

"Aaron!"

"Daddy!"

"Okay, okay but let me tell the both of you right now. I'm not having this double teaming stuff, so don't even start it." Aaron stated and took the bag off Vonda's shoulder ignoring Garrett, and rushed ahead to the building. Vonda placed the bags in her spare room and joined Garrett in the living room. Her father was sitting in his favorite lounge chair that had seen its best days a long time ago, but he refused to get another one. Gina walked in with a tray of cold drinks, and slices of her homemade pound cake and placed it on the coffee table.

"Baby, I made your favorite cake this morning just for you and Garrett," Gina said.

"Thanks, mommy." Pure excitement showed on her face, as she removed two dessert plates and handed one to Garrett. "Garrett, my Mom, makes the best pound cake in the world and if I had my way, I would have our wedding cake made of pound cake," She said as she forks a piece into her mouth.

"Hey, little girl that big piece belongs to me." Aaron protested.

"Look Aaron stop acting like a baby, and let your daughter have that slice. You sure as heck don't need it." Gina reminded him. "You know you're not supposed to have any in the first place." Aaron shot a displeasing glance to his wife, stood and took two plates from the tray, then walked towards the sliding glass doors, and went outside, closing the door behind him with a thump. Gina shook her head at her husband's antics and apologized to Garrett.

330

She explained that he wasn't pleased that she was getting married to a man he felt she hardly knew as he put it. "You know how overly protective he can be about you." Gina sighed and continued. "You don't know how many times I had to talk him out of going and kicking Jerrod's ass. Oh excuse my language," She said putting her hand to her lips.

"No apologies needed," Garrett said. "I know how he felt. I wanted to find him myself and do the same thing." He replied as he looked to Vonda. "That man has no right to live after hurting my baby the way he did." Garrett jaws harden in anger.

Vonda put her plate down and said. "Okay let's change the subject before you and Daddy form a lynch mob and go after him." She laughed then looked up into the hard lines on her father's face, that had been standing just inside the doors. He walked into the kitchen, placed his plates in the sink, and walked to his bedroom. When he returned, he had on his jacket and his keys in hand.

"I'm going to collect from our tenants. You want to join me Garrett?" he asked. A worried expression crossed Vonda's face, as she looked at her father then to Garrett.

"Daddy, he's a little tired from our flight, why don't you wait until tomorrow."

"No baby I'm good. Sure, Mr. Mitchell, I'll be happy to ride with you, Sir." Garrett replied, standing then placed a gentle kiss on her cheek.

"Honey don't stay out too late and don't let the tenants in unit 8 give you any excuses for not having the rent again. They are already behind three months." She warned.

"I got an eviction notice in my pocket just in case," He replied and walked out the door with Garrett close behind.

Neither man spoke a word for at least thirty minutes, then out of nowhere, Aaron said.

"You know that's my baby girl, and I don't want to see her hurt again. That thing with Jerrod nearly killed her. I refuse to let that happen to her again."

"Yes, sir I know, and you don't have to worry about me ever breaking her heart. We've been through too much in the last month for me to do that to her." The car was silent for a moment, then he added, "I love her very much sir." Neither man made eye contact. They just kept looking straight ahead focusing on the road. Aaron gave a quick glance in Garrett's direction and said,

"Then that's all I can ask for."

They pulled into the parking area of the apartments her parents owned. With Garrett by his side, Aaron went from door to door collecting the rent and introducing his soon to be son-in-law. He received many joyful congratulations. Garrett was told what good people Aaron and Gina were. He was glad to hear that since they had gotten off to a rough start. Garrett had had a long day and was beginning to feel tired. He was glad they were almost done, and this was their last unit before they returned home for a good night sleep. They could hear loud music blaring from inside as Aaron knocked on the door but received no answer. He waited a few moments and banged on the door again. Suddenly, the door flung open, and a man that looked like someone Garrett had seen on America's Most Wanted stood looking at them and said in a very nasty tone.

"Yeah, what do you want?"

"I come to collect the three months back rent you owe me," Aaron replied ignoring the tough guy act, which didn't intimidate Aaron or Garrett as they stood their ground.

"Well just like last month and the month before that, I don't have it." The tenant replied and went to close the door. Garrett had seen this type before and could tell his bark, was worse than his bite, and if it weren't, he would have to prove it. Garrett stuck his foot in the door jamb to stop it from closing. "Man, what the hell do you think you're doing? The tenant asked. Aaron held his gaze and took the eviction notice out of his pocket shook it in his face saying,

"Well, if you don't have the rent then you have to vacate the apartment," Aaron demanded.

"Old man, you going to put us out? My family and me on the street? You don't need the money. You have nine other tenants that pay you. Why don't you overlook us and keep moving?

Besides, that piece of paper ain't worth shit. Unless it's served by an officer of the court or the police." He stated with a smug grin on his face as if he had a law degree hanging on his wall. Well, Garrett knew a thing or two about the law, and about street justice. Before he knew what was happening Garrett grabbed the man by the arm, twisted it behind his back, as he slammed him into the door.

"Look, my father-in-law asked you nicely to pay him what you owe. However, I guess you don't understand English. So, let me say it in terms that you will understand." He reached into his back pocket, pulled out his badge, and showed him.

"Now from what I can see, and smell if we decided to call the police I'm willing to bet that they will find at least three reasons, to take your sorry ass to jail. Do you think I'm right Mr. Mitchell?"

"I do believe you are correct Son." Aaron laughed.

"Now I suggest you get the money you owe, and take this eviction notice and find you someplace else to live within a month. Because, if I have to come back here if something unfortunate happened to this apartment, I'm going to take my airfare out of your behind. Do we have an understanding?" He asked as he pressed harder against his neck with his arm. Aaron stood back, watched Garrett, and thought how he and Vonda were so much alike it was scary, maybe they were made for each other from the looks of it.

Chapter

Twenty-Nine

While Vonda attempted to unpack their luggage since they returned home. She realized how much she missed her parents and New York. She had the best time showing Garrett the city, and eating at some of her best restaurants and pizza joints. As she placed the last suitcase in the closet, her body ached in every spot imaginable. She heard the bathroom door open and turned to see her man standing there with a towel over his shoulder wearing a pair of gray boxers. She ran a slow gazed over the length of his body, and unconsciously licked her lips. They hadn't made love in a week, and it was well overdue. A sudden warm feeling rushed through her body, and her nipples harden at the thought of what she wanted to do to him. He recognized that gaze in her eyes, and a slow smile graced the corners of his mouth.

"Hey, baby you looking at me like you want something." He implied, walking towards her.

"Yeah, I want something, but right now I'm too tired to do anything about it," She replied with a slight chuckle, as she stood on her tippy toes and placed a kiss on his lips, then attempted to walk around him.

"Hey don't be starting something and try to walk away. He's up now and ready to play." He playfully rubbed the palm of her hand against his shaft. He was tired, but his friend had other things on his mind. Whether she knew it or not by the fire blazing in her eyes so did Vonda. She giggles, and playfully tries to escape his roaming hands. "Baby no," She said halfheartedly. "I need to take a shower."

"Why? You will just have to take another one after we finish making love."

"Come on, I'm tired baby. Give me a few hours to rest, and I promise I will make it worth the wait." She asked, as she slipped her hand under the waistband of his boxers' and playfully stroked him in her hand.

His train of thought was interrupted when he heard her ask, "What do you say, baby. Two hours and I'm all yours." She smiled up at him with weary eyes.

"Okay, just two hours and it's on baby." He stated and took a step back from her then playfully slapped her on the butt as she passed him.

Vonda awoke to a soul-shaking orgasm, as Garrett pumped his shaft deep into her from behind her. She gripped the sheets and rode out the incredible climax to completion as he reached his too. As her breathing returned to normal, she said smiling. "Wow, what a way to wake up."

"I thought you would like that," He replied as he placed kisses on her neck and shoulder. She turned to face him, and the hunger in his eyes was still as intense as her own. She looked over his shoulder at the clock on the nightstand and remarked.

"Eight o'clock. Man, I've been sleeping for four hours?" She dropped her forehead against his chest and sighed.

"I tried to wait, but you didn't seem like you were ever going to wake up, so I started without you." He laughed and kissed the top of her head.

"Well now that I'm awake don't quit on me now." She pushed him over onto his back and climbed on top of him saying, "Let's get this party started."

♥ ♥ ♥

Their big day had arrived and what started out as a small list of guest, family, and friends ended up being over a hundred people. Vonda had done the big ceremony thing before and could have done without it. This would be Garrett's first time down the aisle, so she let him decide if he wanted to go all out or not. He assured her that as long as he had her waiting for him at the end of the isle, that was all he needed. With the help of Calisa and their parents, the wedding arrangements went smoothly. Her parents arrived a week early to help with anything they could. They came loaded down with gifts, cards that contained money or gift cards from her friends and family from New York that could not attend. Lieutenant LaPointe even took time off from work to attend the nuptial. To Vonda's surprise, she was joined by her fiancé, Lieutenant Michael Potter, from another precinct in New York. He reminded her of Denzel but had those stunning blue-green eyes like Michael Ealy. Besides being good looking, he was smart, kind, funny and most of all, he loved Brenda LaPointe very much. They had been dating for about nine months when he proposed on a midnight stroll on the beach, and she accepted. They had to coordinate their three-week vacations, and planned to marry in the summer of next year. The day before the wedding, Gina stayed busy baking Vonda's favorite lemon pound cake and embellished it to resemble a wedding cake. The lemon pound cake was stacked four layers high and garnished with fresh orange slices, strawberries and drizzled with her unique lemon glaze.

The ceremony was held at A La Carte Event Pavilion in Tampa. The Pavilion was decorated in cream and gold colors scheme. She wanted something classy, yet subtle and elegant because she wasn't a flashy type person. Her bridesmaid Calisa wore a short glimmer gold dress, which she selected. Vonda wedding dress was a cream form-fitting floor-length gown, with a long train that swept the floor behind her. Garrett and his best man, his father, Charles wore the basic black tuxedos and white shirts. Even though Glenda opt out attending the wedding, but offer to let, her daughter serve as a flower girl at the event. She was a beautiful little girl, as she walked down the aisle in her gold and cream dress carrying her white basket trimmed with gold and cream flowers. Vonda remembered how heartbroken everyone was when she had to tell Garrett and his family about Glenda's plan to break them up, at any cost. At the insistence of Calisa, Glenda went to therapy, left Derek, and had filed for divorce. Glenda had gone through a lot but was making good progress. Derek, on the other hand, was serving five years in prison for beating and kidnapping his current girlfriend. He said he refused to let another woman leave him.

The wedding was beautiful, from the first kiss as man and wife to the tossing of the bouquet; it was their dream come true. Even though the party could have lasted all night, they were scheduled to fly out first thing in the morning, destination, California to board a cruise ship to Hawaii.

With all the running around and the slight turbulence of the plane, Vonda wasn't feeling her best and prayed it would pass quickly. She didn't want to be sick on their official honeymoon night, that would put a damper on everything. The flight attendant was kind enough to give her seasickness medication, and after a while, she was feeling better. They made a cute couple and had the air of newlyweds all over them, and the smiles they were getting from the other passengers proved it. They were excited boarding the cruise ship, and once the vessel departed the dock, they clapped along with everyone else. They even stood on the deck and waved goodbye to no one in particular.

By the time, they got to their cabin their bags had arrived, along with a bottle of chilled champagne, which they opened right away. Midnight rolled around, and they managed to leave their room, to take a stroll around the deck. They enjoyed the festive music playing as they took the time to eat. They filled their plates from the many selections on the buffet line, took their plates, and found two seats by the pool. Garrett watched Vonda picking at the food and asked,

"Are you feeling ok? I see you didn't eat much." He asked concerned.

"I'm okay. I think it's just the sea air, and the motion of the boat."

"Baby you can't feel the movement on this big ass ship. What are you talking about?" He asked as he walked over to her lounge chair and slid in beside her.

"I'm all right, as soon as we get back to the room, I'll take a couple more of the sea sickness pills, and by morning, I'll be back to my old self." She smiled up at him as a sudden wave of illness overcame her. She made a mad dash to the nearest restroom and just made it before she lost what little lunch that she had eaten. Garrett stood outside the bathroom waiting for Vonda to come out. She leaned over the toilet praying for the sickness to subside. She stood and leaned back against the stall door, and took deep breaths through her mouth, then another wave hit her, and it started all over again. Fifteen minutes later, Garrett was knocking on the door and calling her name.

"Vonda, Vonda baby answer me. Are you all right?" He asked.

"I'm okay baby. I'll be out in a minute." She answered. She had never felt like this before and wondered what she could have eaten that made her sick. This wasn't her first trip on a cruise ship, and she hadn't gotten ill on any of the others. She washed her face, rinsed out her mouth, and rejoined Garrett who was waiting outside the door. Her eyes were watery, and her face was a little pale, and he knew she needed to see a doctor.

"Oh baby, I'm taking you to see the doctor," He said, feeling her forehead checking if she had a fever.

"No, I just need to lay down for a while. You'll see I'll be as good as new in the morning." No sooner than she spoke the words, she looked at Garrett. Her eyes rolled back in her head and fainted. Garrett panicked, and swept her up in his arms, and carried her inside calling for help as he walked. A member of the crew called the doctor, and within minutes, he was at her side.

Garrett paced outside the doctor's office, waiting for news of his wife. He was just about to open the door, when it opened and out stepped Vonda and the doctor. He didn't like the look on her face, then he looked over at the physician.

"Mrs. Hart, take those pills as directed, and you will be okay," He said and smiled at the couple.

"I sure will Doc, and thanks for everything," She replied. He was baffled as to what was going on and looked to Vonda for answers. She could see the worry etched across his face, so she said, "Baby we need to talk." She looped her arm through his and led him back to their cabin.

Chapter

Thirty

Vonda stood, basking in the warm sun, next to the guard railing of the cruise ship, destination Hawaii. The crisp tropical breeze blew her hair against her face, yet cooled her warm body, causing her to brush her hair back with her hand. The sun reflected in the sparkling freshwater pool as soothing Hawaiian music filled the air. Like her, several guests lingered on the deck or sat in the comfortable chairs taking in the tranquil oasis. Vonda couldn't wait for their evening helicopter ride over the beautiful cascading waterfalls, Hawaii was known for. She was still reeling from the deck party last night, and the tropical rum tasting event, which she thought Garrett enjoyed more than the dancing. If you let him tell it, he was smooth on the dance floor, but she thought he was much better in bed. They would be docking soon, and she wanted to be one of the first people off the ship to start their sightseeing tours. Garrett had signed them up for two tours that day, and she didn't want to miss one thing. She was beginning to wonder what was taking him so long. As if on cue, he walked up behind her, wrapping his arms around her waist.

"Hey, baby how about we skip the tour, and go back to our cabin for..."

"Oh no, we don't. That's what got me in this shape in the first place." She laughed, as she rubbed her still flat belly and turned to face him. The doctor had her take a pregnancy test after he couldn't pinpoint the cause of her illness. It only took ten minutes for her to learn the cause of her sickness. She was pregnant. From their calculation, she became pregnant, after they returned from her parents' house when she was woken up by Garrett's lovemaking. Then she continued; "Besides I'm not going to spend the entire day locked up in our room with you. But I'll be more than happy to spend the entire night locked in your arms." She slowly let a finger run down his chest, then back up around his ear. "We can even have room service bring in our dinner. That way we won't waste one single minute." She gazed at the faint scar over his eye and thought how lucky he was, and that it could have been much worse.

"Mrs. Hart, that sounds spectacular, and I know just what I'm having for dessert." She squeals with laughter, as he tried to discreetly squeeze her butt. The ship's horn blew, alerting them that they would be docking soon. Garrett took her hand in his, then led her to the exit for an exciting, fun day on the island. They both felt as if they were the luckiest people in the world at that moment. They knew their love for one another would last a lifetime, and beyond.

By Sheryl Y. Battle-Maxwell

SloWriters Publishing LLC

Protection by Design (Black Lyric)

Rapped

Say How You Feel

I Believe In Us

Ty The Knot

Las Vegas Connection

Alternate Being

The Age Factor: When Loving A Younger Man Changes

Your Life

www.ingramcontent.com/pod-product-compliance
Lightning Source LLC
Chambersburg PA
CBHW062012170626
46813CB00001B/133